Inked
Death of a Sorcerer

Inked: Death of a Sorcerer by JV Delaney
Published by JV Delaney

1ˢᵗ Edition 2020, paperback.

ISBN: 978-1-925999-56-3 (print)
        978-1-925999-57-0 (epub)
        978-1-925999-58-7 (mobi)

Publishing services by: PublishMyBook.Online

Inked
Death of a Sorcerer

BOOK THREE

JV DELANEY

CHAPTER ONE

THE GLARE FROM the morning sun pours in through my half-open curtains, waking me. With closed eyes and a splayed hand, I reach over to where Lazarus sleeps. The sheets are cool and empty. He's been gone a while.

I listen for the sound of his beating heart and am inundated with the loud thumping of half a dozen dragon hearts beating wildly. The dragons at Nogard Hollow must be hunting together and, by the sound of their overzealous heartbeats, are enjoying their prey. Normally Lazarus hunts before dawn and is back in bed before I wake.

I draw my attention away from the dragons to hear Paul pottering around in the kitchen. He arrived late last night after visiting my father.

Without dressing, I quickly race down in my pyjamas to speak privately with him. With the sensitive ears the dragons have, the best time to talk is when they are all busy consuming their prey. I could use my silence dome, but Lazarus has worked out when I'm using it. He becomes paranoid, resulting in hours of questions as to why I need to speak in private.

'Welcome back, Paul.' I rush to him with my arms open wide.

'Hello, Jazz. How are you holding up?'

As he wraps his arms tightly around me, an emotional lump forms in the back of my throat.

'I have good days and bad days. And even my in those good days I usually end up crying. How was my father?' I quickly wipe an elusive tear away.

'He's putting on a brave face, but I can see he's hurting. I was with him for a week and in that time, it looks as though he's aged ten years.'

I force down the lump in my throat, but it rises back up thicker than before. Fresh tears trickle down my cheeks. I force a smile and nod, encouraging Paul to continue.

He blinks several times, pushing back his own tears. 'I think it was more of the shock that your mother had died. She'd promised him that she was only going to fly by and check on how you were.

'Apparently, she did it quite often and would return home the next day, if not the same day. They would often argue, as he didn't want her to shape-shift and put their lives in danger. When she hadn't returned and then he saw your number appear on his phone, he knew that his worst nightmare had happened.'

'When I telephoned him, I explained she died at the hands of a sorcerer and not a dragon. I could hear the doubt in his voice as if I was lying to him.'

'He's concerned about you and wants to be with you but refuses to be near any of the elite creatures.'

'I knew my mother had sorcery powers but where did she get the power to shape-shift?'

'Your grandfather, as you know, was a sorcerer. But what you don't know is that your grandmother was a shape-shifter. Your father has asked me to answer any questions you may have regarding this.' He takes a deep breath. 'You have sorcery and shape-shifting blood running through you.'

'Wow, I never thought about Granny having any powers. She was such a sweet, fragile old lady. I can't imagine her changing form into a strong creature. What was she?' I jump up to sit on the kitchen table.

'I don't know the answer to that.' Paul smiles before he gives a small chuckle. 'Maybe she only shifted into a Chihuahua.'

'I wonder if I can shape-shift. My mother's powers were transferred to me, as were Sky's and several dragons.' I run my hand up and down my lower leg, trailing over the prominent purple vine. I recall the warm and calm feeling I got when my mother's powers surged into me. Tears fill my eyes and again spill over and down my cheeks.

I look up at Paul through sodden lashes. With a sympathetic smile, he wipes my cheeks with a tea towel. 'It's good to cry.'

'Every time I do, it sends Lazarus into a tizzy. Because we are inked, he's in tune with my emotions. He feels my heart breaking and rushes home to find me in tears. Sometimes I just want to have a good hard cry by myself.'

'Well, you would fall in love with a dragon.' Paul smiles and tosses the tea towel into the sink as if to say, 'no more tears for now'. 'Have you ever tried to shape-shift?'

'No, I wouldn't know where to start. Do you know how I do it? What earthly colour do I draw on?

'My powers are very limited compared with yours. And I have never had the need to ask a shape-shifter. I didn't realise your mother was one. It was a total surprise to me.' He rubs his chin and frowns as if he's deep thought. 'I wonder if Lazarus knew of your mother's shape-shifting powers.'

'I never thought to ask Laz. But I will be furious if he knew and never let on.'

'Hold your horses. Your mother may have confided in him so don't go off the deep end at him.'

'Don't go off the deep end at who?' Lazarus walks into the kitchen with a wide grin on his face.

'You!' I narrow my eyes.

'Morning, beautiful. What have I done to upset you this fine morning?' He slides his warm arms around my torso. He kisses the corner of my eye, acknowledging my recent tears.

'No doubt your big ears have overheard our private conversation.'

'I'll leave you two to talk.' Paul cowardly bows out of the kitchen.

'To be honest, I was listening to your heartbeat and not your voice. So what's up?'

'Did you know my mother was the wedge-tailed eagle who followed me on my trails?'

'I knew the creature had magical qualities but, to answer your question, no. And if I did, I wouldn't have revealed it to you as it is not my place.

'You know the rules of our kind—an elite will reveal themselves to you if there's a need. It's not up to me or anyone else to divulge their secrets. Surely you're one person who believes in this rule.'

'Why?'

'Because you are the most powerful sorceress in Australia. If we don't keep your identity hidden, you will be taken or worse.' He pulls me in tight and kisses the top of my forehead.

'I'm sick of being locked up here with someone always having to know where I am or what I'm doing!'

'Hmm? What's the true reason for you being so snappy?' He stares down at me, locking his eyes deep into mine.

'Tell me how you change form.'

'I don't know. I just do.'

I roll my eyes at him. That was not the answer I was looking for.

Kite and Falcon walk into the kitchen, happily chatting away.

'Falcon, how do you change form?' My tone is a little snappy.

'Good morning, Jasmine.' Falcon smiles.

'It will be a very good morning if you answer my question.'

'I don't know.'

'Oh, sheesh! Kite, can you give me a better answer than these two stupid twits have done?'

'Twit! How did I become a stupid twit?' Falcon directs his question to Lazarus, who shakes his head and shrugs his shoulders.

'I've never thought about it,' Kite says. I roll my eyes and she holds her index finger up, which stops me from saying anything further. 'But when in my natural dragon form, I release the air from my lungs, exhaling every bit of breath I have. I roll my shoulders in and draw my legs in, all under my wings like I am shrinking my large body into my soul. Then I feel parts of me fall to the earth, like my wings and tail; things I don't need in human form.

'And when in human form it's the opposite. I breathe in, expanding my chest, drawing the particles that fell to the earth back up to me.

'It's a warm feeling returning to dragon form and a cooler one to human. But when changing to either, I see it in my mind seconds before changing. I use the earth to help me change; let it take what I don't need and retrieve it when I do. Most creatures of our kind are connected to the earth. It's similar to you and how your powers work.'

'When you say you see the form you're changing into, can you picture something else and disrupt the process?'

'No, we change so very quickly. Keeping our minds on what we are doing for several seconds is easily done and I've never wanted to be anything else.'

'When I was young, I tried to change into another creature. I wanted to surprise my brothers while playing hide-go-seek and attack as a lion.' Falcon sniggers.

'And?'

'And nothing. I changed into a human, but my hair was longer and I had a full-grown beard.'

Lazarus laughs. 'I remember that.'

'Why all the questions, Jazz?' asks Kite.

I ignore her and ask another. 'Do you draw on a specific colour when changing?'

'No, it's not how you draw on your earth powers to create an anoric or an orgle. It's more like my soul is sucking me in then spitting me out.'

'Kite asked you why all the questions,' says Lazarus.

'Call me curious.' I smile before heading out of the kitchen and back towards my bedroom. 'Thank you, Kite.'

I hear Lazarus close behind me as I enter the bedroom. He quickly shuts the door and has me locked in his hot arms. His green slit eyes eye me warily. 'You want to tell me what's going on in that head of yours?'

'Nothing.' I lean forward to kiss his warm, soft lips. He kisses me back, rolling his hands over my back. He groans, pulls me tighter and kisses me harder.

'I have an idea that might cheer you up.'

'Hmm?'

'I want you to meet my parents in England before the engagement party. We could do a low-key trip over there and maybe some sightseeing. What do you think?'

'What about the rebels?'

'Once we are in my parents' home, we'll be safe and under their protection. Your cloaking spell, so far, has been unbreakable and will get us there unannounced. Plus, together we are an extremely strong unit.'

'You know how strong I am, don't you, Laz?'

'That is a matter of opinion, babe. But yes, you are extremely powerful and can bring down an unskilled dragon or two.' He tilts his head with curiosity.

'Good, then you will have no complaints when I go for a ride today *by myself*.'

'You know how I feel about you roaming around out there alone. There are still a few rebels that need to be accounted for.'

'I am protected by every living creature. I'm sure they will warn me if one approaches. And as you said, I can bring down a dragon if need be.'

He sighs and shakes his head at me then takes a breath to continue arguing. But I speak before he can. 'Come downstairs. I need to show you something.'

I grab a pair of jeans, a t-shirt and my boots. He stands with his hands planted on his hips, his lips grim.

'Follow me.' I wave my hand encouraging him to follow.

He follows me down the stairs silently and out to the corrals.

I throw my clothes over the fence and start to remove my pyjamas. 'I want to show you something.' I keep my eyes locked on his.

'Oh, babe. And I want to show you something too.' He smirks, lifting his t-shirt over his head.

'Stop, Laz. Keep your clothes on. That's not what I'm showing you.' I step further away from him. 'Watch my body.'

'Gee, tough job but a man's gotta do what a man's gotta do.' His lustful tone makes me smile.

With closed eyes and my hands on top of my head, I run my fingers slowly down my head, neck, shoulders and torso all the way to my feet. I drag down the black ink that fills my markings. I force it into the earth then draw on a pale colour, similar to the dry grass, and drag it up my body, filling in my markings. When my fingers reach the top of my head, I open my eyes.

'I can conceal my markings,' I gush, happy with my increased powers.

'Why would you want to do that?'

'So I can move around without any creature knowing I am a sorceress. Like when we go to England, I can hide them from everyone.'

'Except for the purple vine you got when your mother died.'

'I don't want to remove that one. Anyhow, so many people have tattoos now, this one will blend in fine.' I shrug.

'Great trick, babe. Put your clothes on,' he orders, turning his head slightly from side to side, as though listening for anyone approaching.

'Trick! I don't do tricks like a well-trained dragon. It's a power. It's sorcery!'

'Well, this well-trained *dragon* is about to bite your head off if you don't lose your snappy attitude.' He growls and blows a puff of smoke out of his mouth and over my face.

The warm heat from his breath instantly relaxes my tense shoulders and smothers the sullen mood that's been brought on by a multitude of reasons. Apart from grieving my mother, I haven't seen the dingoes or visited Nelly's grave in such a long time. I pray every day, wishing I could turn back time and save Nelly from the dragon's murderous tail. The guilt of her death weighs heavily on my soul.

'Sorry, I've got a lot going through my head. I'm going to ride Blue Boy over to see the dingoes. I haven't seen them since Nelly died.'

Grabbing my jeans and t-shirt, I slip them on in record time. I pull on my boots and pick up my pyjamas.

I throw them at Lazarus and he catches them without taking his eyes off me. 'They don't blame you for Nelly's death. I'm sure they will welcome you with open arms.'

'I hope so. I'm not coming home tonight. I want to visit Jet and talk to the angels.'

'I'll meet you over there later tonight,' he says, rolling my pyjamas into a ball.

'I can live one night without you.' I roll my eyes at him and grab Blue Boy's bridle from the hook. I whistle and he trots over to me.

'I'm sure you can, but I can't live one night without you.'

'You're not jealous of Jet! I thought you understood my feelings for him are purely based on our family ties.'

'I'm not jealous of anyone but I don't trust Ash. He never left when all his other relatives did.'

'Oh, he's innocent.'

'What is he hanging around for?'

'Not me, as I'm engaged to be married to an overzealous dragon, remember?' I huff, slipping on Blue's bridle. 'Give me a leg up.' I stand at my horse's withers waiting patiently for Lazarus. I can easily mount him on my own, but I'll use any excuse to feel the warmth of my fiancé.

I feel his heat before his hands run down my shoulders, my waist and eventually my leg. He holds it then hoists me onto Blue Boy's back. I gather the reins and stare down at my jealous dragon. I know he doesn't mean it, but sometimes it's frustrating that he doesn't trust me enough to deal with Ash and his advances. Half of the time it is harmless flirting just to annoy and agitate him.

I lean down and kiss his warm lips. He slides his hands up to cup my face and he holds it there so he can kiss me again. Who am I to argue? He is one fantastic kisser.

'I'll see you tomorrow.' I kick Blue forward, making him jump straight into a canter.

'I will see you tonight at Elyograg Castle,' he corrects.

'If that will make you happy, dragon.'

Lazarus' heart skips a beat before he whispers, 'That it does, witch.'

I'VE BEEN WALKING along the creek bed for the last hour and there is no sign of the dingoes. I use all my senses to try to locate them but turn them off due to the stench of dragon blood. The memory of killing Ethan and spraying his body over this area is still fresh and painful.

I am less than an hour's ride away from the castle with no sign of the dingoes. I decide to give up.

Just as I pull Blue Boy away from the creek's edge, I hear a loud howl breaking the tranquillity of the Outback.

'Ellie?' I yell. 'Rhys?'

Another howl answers me, and another. I inhale deeply through my nose and catch their scent clearly. They're so close. Why didn't I sense them earlier?

Blue Boy's head shoots up high, his ears pricked. I can tell he sees something coming. His muscles are rigid and he leans back with all his weight on his strong hind legs, ready to take off in the opposite direction.

I coo and softly pat his neck with long slow strokes until we both see the dingoes coming along the creek. I watch, mesmerised, as they slowly change form. Recognising them, Blue Boy relaxes and drops his head to the grass underneath him.

'Jasmine, it's so nice to see you.' Ellie smiles.

'We were wondering why we haven't seen you in a while,' Rhys says.

'G'day, Jazz. Can we ride Blue?' Tag asks, with a huge smile on his face.

'Sure, but he is very unfit. I haven't been riding him much. A slow walk along the creek will be fine and see if he needs a drink.' I smile at the two eager pups and slide off his back.

Kip and Tag both move to Blue Boy's side, fussing over him and patting him. I lift both of them onto his back and they slowly head towards the creek.

'So how have you been, Jazz?' Rhys asks.

'I'm good and I'm sorry I haven't been to visit but, since Nelly's death… I didn't know if you wanted to see me again.' I drop my head, guilt flooding my body.

Ellie wraps her arms firmly around me. 'We miss her terribly, but we speak about her every day. Keeping her memory alive helps us to deal with the loss. We didn't want to impose on you mourning for your mother, so we kept our distance.'

'When I rode down here, I couldn't find you and thought that maybe you didn't want to talk to me.'

Rhys places his hand on my shoulder. 'We couldn't live where Nelly died. All we could smell was the blood of that dragon. As Ellie said, we want to remember our Nelly often, without the stench of the dragon that killed her.'

'Come and sit down. We have so much to catch up on.' Ellie guides me by taking my hand in hers and heads towards the creek. 'You must be parched, riding for so long.'

I bend down at the creek's edge and cup my hands, scooping up the cool, refreshing water, lifting it to my lips. The creek water is so fresh and revitalising. I scoop up several large handfuls, slurping them down in record time. I didn't realise how thirsty I was.

I sit down beside the two adult dingoes and start to question them about how they change form.

'Your mother was a shape-shifter, with her original form being that of a human. We are creatures first who can change form to a human,' Ellie explains. 'I told my pups when they were young that, to change form, they must push everything towards their soul.

'It's like diving into a small puddle of water. Picture your soul and dive into it. And do the same to reverse the procedure. It's a cool feeling, turning to human form, so that is why I suggest they picture their souls as water.'

'The dragons have said similar to you. I want to try and change form, but I am worried about what I will turn into. And what happens if I don't change back?'

'You should only be able to change into one thing. It may be an eagle like your mother or it may be something else that runs in your bloodline. But you are different from anyone I know. It might be wise to check what the previous generations became.'

'Knowing my luck, I'll be an elephant!' I chuckle, and it is the first time I have heard the dingoes laugh.

'You won't be an elephant, I can guarantee you that. You will be a creature that is the same size as you or smaller,' Rhys says. 'That's what normally happens.'

'But Laz is bigger than his human size.'

'Because he is a creature first.'

'Hmm, that's another personal concern I have and why I'm going to visit the angels.' I drop my head to stare at my twiddling thumbs. Rhys jumps up, maybe realising I need 'girl talk' and heads over to where the boys have my horse standing in the creek drinking water.

'What concerns do you have?' Ellie asks quietly when Rhys is out of earshot.

'I'm engaged to a dragon. What if... when I have children... what will happen?'

'I have heard of humans and creatures having families, but I am unsure about a human and a dragon. I wish I could tell you it will be fine, but I can't. You'll need to ask the angels.'

'I will, thanks, Ellie. It is so good to see you all again. And just so you know, I miss Nelly so very much. It gives me a punch to the stomach every time I think of her.'

'She was taken by a dragon, not you, so stop blaming yourself. I'd rather your heart sang when you think of her.' She slowly stands and offers her hand for me to pull up on.

'My heart does sing when I picture her riding Blue or when I feel her holding my hand, telling me I am her best friend. It just hurts to know I let her down.'

'Time heals all wounds. Visit us more often so we can reminisce about her time with us.'

'I will. Thank you.' We embrace in a warm, comforting hold. The two pups bring Blue Boy over and hand me his reins. I swing up onto his back and wave goodbye to the dingo family.

I reach the castle as it hits dusk. Jet and Lolana glide above like an unofficial escort. They land with an almighty thud, making Blue Boy jump away. Luckily, I anticipate his reaction and grab a handful of his mane, gripping my legs tightly to stay on board.

After removing his bridle, I am squeezed hello by Lolana in her gargoyle form. She quickly she takes off and climbs the castle's wall, ready to glide off with Corbin, looking for their evening meal. Corbin gives me a roaring growl as they both glide above me. A gargoyle and a dragon—opposites attract! I wave and watch them glide gracefully over the treetops. What a magnificent sight.

'It's about time you dropped in to see me,' Jet says, changing form. He shakes off a few chunks of stone before folding me in his arms.

'Hello, handsome.' I kiss his cold cheek, which slowly changes colour as it warms up.

'You must be talking to me because I'm the handsome one,' Ash says from behind me.

I spin around to see him in only a pair of jeans with his bare chest toned and flexed.

'Hello, Ash.' I smile at him, but Jet keeps me firmly in his arms.

'She is here to see me, Ash, so leave before I rip an arm off.'

I shoot my eyes up to his and frown at his small outburst. 'Can you give me a minute alone with Jet please, Ash? I promise I will catch up with you soon.'

'I will be waiting.' Ash gives me a cheeky wink.

I wait until Ash is out of earshot. 'What is eating you?'

'I heard you're going to England.'

'Gee, news travels fast around here. I only found out I was going this morning.'

'You're not going. It's a death wish!' He growls deep in his chest.

His arms tighten around my torso and I find it hard to breathe. 'You're hurting me, Jet.'

'They will do more than hurt you, Jazz. How stupid are you to even contemplate leaving Australia?'

'I'm not stupid. I can out-power all of them in England!' I push his chest hard with both my hands, breaking his hold. Annoyed, I step back, putting my hands on my hips and glaring hard into his darkening blue eyes.

'You know nothing of their powers. You are guessing. My powers are increasing daily and soon I will be stronger than you.'

'What does that mean?'

'You think because you've covered your markings that they won't know who you are. You stink like a sorceress!'

'I stink! You better calm down and think very carefully about the next thing you say or—'

'Or what? You'll throw an anoric at me, shock me, stab me, lift me off the ground, throw something at me or set me on fire?'

'No, I will calmly walk away from you until you come and apologise.'

His loud growl rattles my eardrums. He takes an angry long breath in but when he exhales his chest stays puffed up and large. He is trying to intimidate me.

We stare at each other without either of us saying a word. He stands still as a statue. He's had plenty of practice at it.

I decide to break the silence. 'Are you feeling better now you have verbally abused me?'

'The dragon can't protect you. He is leading you into a den of death.' His tone is slightly calmer.

'I can protect myself.'

'I agree with Jet. You can't protect yourself. But there's an easy solution. I will go with you,' Ash yells, heading back over to us.

'I will come as well,' Jet says.

'No, you won't. If they get a sniff of what you are, they will capture you or worse. I won't let you go and nor will Lysander. And you must obey your father.' I stomp my foot, trying to make my words final.

'Does that mean I can come?' Ash moves so he is now standing in-between us. 'I'm a gargoyle with no special powers and if killed, won't be missed. Unlike Mr Muscles here.' He pokes Jet with his finger and receives a growl for his efforts.

'Lazarus will not be happy about you coming, but you can sort it out with him. If he says yes, it's fine by me. But not you, Jet. You're too important to the gargoyle clan.'

'So I stay home and do what you say but you won't do what I say,' Jet snarls.

'I didn't come here to argue with you.' I move slowly, reaching my hand out to Jet's arms, which are folded across his wide puffed chest.

'Why did you come?' His eyes narrow, glaring down at me.

'Because you are my family and I love you, even though you called me stupid.' I give him a cheeky smile, trying to break his bad mood.

'Well, if you're not gonna kiss and cuddle her, I will,' says Ash.

'I warned you once!' Jet growls and lifts Ash into the air with the point of two fingers. Ash's shocked face is amusing but I need to defuse the bomb before it explodes.

'You've made your point. Now put him down.' I calmly move my hand up to his pointing fingers and draw them down. I hear Ash's feet touch the ground and turn to him. 'I will catch up with you later. Laz will be here soon, so you can talk to him about travelling with us. But I warn you now, enough of the smart mouth because he won't hesitate to snap you in two. And you are special and would be missed if you died, Ash.'

Ash lowers his head, nods and surprisingly, walks away without a word. Jet walks up behind me and slips his arms around my waist so his chest is against my back.

'You don't know what it's like to be your protector. With Drake screaming in my head and my hybrid powers growing, it makes it unbearable when you continually put yourself in danger. I can't lose you,' he whispers into my hair while taking in my scent.

'You won't ever lose me.' I lean back into his strong chest, rocking slightly, staring out over the gargoyles' lush homeland. 'Come and tell me how your powers are going and what is new.' I lift my head so I can see his glowing blue eyes and smile.

'Sure.' He unravels me from his strong grip and walks me into the castle.

We sit for hours going over any issues he has with mastering his sorcery. He's tapped into the dragon powers he received during the European attack. He is becoming stronger each week and, if his powers keep increasing at this rate, he will be stronger than me in no time. I knew he had drawn on some of the dragon powers which worried me due to their negative outlook and lack of care for life.

AFTER A SCRUMPTIOUS dinner made by the angels, I drag Malachi aside to ask him a personal question.

'I know you can see into our future. I need to know that… that…' I'm unsure of how to word my question.

'I know what you want to ask. Maybe we should head up

to your bedroom where there aren't so many eyes around.' He smiles his angelic smile.

Oh boy, he is one amazingly handsome man. I'm glad Lazarus hasn't arrived as my heart is ricocheting around my chest. 'Many a woman would love to hear those words come out of your mouth.'

He smiles, then nods at Gabby. She returns the nod without a single word.

He shuts the door once we are inside my bedroom and stands confidently in front of me. 'You must ask me what you want.' He moves so there are only a few feet between us.

'Will Lazarus and I be able to have children?'

'There are many elite creature and human relationships where children are conceived. A dragon and a human… I have never met one but that doesn't mean they don't exist.'

'You know my future, Malachi. Can't you just tell me?'

'We can't tell you your future. If I tell you or show you, you can then change the proceedings up to it, changing your life's path. This journey is already decided for you and should not be interfered with.'

'Both Lazarus and I want children. If I can't carry his child, he should be with someone who can, so the dragon race can continue to exist.'

'If Laz doesn't father a child, dragons will still exist. There are plenty of dragons that will reproduce.' He rubs his chin and narrows his eyes. 'Does it worry you that much?'

'It's all I can think of when I'm not crying over my mother.'

'I will help you, but only this once. You must never ask me to look into your future again. When I show you, you must not see past anything other than the answer to this question.'

'I promise. What do I have to do?'

'Hold onto me for balance and close your eyes.'

I move closer and place my hands on his large biceps. He

pulls me in even closer, pushing my arms so they wrap around his taut waist. My stomach and chest are firmly against his. 'Now think only of that one question. What is your question, Jasmine?'

'Will I be able to have children with Lazarus?' I blink up into his hypnotic eyes.

'Remember, that is the only question to search for and when you have your answer open your eyes. Do you understand and promise to do that?'

'Yes.'

'Close your eyes and open your mouth wide.' He leans close so our mouths are several small centimetres away. I can feel his breath on my lips. 'Exhale all the air out of your lungs and when you breathe in, make it slow and concentrate on your question.'

I close my eyes and feel my heart pounding in my chest. I open my mouth wide. I exhale, forcing all the air from my lungs, then I slowly breathe in.

I taste the sweetest taste on my tongue. I flick my eyes open to see a white foggy light coming out of Malachi's mouth into mine. I snap my eyes shut and concentrate on the one question. *Will I be able to have children with Lazarus?*

Like a television being switched on, I see Lazarus playing with a small child, a boy aged about two. I can hear him asking the little boy where Mummy is, and then I see me, with the small boy running over with his arms stretched wide. My question has been answered.

I am about to flick my eyes open but decide to ask another question. *Will we be safe in England?*

A vision flashes before me. There's a dark-haired man down on one knee, placing a ring on my finger. He is asking me to marry him and I agree. I try to see his face but it's a blur. He embraces me before kissing me. I gasp and flick my eyes open and as I do my bedroom door flies open with Lazarus standing angrily before us.

'Someone needs to explain to me what is going on! And now!' Lazarus' voice makes the walls of my room vibrate.

He's glowing red, his body radiating a fierce heat. His chest is rising and falling at a massive speed and I fear he may do something to Malachi before I can explain.

'This not for me to explain,' Malachi says calmly. He looks down to me before continuing, 'You asked two questions. The first question answered the second one if you took the time the think about it. I trusted you to ask one question.' He drops his arms from around my waist and steps back. 'If you will excuse me.' He slowly walks towards the door and the outraged dragon.

'Well someone better answer me and quickly or I will be ripping heads off,' snarls Lazarus.

'It's not what you think, Laz, so please let Malachi pass and you and I can talk.' I keep calm, trying to extinguish the fire burning inside my fiancé.

Lazarus begrudgingly steps to the side of the door, allowing Malachi to exit.

'I'm sorry, Malachi,' I whisper, feeling ashamed for abusing his trust. He leaves without a word.

Lazarus slams the door shut and stalks around me like I am his prey. The heat radiating from his body is intense and his heart is beating out of control.

'Can you stop stalking me and sit down?'

'What am I to think when you're in the arms of the man who makes your heart race? And your mouths were locked together!'

'Our mouths were not locked together.'

In a blink he has his arms around me, drawing in a nostril full, taking in my scent. 'I can smell him all over you!' Then he kisses me. 'I can taste him on your tongue!'

'I didn't kiss him. I asked him to show me our future.'

'You did what? Why on Earth would you interfere with our future?'

'I was scared.'

'Of what?'

'I was scared I wouldn't be enough for you. That I wouldn't be able to give you children.'

'I would love to have children with you but if it's not meant to be… I just want you.' He calms and leans forward to kiss my lips. I instantly feel his temperature cool, along with his temper. 'Don't ever ask the angels to show you the future. It alters everything. Just answer me this—are you happy with what you saw?'

'Yes, very.' I smile and slowly his lips curve up into a huge grin.

'I don't want to know anymore. But promise me never to ask the angels to do that again. Apart from altering the future, it takes five years off an angel's life for every question asked.'

'What? No! Malachi never mentioned that to me. I asked two questions. That's ten years off his life!' I start to pace the room. 'I'm such a stupid idiot!' Why on Earth didn't Malachi tell me? What have I done to him?'

'I hope the second question was worth it.'

'No, it wasn't. It confused me.'

'Speaking of confused, why would you think I would let Ash come on our trip?'

'He asked me and I fobbed him off. I told him to ask you. I don't care one way or another.' I shrug my shoulders, feeling like a black sorceress after what I did to Malachi.

'I said he could come along as another set of eyes and ears wouldn't hurt.'

I spin around and frown. 'You said yes to Ash?'

Lazarus nods and shrugs his shoulders.

'I will remind you that it was *your* idea to let him come. Especially when you are about to rip his head off his shoulders.'

'And I'm guessing you will remind me of this on our flight over because Ash loves to make my blood boil.' He sniggers then inhales my scent, narrowing his eyes and frowning, still unhappy with finding me in Malachi's arms.

Chapter Two

I sleep the whole flight over due to the exhausting arguments I had with the gargoyles and dragons about going to England. The walls of Elyograg Castle had vibrated with Jet screaming at Lazarus for even suggesting that I leave the sanctuary of Australia.

There was no fanfare when we left, just a gloomy castle with angry-looking creatures stalking its exterior.

Lazarus walks confidently around the airport and on the overly-crowded streets of England. It surprises me due to his inability to control himself. He believes being around me has quenched his appetite for humans; forgoing the peppermint oil he normally shoves under his nose masking their scent.

But that's not so for Ash. I can see he is uncomfortable around so many humans. His personality has shrunk, with his posture stooping over, trying to shrink his six-foot frame so as not be noticed. He walks one foot behind me, keeping his eyes on the ground.

A cold shiver floods over my skin, making the hairs on my body stand to attention. I know I'm not scared of humans but something about being here makes me uneasy.

We pick up a hire car and drive through the stunning English countryside for what seems like days.

As soon as Lazarus announces we have arrived, Ash relaxes and grows two feet taller. He is at home amongst the vast pastures, large castles and fewer humans.

There are three large castles close to each other, all sitting beside a fast running river.

Lazarus leads us towards the furthest of the castles. There is no one to be seen except several gargoyles sitting in stone sleep on the roof.

'Are they gargoyles or concrete?' I ask.

Lazarus laughs. 'It's a bit hard to tell the difference.'

'Watch it, leather guts,' snarls Ash. 'They are gargoyles, Jazz. And they are watching us very intently. I can feel their eyes scanning us and not in a good way.' He slowly scans the castle roof then drops his eyes down the walls as if looking for someone. 'You did notify your parents that we were coming, didn't you, lizard?'

'What was I supposed to do? Ring them and let all of England know we are travelling here? It took all the strength Jasmine had to keep the cloaking spell over us for this long. I wasn't going to risk exposing us by contacting my parents over the phone or by any other means of communication.'

'Don't they have dingoes or an elite grapevine?' I ask.

'No, babe. We're extremely lucky to have elite dingoes in Australia,' Lazarus says.

'So they don't know we are coming?' I gasp. 'Do they know that we are going to be married?'

'They will be delighted that we are getting married.'

Ash burst into laughter. 'You're in it deep now, cow breath.'

'Shut up, Ash. They will be ecstatic when they hear of our engagement.' He moves quickly to my side and holds my hands in his. 'They are down in the cave, below the castle. I will go down to them, alone.'

'Why can't I come with you?' I ask.

'Because they'll probably take a bite out of you,' interrupts Ash, laughing.

'Ash, I'm warning you,' he snarls.

'I'm joking. Why on Earth would a hungry dragon want to eat a deliciously juicy human like our Jasmine?'

'Ash!' He growls through a puff of smoke.

'Okay, Puff the Magic Dragon, I'm going. I should introduce myself to the relatives on the roof and check if there are any hot babes up there. Plus, I need to reboot my system.'

I had only just noticed that his skin was changing to a pale grey. He moves quickly to the castle and in a few short seconds has changed form and is climbing its sheer walls.

'Come inside the castle and make yourself comfortable, babe.' Lazarus tugs my arm towards the large front door.

'I understand that you couldn't contact your parents, but I feel uncomfortable about this.'

He gives me a sheepish look and opens the front door.

We step inside and it is stunning. Every arched window is filled with stained glass, shooting an array of colour around the large entry and sitting room. There are large red curtains draping the windows. The furniture is old and well worn, giving the castle a warm, welcoming feel. 'I'm fine, Laz. Go say hello to your folks.'

'I won't be long, babe.' He smiles and leans forward to kiss me before heading off through a set of large doors.

As soon as he leaves, I flush cold and the uneasy feeling returns.

I slowly walk around the room, drawing in the aroma of the house. I'm hit by a nostril-full of a dozen souls. There must be several different breeds of elite creatures living here, as the mixed scent is burning my nose.

I shut my sense of smell down but heighten all my other senses just to be safe.

I stroll the large room and notice that there are no photos on walls or dressers. It suddenly occurs to me that there aren't any photos at home or in Elyograg Castle. How odd!

I stand still in the enormous sitting room, holding my arms

around myself, feeling as though I am being watched. I listen intently and switch my senses to full alert.

There is a smell I recognise… Drake mixed with Lysander and Jarius. I am lifted off my feet, with a large set of wings encasing me. I'm drawn to the chest of a gargoyle with my arms still tightly wrapped around myself.

I struggle against its wings and realise if I get my hands free, I won't be able to conjure up an anoric as my feet are off the ground. I need the earth to draw from.

I stop struggling and notice that the creature is not moving, just holding me still and off the ground.

'Hello, Jasmine. It has been a long time. I recognised your scent as soon as you crossed the threshold. Your cloaking spell has worn off.' The gargoyle inhales me before continuing. 'You have strong sorcery powers, just like your mother. I can smell them. But you have added powers, which have not all been given to you freely. My sweet Jasmine, you have killed.'

'Please put me down.'

'So you can put a hole in me?' The creature chuckles.

'I promise I won't.'

'I'd be disappointed if you didn't try. Let me introduce myself before I put you down.' He spins me around in his oversized arms and wings. He stares his bright blue eyes down at me. His teeth are sharp, with several of them sticking out of his large mouth. 'Don't you recognise my scent?'

'A small part of your scent smells like someone I used to know.'

'Used to know?'

'He was someone I loved… well, I still love him, but he died in my arms, saving my life.'

The gargoyle slowly drops me to the ground, his posture vulnerable. 'My son is dead?'

'Drake is your son?'

He nods.

'You're Hudson?'

'Tell me what happened. Is the rest of my family alive?'

I sit in a chair closest to me while Hudson changes form. He is a strikingly good-looking man and I instantly see the resemblance to his sons.

'Hudson?' I whisper and he nods. 'Everyone at Elyograg Castle is frantic about where you are. Some have predicted you've been taken by the rebels or worse, that you're dead!'

'There is more going on over here than just the battle between the dragons and gargoyles. Many of us elite creatures have banded together, staying hidden amongst these three castles. I couldn't take the risk of contacting anyone in Australia in case I exposed our whereabouts.'

'My mother told me that she and you had a relationship, but you never changed form, which made it difficult. But you just changed form in front of me.'

'We found our way around it. There were other factors that interfered with our lives that made it impossible to be together. But she is happy living a human lifestyle with your father.'

'My mother died in the fight with the rebels. She shape-shifted into an amazing wedge-tailed eagle and was hit by a dark sorcerer's anoric. She died beside me.' An elusive tear trickles down my cheek.

I look up and see his eyes filling with tears. 'She went to such long lengths to keep that side of her life hidden. Why would she reveal herself after all these years? It makes little sense.'

'To watch over me. If I had known her life was in danger, I'd...' My words stick in my throat.

'My other two sons and my wife, are they alive?'

'Lysander, Jarius and Demona are all well. My cousin

Raven, Sky, also passed away but before she did, she had a child with your son, Lysander. You have an amazing grandson, Jet. He has the strength of two gargoyles and soon his powers will match mine. He took Drake's soul when he was born which has made him into a remarkable creature.'

'I have a grandson who is a hybrid?'

'Yes, you have a fine grandson. Who is very overprotective of me.' I shake my head, remembering his tantrum before I left.

'Who is the young gargoyle climbing over the roof of my castle?'

'That is Ash. He is a relative of yours who came to help fight the rebels back home.'

'And you are in a relationship with him?'

'No, Hudson. I am engaged to Lazarus.'

'No! You can't be with a dragon! It's not your destiny. I will not allow it!'

'Sorry to burst your bubble, but I am and will marry Lazarus. You have no say in the matter.'

'Does your father know of your decision to marry a dragon?'

'My father? Why does his opinion matter to you?'

'Both your mother and father went to great lengths to keep you and their sorcery hidden.'

'What do you mean "their sorcery"?'

'Hudson, you've said enough!' Lazarus bellows from behind me.

I hadn't felt his presence as I had been too engrossed in what Hudson was saying. I flick my head around to see Lazarus standing with two people who I presume are his parents.

'Her father would never let this union happen,' says Hudson.

'He and I have spoken. And he is more than happy for us to be—' Lazarus argues.

I interrupt him. 'Answer me, Hudson. What do you mean "their sorcery"?'

'It's not your place, Hudson,' Lazarus' father says with a deep, threatening tone.

'Don't give me the line where "a creature has to reveal itself to me" crap! Tell me or I'll…' My palms start to heat and I feel a small anoric swirling at the tip of my fingers.

'How dare you threaten a creature in our castle?' snaps Lazarus' mother.

'Jazz, you need to calm down and remember where you are. The creatures here don't understand that your threat is harmless.' Lazarus comes to stand beside me.

'You need to put a leash on your little witch, Lazarus darling.' I spin around to see a stunning young woman step out from behind his parents. I inhale her scent and smell Lazarus' scent on her. She smirks.

'Oh, bite me, dragon!' I snarl.

'Well, if you insist!' She licks her rosy lips.

Ash appears in gargoyle form. 'Move one muscle towards her and I will rip your head off your shoulders, as beautiful as it is.' Behind him are another six gargoyles with eyes glowing bright blue. 'Having a problem with the in-laws, Jazz? It's never too late to switch sides. I'm always available.'

'Not now, Ash!' snaps Lazarus.

'Oh, lighten up people. Is this how you welcome all your guests?' Ash smiles at them, his sharp teeth poking out of his mouth.

'Guests are invited. She is not a guest, hence not invited,' says the pretty dragon.

'This is my fiancée, Keira. I'd appreciate you showing her some respect,' Lazarus says.

'Respect! When she openly holds an anoric in both hands! Huh!'

I glance down at my hands. They are shimmering with white swirls. Embarrassed that I'd forgotten they were still brewing, I clench my fists, extinguishing them, my cheeks reddening.

I shoot a look at Hudson, whose eyes slowly lift from my clenched hands.

'I apologise for… I didn't realise…' I'm ashamed I didn't realise my body was automatically protecting itself with live ammo.

'As I said before, you have powers you've yet to tap into. You can't uncover them or learn to control them living with a dragon. Dragons have hot tempers and you need to keep a cool head.' Hudson holds firm eye contact with me.

'Hmm, I can guarantee we dragons are hot. Isn't that right, Lazarus darling?' Keira purrs.

I spin my head around to glare at him. 'God help me, Laz, shut her up!'

Lazarus moves like lightning to slip his heated arm firmly around my waist.

'Hudson, it's great to see you again. It is unfortunate that you're not happy with our news as I have always valued your opinion in all situations. But you are wrong when it comes to Jasmine and me. We are inked and will be married with or without your blessing. It is my parents who we came to seek a blessing from.'

'Ray and Loretta, do you give your blessing?' Hudson asks.

'I think we need start all over again.' Loretta says, moving cautiously with her hand held out. 'I'm Loretta. Welcome to our home.'

Lazarus takes one small step backwards while Ash moves several steps closer.

Loretta smiles and my senses tell me her welcome is legitimate. I return the smile and open my arms as if to embrace her.

I hold my breath, hoping she doesn't reject me after my

uncontrolled display of anger. Her movements are slow; uncharacteristic for a dragon. I presume she does not want to alarm me with her quick actions.

'G'day Loretta, I'm Jasmine, your son's fiancée.' She pulls me in for a hug. Thankfully, it's a warm and genuine embrace.

She slowly pulls back and for the first time, I notice her green slit eyes. I tilt my head, taking in her features, noticing they are similar to Lazarus'. She smiles, standing still for my appraisal.

'And I'm Ray.' I jump, not noticing he had moved to one side of Loretta. 'Sorry, I didn't mean to startle you. It's rare that we have humans here and I forget to move slower.'

'Not a problem. Laz often forgets or does it to amuse himself.' I move to embrace Ray. He kisses my cheek, his lips hot on my skin. I take in his features and realise that Lazarus looks more like his mother than his father.

'And this is Keira. She has been living under our protection since her family were murdered several months ago. She grew up with Lazarus before he left for Australia.'

'Yes, we were inseparable and such a cute couple,' Keira purrs. I feel my hands heat with jealousy and grit my teeth, trying to think of something other than blowing a hole through her.

'You must be tired after such a long trip. Let me show you to your room, Jasmine,' Loretta says, gripping my hands in hers and squeezing them to gain my attention. I pull my eyes away from the beautiful dragon to find her calm gaze. She blinks then squeezes my hands again as if signalling me to ignore Keira. I take a deep breath and do so, smiling at her.

'Thank you, but I would like to speak to Hudson in private.'

'Why don't you freshen up and I will visit you in an hour.' Hudson smiles.

'Great idea, Jazz. Go put your feet up and then while you're

safely locked in your room, I can reboot, ready for round two,'
Ash adds, giving a wink and a reassuring nod.

I return the nod and do as everyone suggests but not before glaring at Keira on the way past.

Loretta politely shows me into an enormous room—one end being the bedroom and the other a sitting room. She gracefully leaves me and Lazarus, kissing her son's cheek before departing.

'Well, that seemed to go down well,' he says with narrowed eyes.

I can't tell if he is disappointed with me or angry, so I decide to turn the tables on him before he can start on my behaviour. 'Who is Keira?'

'My mother explained who she is.'

'You forget I can smell your scent. Especially when it's wrapped around another woman.'

He wraps me tightly in his arms, my hands pinned behind my back with his. Our bodies are pulled tightly together.

His body heats up. Oh boy, he's angry. Luckily, I find him very sexy when he's angry. 'I leave you for five minutes and you nearly start a war between the elite.'

'You left me for five minutes to spread your scent over another woman.'

'You're being jealous and I don't like it.'

'You're deflecting from what you did.'

'What I did was hug a woman I grew up with. A woman who has just lost her parents!'

'Who happens to be beautiful and obviously attracted to you. Be careful in your reply, Lazarus. Remember I can hear your heart if it skips a beat for her.'

'You're being ridiculous! Yes, she's beautiful but there's been nothing between…' He stops mid-sentence.

I listen intently to his heartbeat. It fails him and skips a beat. I draw small angry energy from the ground and zap him.

'Ouch!' He jumps back, letting my wrists free from his hold.

'How beautiful, Lazarus?'

'We were together many years ago, for a short time only. We decided we were better suited as friends than—'

'Than what? Lovers?'

He runs his hands through his hair, blowing out an exasperated breath. 'I never loved her as I do you. She was a part of my life growing up, that's all. She is in the past.'

'Looks like your past just caught up with you.' I walk towards the door, not sure where to run to.

Before I can reach out for the door handle, Lazarus is leaning up against it, stopping me from leaving.

'I thought I was the jealous one. It's you I'm marrying.' His fingers tilt my chin up so I am looking up at him. 'I am in love with you, witch.'

'I have a bad feeling about being here. I think we should cut our visit short and leave by the end of the week. I don't feel in control here.'

'I agree. As much as this used to be my home, I feel the unease amongst the elite creatures. Make sure you're with me or Ash at all times, just to be safe.'

I slip my hand up and uncover the left side of his chest. I want to check to see if Keira's name has appeared, inked over his heart like mine is.

Lazarus grabs my hand and squeezes it. 'I'm hurt you don't believe me when I say she means nothing. My markings, or tattoos, as you humans call them, are not done by a vibrating needle, but come from within us. Our soul imprints our life's mate over our heart. It can never be removed.'

'I'm sorry, it's just… I'm jealous knowing…' I can't finish my sentence and my face heats with embarrassment.

He loosens the grip on my hand. 'When I was jealous about

your ex-boyfriend I burnt his car.' He shrugs his shoulders and I can see the corners of his mouth curving up into a cheeky smile.

'And the garage it was sitting in.'

He pulls his shirt to the side, revealing the ink over his heart. There are two dragons in the shape of the yin-yang symbol with my name delicately written amongst it.

'I have another marking wrapped around my bicep and I'm more than happy to strip down naked so you can scan me for any other markings. Actually, I definitely think I need to strip naked for your appraisal.' His voice is low and husky.

'Keep your clothes on or I'll do more than appraise, babe. Hudson will be here soon and I don't want him walking in on us making love.'

'You forget that I'm a dragon and can move very quickly.'

'As tempting as your offer is, I'd rather make love to you slowly and romantically, not like Speedy Gonzales.'

'Are you calling me a mouse? Wow, talk about an ego crusher.' He chuckles, scoops me up into his arms and puts me on the edge of the bed. He stops laughing and a serious look floods his face. 'I love you, babe. No creature will ever come between us. We're inked.'

He gently lays me down on the bed, leans down and places his heated lips on mine. His kiss is soft but passionate, just the way I like it.

Hudson arrives exactly an hour from when he said and thankfully in human form. He has a young woman, who I presume is the clan's chef, bring up coffee and cake.

He paces the room until Lazarus excuses himself to go hunting with his parents.

Before Lazarus leaves, I hear him telling Ash to keep close

by me. I laugh when I hear him plonk himself outside my bedroom door in full gargoyle form. I must admit I feel calmer knowing he is close by when Lazarus is off hunting.

'Please sit, Hudson. Your pacing is making me dizzy.'

'I'm sorry, but your father should have never accepted your union with a dragon.' He moves so he is sitting close. 'Use your silence spell. There are too many ears listening in on our conversation.'

'I can feel every creature holding their breath so as not to miss a word we say,' I add. I lift my hand, which is holding my imaginary crayon, and draw a rainbow over both of us.

'You are stronger than your parents and I predicted, especially if you can feel all these creatures' senses,' he says.

'What did you mean by both my parents having sorcery powers?'

'You are so like your mother—straight to the point.'

'You haven't seen my mother in years. How would you know?'

'I'm in contact with both your parents and have been since long before you were born.'

'I've never seen you before.'

'Just because you've never seen me doesn't mean I'm not around. Your mother was a shape-shifter and you never knew, and she lived under the same roof as you did.

'I watched you grow up under a protective spell. It kept you hidden from any creature that searched for you. A protective spell was cast over you by Australia's strongest sorcerer.'

'My grandfather?'

'No, Jasmine, not your grandfather. Your father.'

'My father has basic sorcery powers. My mother is the sorceress and shape-shifter and that's where I get it from.'

'There is a mixture of creature bloodlines that run through your family. Your grandparents on your mother's side are shape-shifters, sorcerers and I also believe you have links to gargoyles.

'Your father's side is pure sorcery. Both his parents were talented witches, and when they united, were labelled as the strongest pair in history.'

'My father?' I'm unable to process why my father hid this important information from me. 'Why would he lie?'

'He didn't lie to you, Jasmine. He was protecting you.' Hudson leans forward and takes my hand in his. 'When you and Sky were young it took every bit of your grandparents' energy to keep your identity hidden from those who wanted to kidnap you both. Together, you would be unstoppable.

'When Sky went missing, we presumed she was taken by dark sorcery and we had to protect and hide our greatest weapon—you!'

'Me?'

'Yes, you. Your father took over the spell your grandfather created that protected you from creatures outside our clan. It allowed a few chosen creatures to see you and blocked all others. With Paul's help, they couldn't locate you as the spell was created and held by your father, the strongest sorcerer alive.

'Somehow you stumbled back into our world, breaking your father's spell.'

'Have I taken my father's powers?'

'No, sweet girl, you haven't harmed your father in any way. He promised his parents, on their deathbed, that he would only use his powers to protect his only daughter. Your father is a good man and will never break his promise.'

'You speak as though you and he are great friends.'

'We were both in love with the same woman.' Hudson releases my hand. 'Your mother would always have been in danger being with me. Your father was the best person to keep her protected. I did the honourable thing and stepped aside. He was, in her case, the better man.

'Your father knew of my feelings towards her and respected me for stepping aside. That respect turned into a loyal friendship between us.'

'If you respect my father, as you state you do, respect his decision to allow Lazarus to marry me.'

'A dragon is not a good partner for a strong sorceress like you. He will be your undoing.'

'You're wrong! We are inked; our souls are joined forever,' I say, gritting my teeth in defence.

'Time will prove one of us wrong. I pray you are right as I wish you nothing but happiness for your life.'

'You'll see. We are meant to be together.'

'You haven't tapped into half of what you can do.'

'Can I shape-shift like my mother?'

'Yes, of course. Don't tell me you haven't tried yet?'

His wide smile slowly takes over his face. I think this is the first time I've seen it. 'There is one particular creature you can change into easily, as it's floating around in your blood. And I bet your fiancé will be… amused. Well, maybe horrified when he sees it.' He breaks into a boisterous laugh. 'How long do we have before your dragon returns?'

'His name is Lazarus and he will be…' I quickly remove my silence spell and listen for his heartbeat. I fight through several other excited beats, finally finding his. 'He will be some time yet. He has just found his prey. Why do you ask?'

'I can help you to change form if you would like to try it.' Hudson stands up and holds out his hand.

'Will I be able to change back?'

'You will. Do you trust me, Jasmine?'

'Yes, but I'm curious to know what I will change into.'

His face cracks a large smile, showing me his white teeth. 'The mightiest creature that roams the Earth.' He chuckles and puffs his chest out. 'Do as I say. Now close your eyes.'

I stand up and follow his instructions. 'I better not turn into a spider or some creepy critter.'

'Trust me. Open your mind to all the colours of the earth, similar to when you draw on your anorics, but push that colour away. I don't want to be blown up today.' He sniggers, making me relax slightly. 'Imagine a gargoyle standing at its full height.'

'A gargoyle!'

'Concentrate or you will shape-shift into a creepy critter.' He squeezes my hand.

I draw my mind back so I am picturing Drake standing tall and strong in front of me.

'Good girl. Now blow out all the air in your lungs, emptying them completely. When you draw in, make it long and slow and pull in the Earth's rocks, the Earth's blood and the Earth's strength. Don't question, just do.'

Keeping Drake's strong gargoyle frame in the front of my mind, I draw my breath in, pulling with it the Earth's rocks and boulders. I see Drake's frame filling like his body is a puzzle and the pieces are slotting into place. My body and skin feel as though it's been stretched and starts to tighten uncomfortably.

I search the Earth for what Hudson describes as blood and strength. As soon as I ask for it, I feel a cold trickle running into my toes, up my legs, through my torso. It continues down my arms and finally fills my face. The vision I have of Drake disappears and I blink my eyes open to see Hudson's shocked face.

'Holy moly! You are a lot bigger than I predicted. What gargoyle did you picture?'

'Your son, Drake.'

'Well, that explains it. Most shifters change to a smaller size creature but you, my dear girl, have doubled your size. Remarkable!'

'What? I don't want to be double my size! What woman in their right mind wants to be bigger? We all want to be smaller when stepping on the scales!'

Hudson laughs and runs his hands through his silver hair. 'You're remarkable! It only took you thirty seconds to change form. Imagine with practice how quick you can change. Tell me, did you find it easy searching for the right tools? Did the Earth give freely to form this elite creature?'

'It was easy. I did exactly as you said. I found everything I needed lying at my feet.'

'No pain?'

'No, should there be?' I panic, wondering if there is pain still to come.

'There is for some creatures but obviously not for you. Your mother could only change into an eagle without pain, hence she stuck to that.'

I look down at my body and legs, then hold out my arms. 'I'm naked!'

Hudson lets out another boisterous laugh. 'As you know, gargoyles display no genitalia in this form.'

'What happens when I change back into human form? Am I going to be naked in front of everyone?'

'When you draw down into your human form, make sure you imagine yourself with your clothes on and you will appear that way. If you appear naked, it's because you forgot to dress. It might be wise to transform in private the first few times, just in case. Why don't you try your wings out and get the feel of being a gargoyle?'

I lift my hand to my mouth, embarrassed about the

conversation I'm having, when I feel a set of large teeth protruding from my mouth.

'Whoa!' I jump back in fright and my wings automatically spread wide open, sending all the cups, plates, chairs and tables flying across the room with a loud crashing sound.

The bedroom door flies open with Ash bolting inside, still in his gargoyle form. 'What the hell is going on?' He roars with his chest puffed out.

'Nothing is going on. I presume you are Ash, Jasmine's friend.' Hudson still has a huge grin plastered on his face.

'I am. You best tell me where she is before I break you in two.' Ash takes an aggressive step towards him.

'Calm down, Ash,' I say, trying to pull my large wings in against my solid body.

His head spins around then tilts in a questioning motion before he moves in my direction.

'Say that again.' He eyes me up and down.

'I said calm down, Ash.'

'Jasmine?' He moves close enough to reach out and touch my arm, running his fingers down to take hold of my hand. 'If lizard-guts could see you now.' He bursts out in laughter.

I squeeze his hand hard.

'Ouch! Yep, that's definitely my Jasmine.'

'This is her first time changing form. I wanted her first shifter-change to be a gargoyle.' Hudson says as he walks around me, passing his eyes over me. 'She can choose many forms in which to change into, unlike us.'

'Trust me, I'm enjoying this form. You rock the gargoyle look, no pun intended.'

'I feel clumsy and…' I suddenly realise I may offend the two gargoyles before me.

'And what, Jazz? Ugly?' Ash asks. I don't answer before he continues, 'You're a lot bigger than I thought you'd be.'

'Gee, make a girl feel good!' I shake my oversized head.

'Coming from a gargoyle, it's a compliment. How about we test-drive those wings and glide around for a while?' Ash nudges me with his rock-solid arms.

'What if someone sees me?'

'Are you ashamed of being a gargoyle?'

I look into Ash's eyes and am careful in choosing my words. 'No, Ash, I'm not ashamed to be a gargoyle. I'm worried that everyone will understand the volume of my powers.'

'You look nothing like your human form which is the bonus of being a sorceress. Look in the mirror over there but remember to keep your wings in check.' Hudson points to a full-length framed mirror which is leaning up against the wall.

'It might be an idea to walk behind her, Ash, in case she gets a shock seeing herself for the first time.'

As I walk over I'm careful to not break any of the remaining furniture.

Ash's cool hands clasp around my wings as I approach the mirror. I try with all my might not to yell out in shock or pull a disgusted face as I don't want to hurt either of their feelings, but it's a dismal failure. If it wasn't for Ash holding me, I would have smashed the room to pieces with my wings flying out in despair.

I am a huge lump of rock! I don't recognise myself in this creature, except my eyes—they are the same colour but have the trademark gargoyle glow.

After taking a good long look at my form, my eyes catch hold of Ash's. I can see I have hurt his feelings by being disgusted by my form.

'I'm sorry, Ash. I hate being anything more than a size ten. It has nothing to do with being a creature.'

'How about that glide?' He tries to cover his disappointment.

'It would be a good idea to learn everything you can about any creature you change into but stay close to the castles. And limit the time you're in this form. Being your first time, you will tire quicker than normal.'

'How will I know what to do?'

'Your elite instinct will cut in. I can come along if you wish but I'm sure Ash can show you everything you need to know.'

'I'll be your wingman. Let's hit the rooftops.' Ash flicks his eyebrows several times with the largest smile I've seen on his face.

As I STAND at the bottom of the castle looking up the straight and long wall, my stomach rolls upside-down.

Ash instructs me to concentrate on gripping onto the castle wall, grabbing any protruding brick, ledge, window or frame. He stays beside me all the way up.

I notice out the corner of my eye that he has one of his wings open underneath me. He doesn't have the confidence in my climbing ability he had expressed at the start.

I blow out a sigh of relief when I stand on top of the castle. We creep to the edge of the roof and open our wings. I feel the soft breeze fill them, gently trying to pull me back, but my rock-solid legs keep me grounded.

I look down at the ground and feel like I'm jumping to my death. 'I can't do this. What if my wings can't hold my heavy weight?'

'Do you think I would let you do this if there was any chance of you getting hurt? Gee, it took me this long to get you to look like me. I'm not losing you now, beautiful.'

'I can't do it. Maybe another day.' I quiver, staring down at the rocky ground. 'What if I fall?'

'Oh, but beautiful, what if you fly?'

He's right. If I can fly what else can I do?

'Do you trust me, Jasmine?'

'Yes, but—'

'Do you really trust me?'

I look up into his glowing blue eyes. 'With my life.'

'Good.' He smiles before pushing me off the top of the castle with his outstretched wing.

I don't have time to scream or yell abuse because I am gliding like an eagle over the top of the castle. Ash glides next to me with a grin that should have cracked his hard rock face.

'Looking good, blue eyes.' He smiles and gives me a wink. 'Curve your right wing slightly and roll under the same shoulder. Like this.'

I watch him as he glides to the right. I do as he says and drift to the right.

'Now push down both wings like you're going to clap your hands but stop at about your body's width then pull them back up above your head. Like squeezing your shoulder blades together.'

I do and let out a small squeal of fright when I shoot up a metre higher into the sky. Ash laughs and I can see he is enjoying showing me this new world of his. He keeps close to me at all times, directing me to turn left and right or up and down until my feet are firmly back on the ground.

As I land, I notice Lazarus in dragon form with several other dragons. I presume they're his parents and probably Keira.

Ash walks over to me, happy with himself.

'I told you to trust me.' He beams. I swing my large right rock hand and connect it with his jaw. Smack! 'What was that for?'

'You pushed me off the top of a castle. Never do that again.'

I rub my fist, surprised it doesn't hurt. I look over to Lazarus and he is staring his bright green eyes at me. His head is tilted slightly. I can see he is struggling to work out if it is me or not.

One of the other dragons walks over to him and nuzzles him as a horse would do. I feel my frame increase in size, my chest puffs out and my wings fly open in a defensive stance. Lazarus raises his head and his eyes widen when he realises it is me. He flicks off the other dragon with a powerful bump of his neck before billowing a mouthful of flames into the air.

'Jasmine, I think it's time for you to change form. You've been out here gliding for over an hour. By the look on his face, I'd prefer you in your sorcery form to deal with his temper.' Ash forces my wings down and closes them into my body.

'It looks like he has been too preoccupied with that dragon to worry about what I've been up to!'

'Since when have you been the jealous type?' he whispers. I nudge him hard in his stomach. 'Ouch! I think I want you in your human form before you break me in two.'

I take off, leaving both the dragon and gargoyle behind to find no one in my room when I return. I lock the door and pace the room, trying to remember Hudson's instructions on how to turn back. It doesn't take me long to figure it out and, in seconds, I am standing in my original form but only partially dressed. I am standing in my underwear which I now realised was what I was picturing. I must remember to concentrate on the outer garments instead of the minor factor of the undergarments.

Moments after changing form I hear the door handle being turned then a loud banging on the door.

'Open this bloody door, Jasmine!' yells Lazarus.

'Give me a minute.' I don't know who's with him and want to put clothes on.

'No!' The door flies open and there stands a furious man. 'Where are your bloody clothes?' His growling voice sends a chill over me.

He is beyond angry. His eyes are changing to a fiery red and his stance is ready to pounce. I've seen him like this before, ready to attack, and it didn't turn out well. I decide the best thing to do is to calm him down before I question him over hunting with Keira.

'I locked the door so I could get changed. As you have just mentioned, I am in my underwear, so could you please close the door.'

He slams the door shut and, in a blink, is standing in front of me, breathing steaming hot air over me. I see his eyes dart from side to side. He is checking to see if anyone else is in the room.

'Do you really think I'd lock the door with someone in here other than you?'

'I don't know what to think anymore.' He puffs a lungful of smoke in my face.

'What?' I know he is angry, over what I don't know, but my veins are beginning to bubble. This will not end well. 'You better calm down or we will have a problem.'

'Dragons don't take to kindly to threats,' he says, exaggerating the 's'.

'Nor do powerful sorceresses.'

I drift away from him and pick up my clothes. In slow movements, I slip on my jeans and t-shirt, conscious not to make any sudden moves. Even though he is in human form when he is this wound up, he can accidentally hurt me.

'I'm going for a walk outside until you calm down.' I go to move but within a second he is in front of me, glaring down fiercely at me.

'You're not going anywhere.' I notice that several of his teeth have changed and are becoming razor sharp.

I contemplate giving him an electric shock to snap him out of this mood but fear it may enrage him more and I may not walk away with my head intact.

'Okay, Lazarus, I'll stay here with you. What would you like me to do?'

'Not change into a hideous bloody gargoyle would be a good start,' he spits. 'The first creature you change into is a gargoyle! How do you think that makes me feel? And how do you think it looks to my parents if I can't control you?'

My veins fill with white electric energy. I clench my fists together, forcing back the anger building inside of me. 'Control me! Neither you nor any man will ever control me! Get out of here before—'

'Don't you dare threaten me. I can see you glowing white, witch!'

Lazarus lunges forward, grabbing both my arms, holding them down by my sides. I feel his anger burning into my skin, enraging me further. I try to stop before it builds, but our energies connect and explode.

With a violent jolt, we're flung backwards in different directions. My back hits the wall with brutal force before I drop unceremoniously to the ground. The air's been knocked out of my lungs, making it hard to catch my breath.

Hudson bursts through the door, with Ash two feet behind, still in gargoyle form.

'You!' Lazarus yells at Hudson as he gets to his feet. 'This is entirely your fault!'

I try to speak but my lungs refuse to give me the air I need. I tremble, fearing that my back may be broken. My gasps for air are panicked and I feel the room spin.

'Ash, keep your eyes on him and protect my back.' Hudson says pointing to Lazarus. 'This is why you shouldn't be in her life, dragon. You will kill her.'

'If you hadn't changed her into a gargoyle this would never have happened. Get your hands off her.'

The last thing I see as I'm lifted into Hudson's arms is Ash holding Lazarus down and the familiar red particles as he changes into his dragon form. I have no time to fear what Lazarus will do to Ash as I black out.

CHAPTER THREE

I blink several times before focusing on a pair of green slit eyes.

'There you are. Welcome back, Jasmine.' Loretta's smile is warm and friendly. 'You had us worried for a while. Your heart-beat was erratic and unbalanced. How do you feel, darling?'

I inhale a deep breath and am rewarded with a sharp pain in my back. I cringe and groan.

'You hit the wall hard, my dear, as did my son.'

'Lazarus? Where is he? Is he—'

'He is fine, but he's worried about you. Hudson refuses to let him anywhere near you.'

'Hudson can go and—'

'Go and what, Jasmine?' Hudson says, peeking out from behind Loretta.

'You can mind your own business. I'm not yours to protect. I can look after myself.'

'Yes, I can see that.'

'What happened between my fiancé and me is personal and has nothing to do with anyone.'

'It has everything to do with me when he threatens you,' he growls.

'I want to see Lazarus.' I look directly at Loretta. 'He is your son. Please let me see him.'

'There are rules for a reason. While you are all here you must abide by them.'

'Fine, I'll leave!' I go to stand up but as I do the room spins again. I stagger back down to the bed. 'Lazarus!' I yell as loud as I can then realise my head is throbbing. I hear his roar and locate his heartbeat to be on top of the castle. 'Where is Ash? No, don't tell me, I'll locate him myself.' I listen for his heartbeat and quickly work out he is stationed outside the door. 'You have Ash guarding me against Lazarus?'

'He is guarding you, but not only from Lazarus,' replies Hudson.

'Who else would he be guarding me from?'

'You forgot when you were fighting that every other dragon can hear your argument. Everyone here knows what and who you are, Jasmine. Your arrival is no longer a secret.'

'But everyone under the protection of these three castles wants the same thing—peace. So why would I be in danger?'

'You would be a rich trophy for any clan, or you could be a queen to a dark sorcerer. Someone may trade you to get one of their family members released or to gain a kingdom of their own in return.

'So, my dear Jasmine, your rather loud outburst with your dragon has put you in more danger than ever,' he explains through gritted teeth. 'All these years, your parents kept you hidden and in one stupid outburst you reveal your identity to all Europe!'

'He is not my dragon. He is my fiancé and I need to be with him now!' I snap. I force my legs to hold me upright. The room stays steady. 'Lazarus, change form and come and take me home. Please, babe,' I whisper low enough that only a dragon's ear would pick up. I flick my eyes to Loretta to see if she gives me away, but she drops her gaze to her hands and smiles.

I hear a small commotion before the door flings open and Lazarus is standing there, his eyes locked on me. Ash is several long seconds behind him.

'Geez Laz, I nearly took you down. You should have let me know it was you,' Ash pants.

'In your dreams, mate. You could never catch me.' The corners of Lazarus' mouth slightly curve up. 'Hello, babe. I hear you're ready to leave this place.'

He moves cautiously towards me. I can see him scanning the situation, eyeing Hudson from the corner of his eye as well as his mother.

'You're making a big mistake, Jasmine,' says Hudson.

'I told you before that you are not my protector. Lazarus is.' As soon as the words leave my lips, Lazarus is by my side, radiating the warmth I've missed.

'There is so much more I need to teach you and more powers you need to tap into. You need to learn how to control your emotions so what happened two days ago won't happen again,' explains Hudson.

'Two days?'

'Yes, my dear, you have been out for two days, with the help of medicine. We predicted you'd want to leave and made the decision to sedate you so you could heal.' Loretta smiles.

'Please reconsider your departure and stay for the week so I can help you to deal with your powers properly. After that time, I will happily wave the three of you goodbye knowing you are not dangerous to yourself,' pleads Hudson.

I look up into Lazarus' eyes for the answer, but he smiles softly down at me, letting me make the decision.

'On one condition.' I turn to face Hudson.

'What is that?'

'Actually, I have two conditions. Firstly, you will refrain from calling my fiancé "dragon". His name, as you well know, is Lazarus. Secondly, Lazarus is to be with me at all times.'

'I'd prefer you kept the quality and strength of your powers to yourself. You can, and may, one day fall out of love with the… with Lazarus and it would be detrimental to you if he used your powers against you.'

'He won't do that and we won't be separated. Great, then we have an agreement,' I clap my hands together, instantly feeling the pain shoot up my sore back. I feel Lazarus grasp my arm for support. I smile and head for the door, which is filled with Ash's giant form.

'Rest tonight. We will start fresh in the morning,' says Hudson, defeated. 'Your mother was right when she said you are one of the strongest women she knows. You remind me of her.'

I stop and turn around so I can see his face. He gives me a gentle smile and nods. I return the smile before leaving.

Returning to our room, I notice that someone has fixed the broken latch on the bedroom door. Lazarus closes the door and moves slowly towards me, nearly at his stalking pace. I eye him warily, unsure of his actions.

'We need to talk about what happened,' he whispers. 'In private, please.'

I pull the silencing dome over us before gently sitting down on the couch. I realise as I sit that all the furniture has been replaced from when I broke it in my oversized gargoyle form.

'You don't and will never control me.' I start the unavoidable discussion.

'I know. I was furious and way past boiling point when I said that.'

'I've seen you grumpy with me but never this angry. It didn't help that I too lost control. As much as I tried to rein it in, it grew. I was jealous that you were with Keira and then when she rubbed up against you I just…'

'I'm not rehashing that again. I told you before that I don't like your jealous side and she means nothing to me. But what *does* mean a lot to me is you changing form. It gutted me to see you as a gargoyle. Why would you change to that form when I am a dragon? Why wouldn't you want to be like me?'

'I didn't think about it until I had already changed form. Hudson showed me what to do and I followed. To be honest, I was too intrigued to stop and think clearly. That's why I asked for you to be with him and me in the future, so I don't offend you again. I never meant to hurt you.'

'It gutted me to see you gliding around with Ash. The only pleasure I got was seeing you punch him in the mouth. And even then, I was past listening to any excuses.'

'I don't need permission from you or Hudson to use my powers.'

'I agree but I had just returned from hunting and then I see you. The adrenaline was already pumping fiercely through my veins. Seeing you as a full-blooded gargoyle was not what I needed.'

'Are you sure your adrenaline wasn't being spiked because you were hunting with Keira?'

'Well, maybe if you decided to change into a dragon, I could have shared that moment with you instead of her.'

'Don't let me stop you! I'm sure you haven't had your fill yet and, by the way, she was rustling up your scales she hasn't had enough of you!'

I instantly regret saying it. I don't want him to be anywhere near that dragon. I try to stand up and feel my back pinch, making me gasp in pain. Lazarus comes to my side. His eyes narrow and I can see a small red flicker in them. My comments obviously hit a nerve.

'I never want to be apart from you. You are my life. I live and breathe for you.' He rips off his shirt and punches his left pectoral muscle. 'No one can break this link. We need to trust one another or this will keep happening. We decided, long ago, not to doubt our love.'

A tear runs down my cheek. Lazarus leans forward and catches it with his warm lips. 'Hmm, salty tears are delicious, babe.' He flicks his eyebrow before his face becomes serious. 'Can you make me one promise? Never shift into a gargoyle again.'

'It's not on my current agenda and I can't predict what the future holds. But for now, I promise.'

'Tell me you love me and that we are going to be okay.' He runs his warm lips slowly up and down my cheek. 'Tell me.'

'What doesn't kill us will make us stronger.' I know full well that's not what he wants to hear. He leans back, his green eyes narrowing and brow creasing. He blows a small puff of smoke over my face, something he'd normally do as a threat, but this is more like a tease.

I lean forward so I can kiss him, but he pulls slightly back. His eyes are still asking for a reply.

'I shouldn't have to tell you how much I am in love with you. Use your senses, dragon. That's what you keep telling me to do. Or maybe you're getting old and forgetful.'

Within a millisecond, Lazarus lifts me up on the bed and on top of his prone body. 'I am neither old nor forgetful, witch! Hence you are on top of me instead of me pinning you down, which I am still tempted to do. I remembered your back is sore.

'And regarding my senses, I am fighting every one of them right at this very moment as they are screaming at me to devour you.'

'Devour me with kisses or with your razor-sharp teeth?'

'Both, so play your next card very carefully, babe.'

'Maybe you should remember that I now know how to produce my own set of razor-sharp teeth.'

He pulls me in tightly and I can feel his body heating up. He inhales my scent then nuzzles my earlobe before nipping at it. 'This game just got interesting!'

THE MORNING LIGHT pours through the open bedroom window, alerting me to the new day. I slept solidly through the night after making sweet love to my fiancé. I reach over, expecting his side of the bed to be empty but find my hot-blooded fiancé beside me.

'Good morning, babe,' he purrs. 'You slept like a log.'

'A log? Not a princess or an angel but a log! You're such a romantic.'

I snuggle into his warm side. I rest my head on his chest and, with my index finger, trace the outline of his yin-yang dragon marking.

'I should get a tattoo over my heart with your name on it, then everyone who sees it will know I'm inked to you and only you.'

'Don't you think you have enough markings?' He pulls back the bedsheet, exposing my legs, which have vine-like markings running up them. The single purple vine I received when my mother died is prominent on my left leg.

I run my hand over my face, remembering the one that creeps over one side.

'I love your markings,' he says, 'and if you decide to mark my name over your heart, I would be extremely honoured.'

'I'd do it, so you'd know that you're the only one for me. There will never be anyone but you. I love you, Laz.'

'As I do you. But I need to be truthful about something.'

'What?' I lift myself up so I can see his eyes.

'I need to go on another hunt. The flight and car trip here really took its toll on me. I didn't hunt while you were out cold for those few days.'

Being mindful of my back, I jump up and stand above him. I slowly sway to imaginary music playing in my head. 'Do I look tasty to you, babe?'

'You look like two delicious chicken legs rocking back and forth, teasing me. I'd love to sink my teeth into those legs.' His tongue slowly rolls over his lips.

'Keep those teeth in your mouth, mister!' I jump off the bed, instantly regretting it.

'You know you should never run from a dragon, babe.' I turn around and he is in his stalking position. 'If only I had some salt and pepper.'

I keep my focus on him and draw up the same earthly energy I used when I focused on the gargoyle, except this time I instantly feel the heat. I stop it flooding any further than my legs as I don't want to change form totally. I just want to play with a little bit of dragon juice running through my veins.

I blink several times as my vision becomes obscured. I can see less beside me but everything in front of me is becoming magnified. I twitch my hands and they move like lightning, then I do the same to my feet, finding that they are just as quick.

Lazarus clicks onto what I'm doing, his grin taking over his entire face. 'I'm impressed, babe, not to mention turned on.'

I think about stalking and immediately my body mimics his. 'You know, Lazarus, you should never run from a dragon.' I smile seductively.

I'm rewarded with a boisterous chuckle. 'You've got my full attention. Show me what you've got, babe.'

Before he can finish speaking, I pounce on him, knocking him back onto the bed.

His eyes go from pure shock to excitement. 'Oh yeah, this is gonna be fun.'

LAZARUS TAKES HIS father and goes hunting in a nearby forest while I head down to find the kitchen. I can hear whispering voices from all over the castle. Everyone is discussing me, my powers and the relationship I have with Lazarus. You'd think they'd realise I can hear every darn word they're saying.

By the time I smell out the kitchen I have lost my appetite.

'Good morning, Jasmine.' Hudson walks up behind me in human form.

'Shouldn't you be up on the roof during the day?'

'I have mixed creature blood flowing through my veins. The sorcery side allows me to reboot my system whenever I feel like it.'

'Drake was pure gargoyle.'

'Yes, as was his mother. Demona's sorcery was taught to her by Sky. It was not in her blood and only very basic. Drake never received any of my sorcery. Sometimes it doesn't always flow through to the next generation.'

'Oh, I see.'

As if on cue, my stomach growls embarrassingly.

'You haven't eaten since you got here. You need to keep your strength up or you may become confused while shifting forms.'

I give a shy smile, embarrassed over my behaviour since I arrived.

'I'll make us both something to eat and then we can talk.'

Hudson and I eat, or I should say demolish, several sandwiches made from fresh home-baked bread.

He takes me to a large sitting area filled with comfortable lounge chairs and a stunning open fire. We sit and talk about my parents and I find myself drifting off, remembering them both while staring blankly into the crackling fire.

'Jasmine?'

'Sorry Hudson, you were saying?'

'You obviously miss your family.'

'I do, very much, but I have a new family back at Nogard and Elyograg Castle.'

'It may not feel like it, but we are also your family.' He smiles, and I sense he's genuine. 'Anyhow, you were telling me how you drew on the dragon powers while starting to shift but stopped halfway. Why?'

I feel my cheeks blush and decide to tiptoe around this question. 'Laz was playfully stalking me. I wanted to see if I could do the same.'

'And could you?'

'Yes, very easily. My vision changed first by blocking off anything that was either side of me, like blinkers on a bridle. It then magnified everything in front of me. I tested my hands and feet for speed and the next thing I knew I was zooming around the room in a microsecond.'

'That's very impressive. My concern is, when a dragon is in human form, we can have somewhat of a level-headed conversation with them. But when in their natural form their instincts are to eat anything in front of them, which sometimes includes humans. Others burn or attack without realising how deadly their sphere-like tails are.

'I would ask you to refrain from shifting completely to dragon unless you have someone you can trust who will help you control these senses.'

'I understand what you're saying. When I first met the dragons, they had trouble refraining from eating me. It took a lot of control and patience. What about Loretta? Is she a controlled dragon?'

'She is one I would trust but that's something you would have to ask her personally.' He places another log on the fire. 'Thank you for staying. I'm enjoying having you here. It's been a long time since I have been with you. It was difficult to watch you from the sidelines.'

'You're welcome, but our alone time is coming to an end. The dragons are on their way back and the gargoyles are starting to warm up.'

'Wow, it can't be that late in the day already.' He moves to look out the window. 'I can't see the dragons. Are you sure they're heading back?'

'Positive. Lazarus just spoke to me and, within the next five minutes, I will be able to tell you what they have eaten. He never tells me as he likes me to use my senses to work it out.'

'You are a very powerful young woman. Promise me one thing—never draw on dark negative energy.'

'I have promised so many people before you and I will again promise you. It will never happen. No matter how grim the situation seems I will never turn to dark sorcery. It's killed too many of my family and I will fight it with all my powers.'

'Thank you.' He smiles then quickly turns his head to look out the window. 'The dragons are on the horizon. I could help you cheat and tell you what animal is plentiful in the local forest.'

'I do believe that deer was on the menu.' I laugh.

'As I said, you are one powerful woman. The more you practice the easier the earth will release new powers to you.'

It's not long before the lounge area is filled with different creatures in human form so they can interact with Ash, Lazarus and me. I decide to sit back and concentrate on each individual, using my senses, to work out what elite creature they are. I make sure I don't look them in the eye because that would give it away.

Becoming bored, I decide to draw on the same dragon energy I'd used earlier that morning. I feel the warmth flood my feet then my legs, stopping before it passes my hips. My eyes start to change. I blink several times, helping them adjust to the dragon vision.

The whole room changes. The humans standing in groups around the room have all changed. I gasped out loud. 'Oh, my goodness. Oh, my. Oh, bugger.'

'What is it, Jasmine?' Lazarus asks.

'Nothing.' I drop my head so I can't look at anyone.

'Look at me, babe. What's wrong?' Lazarus persists.

'I think I need to get some fresh air.' I try to stand up without looking in anyone's direction.

'Ha ha ha,' roars Ash. 'You cheeky girl.'

Ash quickly stands before me, not letting me move. I drop my head. I don't want to look at him

'Look at me, beautiful.' He sniggers then leans close to my ear. 'I know your secret.'

'What is going on? What secret is he talking about, Jasmine?' snaps Lazarus.

'Why don't you tell your fiancé what power you have just tapped into, beautiful?' With his fingers, Ash lifts my face up to him. I hold my eyes tightly shut until I am happy that I will be looking at his face.

'I'm gonna kill you for this, Ash,' I whisper, but unfortunately, most of the creatures can hear me no matter how softly I speak.

'I'll ask once more before heads start flying,' snarls Lazarus.

'Your beautiful fiancée here has just worked out how to use her x-ray vision.' He laughs.

The room erupts with laughter and everyone starts calling my name, hoping I will look in their direction.

'Stop it! This is not funny!' I yell.

I feel a set of warm arms around me, recognising Lazarus instantly. He pulls me into his firm chest, covering my eyes. I slowly peek one eye open and instantly see through Lazarus' shirt, spotting his marking over his heart. Then his marking starts to disappear, and I can clearly see his heart beating within his rib cage.

'Oh boy, this is not good. I think I need to lie down, babe.' I blink and shake my head, trying to remove the power I have just found.

'Tell me what's happening, Jasmine. What can you see?' Hudson is close; I can smell and even taste him in the air.

'Firstly, everyone's clothes disappeared. Then I saw through Laz's clothes and skin until I saw his beating heart.'

'Well, there you go, bro. Everyone back home thinks you don't have a heart and now Jazz just proved them wrong.' Ash chuckles.

'Please, Ash. Not now. I'm freaking out here.' I pant and push my face harder into Lazarus' chest.

'Jasmine, you know how to shift back so do it and you'll be fine.' I feel Hudson's hand on my shoulder as he speaks, and I do as he suggests.

I slowly push the warmth down and out of my feet, returning it gratefully to the Earth. I feel Lazarus' body heat against mine and that's when I know I have succeeded in shifting back. I lean back and blink several times to focus on a room full of amused faces.

'Not funny, people,' I murmur. They all burst into hysterics. After a few minutes and a few deep breaths, I join in the laughter.

Thinking about what I had just achieved, I realise that this is how dragons see things. I turn to Lazarus with my hands firmly plastered on my hips.

'Oh boy, watch out, she's back to her normal self,' says Ash.

'Zip it, pebbles!' I playfully snarl.

'Yep, that's her alright.' He backs away with his hands up in surrender.

'Lazarus, I have just thought of something.' I swear if I look down to my foot it would be tapping.

'Hmm?'

'The x-ray vision I've gained. You can use that at any time. Is that not true?'

'I know what you're thinking, babe.'

Ash claps his hands together before saying, 'Come on cow breath, let's see you get out of this one.'

'After seeing a room full of naked men, I don't think you know what I am thinking at all, my dear fiancé.' His eyes narrow. He's not impressed that I can strip the clothes off people using my dragon eyes. 'But what I'd like to know is how often do you use your x-ray vision?'

'Most teenage dragons use it for things other than seeking our prey. But I use it to see through the forest in search of prey.'

'Oh, good save, dragon!' Ash is enjoying this.

'Shut it, boulder brains,' growls Lazarus.

'When I was captive at Nogard Hollow and you threatened me with your x-ray vision, did you—'

'Hang on a minute! When were you held captive?' says Hudson.

'Come on, man. Keep up with the story,' Ash says with sarcasm dripping from his words. 'She found an injured gargoyle—Drake, your son—then accepted an invitation to the dragons' lair where they blackmailed her into drugging the angels at Elyograg Castle, but she didn't and instead she was attacked by Falcon, who Lazarus fought to keep her alive.

'Drake and the angels healed her wounds. She was then kidnapped, together with Demona, and locked in a cave by Attor, Falcon's father. They escaped and were found by Drake and her now fiancé, who bonded.

'Jazz killed Attor but not before he killed Drake. Distraught, Jazz left only to be tracked down by a dark sorcerer. Laz came to her rescue and returned her home but was followed by the dark sorcerer who sadly killed Sky.

'The European dragons arrived in Australia and this is the good part because this is where I arrive. A fight broke out with blood, guts and goop everywhere. We kicked some serious butt! But again, we lost too many lives, including Jazz's mother, Gloria.

'After an earth-shattering fight between Laz and myself, she chose to settle down and marry leather-guts. And that was only after I told Jazz she and I would never be.'

'In your dreams, Ash,' I say.

'I think I need a drink,' says Hudson, shaking his head.

'On that note, I think I will retire for the night,' says Lazarus, staring down at me.

I nod then glance around the room. Everyone is quiet and still staring at Ash.

'Goodnight, everyone,' I say before leaving. There are several polite replies but they're too busy whispering questions to Ash about the fight with the Europeans.

As soon as the bedroom door is shut I resume the stance I had downstairs—my hands planted on my hips. 'You avoided my question.'

'Would it matter if I used it?'

'Yes, it would! I asked you not to.'

'Well then, I didn't use it.' In a quick move, he lifts me up and onto the bed.

'I don't believe you.'

He kisses my nose then trails soft wet kisses all over my face until he reaches my ear. 'Maybe I had a tiny look.'

'Lazarus!' I try to pull my hands out from underneath him so I can playfully hit him, but he pins both of them above my head, holding them together with one of his.

'I've only done it with you. You were so delicious and irresistible, just like you are now.'

With slow seductive kisses, he trails down then up my neck, spreading his heat over my body, only stopping when his lips kiss the side of my mouth. 'You taste like heaven, babe. I could kiss you all day.'

He pounces on my waiting lips, kissing me like he's possessed. I don't complain.

It's not long before I feel his body heat, with the blood in my veins doing the same. I know the electric current is close by and I try with all my might to extinguish it. As we connect as one, it hits us, but this time it's different. There is no pain. Instead, it's a pleasurable feeling.

Lazarus stops kissing me and looks as baffled as I feel. A smile creeps across his face, matching mine. 'Now that's what I call fun!'

THE NEXT FEW days fly past, and I spend most of my time with Hudson learning how to control my powers. So far, I haven't burnt down the castle. But this morning Loretta promised me she would help me shift into a dragon.

I race downstairs as soon as Lazarus leaves to hunt and help train the younger dragons. I don't want him around when I change, as I can guarantee he will try to interfere.

Loretta is patiently sitting on a large boulder out the back of the castle. Her smile is warm as I approach.

'I don't know if I'm nervous or excited,' I say, before kissing her cheek.

'You wouldn't be human if you weren't a little anxious, my dear.'

'How will I communicate with you when I'm in dragon form?'

'That will be revealed when and if you change form. I'm still not sure you can change into such a large creature but I'm willing to try if you are.' She grasps my hand in hers and tugs me to a large clearing.

'I'm ready to try.'

'Very well, Jasmine. Clear your head and concentrate on the outline of a dragon. Make sure you only concentrate on an outline as if it is drawn on a piece of paper.'

'That's easy.' Lazarus' magical form pops into sight. With a reluctant sigh, I push away his magnificent colour and alluring green eyes, leaving his huge outline.

'This is a large creature. Everything should be done in slow, calculated moves.' She steps back before continuing. 'Breathe out. Empty your lungs; force every bit out. Open your mind but most of all, your soul. Accept what the earth's energy is giving, similar to what you did while changing into gargoyle form.

'With a slow, controlled breath, fill in the picture using the earth's natural resources. Remember, if things don't go as planned, do the reverse to return to your original form.'

I blow out, squeezing my lungs of any oxygen. I try to keep calm as a feeling of suffocation falls over me. Closing my mouth and breathing in through my nostrils, I draw in from the earth underneath me.

Like a shower being turned on, my blood heats to an uncomfortable temperature. Glancing down at my limbs I see no change. My lungs are nearly full! I should be part-creature or show some sign of being one. In a panic, I squeeze my eyes shut and fill my lungs with a sharp, satisfying breath.

There are millions of small particles circling around the vision I have in my head, similar to what I see when a dragon changes form. The only exception is that the particles are a golden colour and not red.

I feel my arms stretch, as does my body. There's a dull pain in my back as it lengthens. My body flushes with intense heat. A loud crack, similar to the sonic boom a stock-whip makes, bellows from behind, taking my mind away from the pain. I wonder if I'm growing a tail.

It's taking too long. I fear the transformation has gone haywire.

Loretta's calm but impressed tone interrupts my panic attack. 'Open your eyes, Jasmine.'

I open my eyes. I have to blink several times to get my vision under control. I remember back when I partially drew on the dragon form how my vision changed and how everything was enhanced. I blink again and look around for Loretta.

'Down here, my dear.'

I drop my eyes. She is so small and is waving her hand in slow motion.

The first thing I feel like doing is taking a bite out of her arm. My tongue licks my lips, catching the saliva dripping down them.

I run my tongue over my teeth. They're sharp and large but not too big for my mouth.

'In time, you'll learn to control the predatory side of a dragon. Humans will always look like candy. Unfortunately, dragons' actions are very childlike. Their hands are usually caught inside the candy jar. Everything that moves will look like a temptation. So this is number one on your priority list—learn control.'

She approaches me at a slow pace. I realise my head is up high and my wings stretched out wide. This is the stance a dragon uses when threatened or about to attack.

Keeping my movements controlled, I fold in my wings, pulling them to my sides. My tail is high and curving over my back. I fear I may puncture myself with it and lower it slowly, happy when it touches the ground.

I drop my head to Loretta's height. Without thinking, my large nostrils inhale her scent, her body slightly tipping towards me. I know her scent well and the urge to bite her dissipates.

'Good girl.' She smiles up at me. 'You are an amazing creature and your colour is one I've never seen. Lazarus will be even more besotted with you when he sees your dragon form.'

I wonder how I can speak to her and open my mouth. An awkward growl escapes. I try again only to puff smoke over her. In my head, there are so many buttons I can push but I fear I may push the wrong one and burn Loretta to a crisp.

She laughs. 'Are you telepathic, Jasmine?'

'I am. Can you hear me?'

'Loud and clear. This is how we communicate. Dragons have their own telepathic wave which differs from that of a sorcerer or other elites. I was unsure if you would get that ability on your first change.'

She slowly runs her hand over my head and my eyes watch every move. I trust her but, for some reason, my dragon instinct is telling me to always be on guard. *'Lazarus told me how you helped Kite overcome her need to devour a human. Maybe she can return the favour and help you understand the powers a dragon has.'*

'I'm sure Laz will want to show me the ropes.' I chuckle and puff more smoke. There's a hot feeling inside my throat when it happens.

Loretta continues to run the palm of her hand down my neck. I turn my head when she reaches my front leg.

'Don't go any further. I fear my tail.'

'Of course. "Slow going" is the best policy when it comes to dragons.' She touches my wing before turning back towards my head. *'Your colour is as bright as a gargoyle's golden soul. I wonder if you have gargoyle blood in you.'*

I don't answer. Again, my dragon instinct is to protect me and my soul. I wonder if Lazarus feels he must protect himself against me when he is in his true form.

'It might be wise to return to your human form. When you return home, learn how to fly and hunt in the areas you know are safe. I'd hate you to try here and accidentally fly into rebel territory.'

'I'm happy to learn the traits of the trade, less the hunting. I'd rather eat my steak from a plate.'

'You don't know what you're missing out on. It's a huge adrenaline rush.'

She runs her hand all the way back to my head. I gently nuzzle her away with my nose before drawing back down to my human form.

WE ARE LEAVING for Australia tomorrow and I'm desperate to see England's famous attractions. I doubt I will ever be able to afford to come here again so this may be my last chance.

'There's been no threat to the castle and no word on the sorcerer called King. I see no reason to stay hidden,' I say, driving with Ash towards London town. 'Hudson wouldn't have convinced Laz to let me go if he thought there was a threat. All he asked was for me to keep my senses and my cloaking spell switched on.'

'Lazarus is unhappy you're heading into the city. He's annoyed they need him to stay at the castle and help train and ready the young dragons. But they need to be prepared if the castle is attacked,' Ash says. 'Just to let you know, he's forcing me to go with you. I didn't willingly get in this car with you.'

'I suppose an extra set of eyes and ears wouldn't hurt. It's nice to see that Lazarus finally trusts you with me. He now accepts and sees you as a friend.'

'I can show you what London looks like in a geography book,' Ash grumbles, folding his arms across his chest while keeping his eyes peeled for anything unusual.

'Shopping with the girls is fun, Ash.'

'You're one girl and I don't like shopping. I did it once and hated it.'

'Were there too many people in the Outback store for you?' I tease and poke him in his side, making him jump.

'There are plenty of locals and travellers, smarty pants. I feel uncomfortable amongst humans.'

'I can pull over and you can head back home. We're only a few hours out.'

'I've just got the oversized lizard liking me. If I return without you, Lazarus will bite my head off without letting me explain.'

'It looks like you're stuck with me. I promise I won't drag you into any dress shops. Just the touristy stuff, like churches and castles.'

'Haven't you seen enough castles? Or are you attracted to the handsome gargoyles protecting them?'

I quickly turn my head as he flicks his eyebrows. 'I find

them interesting. Nothing more and nothing less.'

The road narrows and on the bend ahead is a car pulled over with a small woman leaning up against it. She has several tools laid out on the road and a spare tyre. 'Looks like she's got a flat tyre.'

'She can deal with it. Let's keep to our plan.'

'Look at the size of her. She's a pretzel. If you hold the car up, I'll change the tyre for her.'

'Doing a good deed will always get us into trouble.'

'It will not! Stop being so negative.'

'Don't you think she will be curious if I can hold up her car?'

'It's a tiny car and you're a big strong man. I'll use the winch if that makes you feel better.'

'I'd feel better if you drove past and ignore her.'

'That's not the Aussie way. What's got into you?'

'It doesn't feel right, Jazz.'

'Oh, stop it. You're turning into Lazarus.'

'Am not!'

Ash sighs when I pull over behind the other car. She waves, smiles and starts to walk towards us.

'Her skin is too pale. She's not human. I don't like this.'

'For goodness' sake, Ash. Look at the size of her. We could blow her over with one big breath. And everyone in England is pale. They don't have summers like us. Now stop being silly and help me change her tyre.'

I open the car door and step out, with Ash doing the same.

'Hello! Thank you for stopping,' says the young redhead.

'Hi! Looks like you need a hand.' I smile, meeting her in front of my car.

'I tried to change the tyre myself, but I must admit, I don't have a clue what to do.'

'Well, you are in luck because we do. Don't we, Ash?'

Ash is standing with his arms folded across his chest,

his head scanning the area. 'Something's not right, Jasmine. Listen to the birds.'

'Stop it, Ash! It's quiet.'

'Exactly. We're in the countryside so why don't we hear the creatures?'

I flick my eyes back to the small redheaded woman. She blinks several times. Her eyes are uncomfortable and watering.

'I'm sorry,' she whispers.

'For what?'

Ash's stance broadens and his skin starts to dry and turn to his true form. But before he can transform several tall figures appear from nowhere to circle us. In an instant, my hands fill with anorics ready to fire, but my senses are confused as to what creatures they are.

'Relax, Jasmine. We mean no harm,' says a voice, from underneath a black cape.

'Is that why you cover your face?'

I do a headcount, checking to see if anyone is behind me but as I do, Ash is struck to the ground, his transformation still incomplete. It baffles me why it's taken him so long to change form.

I lift my hands which are full of deadly fuel and as I spin around to fire I am face-to-face, nose-to-nose with the devil himself. Then black!

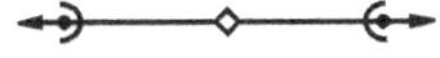

Chapter Four

I blink several times, waking from what I thought was a bad dream. The first thing that hits me it the agonising pain in my hands.

'He let your anorics burn out in your hands to teach you never raise them at him again,' a voice says beside me.

'You! What and who are you?' I frown at the young red-headed woman.

'My name is Emily and I am a vampire.'

I question the word by saying it out loud. 'Vampire?'

She nods with a sympathetic smile. 'Put this cream on your hands. It will help them heal.'

'Where's Ash? Am I a prisoner here?'

'He is still out cold. It will take him a little longer to recover as he was in the middle of transforming.' She points to a corner of the room where Ash lies slumped in a pile, his face half-stone, as is his body.

'He will recover fully, as you will if you apply this cream.' She hands me the jar. I hesitantly scoop a large amount into my palms. 'To answer your last question, yes, you are a prisoner, as am I.'

'You? I'm confused. Did you know the creatures who ambushed us?'

'Yes, it was King and his men.'

'King the sorcerer?'

'He is a sorcerer and the mightiest of vampires. I was not born a creature. I am human first. King turned me many years ago and uses me to lure his prey. Even though he doesn't need my help, he finds me an amusing toy.'

'Have you tried to escape?'

'And where does a vampire run too, Jasmine? All elite creatures fear me, even when I show I'm no threat. I have tried to kill myself by starvation and stabbing wooden stakes into my heart.'

'And?'

'Let's say a lot of the books have got it very wrong.'

'I've got a few powers we can use to get out of here.'

'We know of your powers, but they are useless in here. Many of the rooms have spells on them where they quash, demobilise if you will, all elite creatures' powers. If you try to rebel, King will punish you or your servant.'

'My servant?'

She nods and looks at Ash. 'I must speak quickly as these walls have ears. All gargoyles here are servants to all others. If they disobey, they are killed. If Ash is your friend, the best way to keep him and you alive is for him to be your personal slave.'

'No way!'

'Yes way,' murmurs Ash. He staggers to his gargoyle feet. His body has transformed into his true nature, trying to repair.

'Are you OK?' I go to move towards him and cringe in pain when my hands touch the cobblestone ground.

'I'm better than you. What happened?'

'Explain that to him later. You better be a good actor, Ash, because King can sniff out a bad one. He has killed and smashed at least eighty gargoyles. He uses their golden souls to light up the hallways,' Emily says.

'How can we trust her?' Ash growls as he squats to look at my burnt hands.

'You can't, and you shouldn't trust a vampire. I only lured you because King uses my human sister's life as a pawn. He will snuff her out, or worse, turn her in front of me. My sister is my life. I love her.' The pain is evident in her voice.

'I believe her, but I don't want you to be my servant.'

'Huh! You've been dying for me to kiss those feet of yours,' scoffs Ash.

'If Jasmine displeases King, you will receive her punishment. It's not a pleasant life, believe me.'

Interrupting our conversation, the door violently swings open. Emily jumps to her feet and bows her head. A tall slender man glides in as if on roller-skates. Emily takes several steps back.

'Good morning, my queen.' He sounds like a character from a Dracula movie.

'You must be King.' I roll back my shoulders to stand tall, not wanting to show fear.

'Ah, you have heard of me.'

'Only that you're a leech and a monster.'

Before I can snarl, a crippling pain rakes my body, forcing me to fall to the floor. Ash runs to my side but as he reaches me, he is flung to the ground.

'Emily, I had hoped you'd explained to my guest why she is here. Have you disobeyed me, sweet Em?' He says, changing his voice to an English accent.

My pain subsides but Emily screams and drops to the floor.

'She explained everything. It was others that call you a monster as I do,' I yell before staggering to my feet.

I spot Ash getting to his feet and remember what Emily said about gargoyles being killed unless they're a servant.

'Ash! Stay where you are and fold in your wings!' I turn my head to give Ash a hidden wink.

He bows his head, kneels and folds his wings into his sides. 'As you wish.'

I flick my eyes back to King, 'Your accent changed.'

'When everyone meets a vampire, they expect us to have

Dracula's voice. So I give it to them before I devour them. It's a game that keeps me amused.' He gives a synthetic smile.

'So I'm to be devoured?'

'No, sweet Jasmine, you are to become my queen.'

'Your queen? I'm engaged to be married next month.'

'I thought you said Emily explained everything to you.' He lifts his two narrow hands up, pointing his fingers towards her.

She grabs at her throat as if she's being choked. Her body is being lifted, her feet dangling in the air. Her fangs drop down and blood runs down them and onto her chin.

'Stop it! Stop it! You came into the room before she could tell us anything.'

'Oh, I'm sure sweet Em told you plenty, but she forgot the most important thing and that is you will be my queen.'

He turns his dark red eyes away from Emily and locks with mine. He smiles and looks back at her before he snaps her neck, using the twisting of his fingers to do so. She drops heavy and lifeless to the ground.

'What the hell? Why would you kill one of your own?'

'I'll explain this once and once only. So listen carefully. There is no escape. Your powers are void here until I require them, and I will. And you will be my queen and rule beside me as one.'

'And if I refuse?'

'Simple. You die.'

He glides towards me and lifts his hand to my face. I flinch and pull back. A second later, Ash is on his side, writhing in pain. King lifts his hand again but this time I stay still. He cups my cheek; his hand is cooler than a gargoyle. I force myself to not show any expression, even though his touch revolts me.

Ash's pain disperses and he returns to a sitting position. King leans in and inhales my scent long and slow. He then presses his lips against my cheek, leaving them there too long.

'Good girl. If you displease me your servant will be punished.'

'I understand.'

He leans back and stares into my eyes. His ruby-red eyes circle with black swirls, like a storm is brewing in his head. He frowns and tilts his head. 'Open your mouth wide.'

'Why?'

'Ha!' He laughs. 'I can't hypnotise you. What an interesting woman you are.'

'So it seems.'

King smiles before turning and heading for the door. 'You do have full control over the gargoyle?'

'Yes,' I'm quick to say.

'If he steps out of line I will kill him and use his soul to light your room.'

'Fine. Then I will find another gargoyle to replace him.' I try to sound blasé as if Ash is no value to me.

'Ah, we are going to get along famously, my queen.'

'Am I a prisoner here?'

'At the moment, yes. Once you are my queen and I have turned you, you can roam around as you wish.'

I gasp at the thought of being turned into a vampire.

'Oh, my dear beautiful bride. Did I forget to mention that part?' He chuckles. 'These men will take you to your room. Your servant can go down with the other gargoyles in the basement.'

'My servant sleeps in my room as my protector. He has done this all my life and will continue to do so.' My heart thuds at the thought of being separated from Ash. I pray King can't hear it.

'I do believe you're dictating to me, my queen. You will refer to me as King, or be punished.' He eyes me up and down.

I stand tall, pretending he doesn't intimidate me, even though internally I'm shaking like a leaf in autumn. 'Are you telling me you never slept in the same room as your ex-fiancé?'

'That is exactly what I am saying. I have been brought up with strict morals and will die before breaking them.'

'So you won't lie with King before marriage?'

'No and if you were any kind of gentleman you would respect my wishes.' I speak as if insulted, praying I haven't overstepped the mark.

'Oh, my sweet sorceress, you are going to taste better than I have ever imagined.'

Faster than Lazarus, he is back in front of me, both of his hands cupping my face. His eyes widen as he rolls his head on his neck, observing my features. 'You intrigue me. I pray, for your sake, you are speaking the truth.

'I will respect your wishes, for now, and allow your pet to protect you as we are a castle full of vampires. If any of them realise how sweet your blood is, you will need the gargoyle's protection. He can easily kill one single vampire but remember, I am no ordinary vampire. Do not underestimate my powers.'

He leans forward and I hold my stance. I refuse to let Ash be punished for my selfish acts. King kisses my right cheek then slowly moves across my cheek, dragging his lips across mine to the other one. I hear him inhaling me as he does. I do the same, taking in his hideous scent and locking it down into the pit of my stomach.

In a flash, he turns and heads for the door. 'When we meet again, I expect you to remove any emotions you have for the dragon. Remove it or I will hunt him down and kill him. His scent is on you. He will be easy to find and kill.'

I keep my heart beating at a slow steady pace even though it wants to run faster than an emu. I don't know what King's powers are, but by the way he easily killed Emily I'd gather he's killed many creatures and gained their powers.

Before I have time to think further, two vampires approach me. 'Please follow us, my queen,' one says, his eyes as red as blood.

I nod before demanding Ash follow me.

We are taken to a room and handed a key to the door. King is the only other person who has a key, I'm told. I can move around the castle if I wish but I'm warned that I leave my room at my own risk as vampires roam freely. All vampires have been told that I'm forbidden fruit, but I may be too tempting for some.

'King has given me permission to use my powers to deter any unwelcome fangs. So that means there are no spells in some part of the castle. I may be able to use my powers,' I say as soon as the door shuts.

'Shh!' Ash whispers.

'There's no one here. I'd sense them.'

'Can you use all your senses?'

'Yes, they never left, just the power to do anything.'

'I wished you'd had them switched on when you decided to stop and help poor helpless Emily. Stop thinking like a human and be more like the elite sorceress you are.' He shakes his head. It's the first time I've seen him annoyed with me. 'Can you use your telepathic waves?'

Closing my eyes, I concentrate on anyone outside the castle. It's blocked solid. I try again and hear one, then two, then more echoes. It's the golden souls I'm hearing. I ask them to quieten so I can concentrate on the outside. The same solid wall stops me.

I try a different approach and start to transform into dragon form. If I can connect to Lazarus he will be able to trace us. But as I heat up and connect to my dragon form,

I'm blocked again, seeing a cave wall similar to the caves at Nogard Hollow.

'I don't think we're in a castle, Ash. We're in a cave of some sort. I can only hear what's inside.'

'And what's inside?'

'I'm sorry to tell you this, but all I can hear is the screaming from golden souls.' I wrap my arms around his gargoyle waist. He brings his large arms around me, wrapping his wings to cocoon us.

'You don't need to be sorry. You didn't kill them. But we saw how inhumane King is and need to keep our wits about us. We need to devise a plan on how we can bring him down. A sorcerer and a vampire are a mix I've never seen.'

'I'm sorry I got you into this. I feel terrible speaking to you like you don't matter.'

'I appreciate your quick thinking as I didn't like the idea of us being separated.'

'I'm amazed he's giving me the respect I've asked for, especially as he can take what he wants at any time.'

'Yeah, that shocked me as well. It may be a loophole out of here. What do we know of his powers?'

'Hudson said King was born a vampire and gained his powers from killing sorcerers and drinking dry his victims. His powers are equal to mine, with the added vampirism. Does the sunlight burn them or is that a fairy tale?'

'I've never met one before this, but it was daylight when we met them today, so I think that wipes out any idea of pulling back the curtains.' Ash goes quiet, hesitating.

'What is it?'

'King lifted Emily and strangled her. Are your powers that strong?'

'I can lift a person or creature with ease, but I've never strangled someone.' I remember the European fight back at home when I lifted a dragon off the ground and pounded him, over and over, breaking his neck. 'Yes, I can and have killed that way.'

'The only thing we need to work out is what powers his vampirism holds.'

'Emily said she staked her heart and starved herself, but she didn't die.'

'I hate that I'm saying this, but you need to get close to him, play his sick deluded game. Figure out his weaknesses.'

'You want me to pretend to like him?'

'More than that, Jazz. You need to pretend to love him, to become his queen. We need to have the upper hand and find his weakness. Then we can draw him away from his henchmen and kill him.' He opens his wings. 'We've been quiet for too long. If King has sorcery powers he will be listening and know we're silencing our conversation.'

'I don't think I can pretend. His touch makes my skin crawl. Maybe we should have faith that Lazarus and Hudson will find us.'

'You said yourself, we're in a cave, or worse, we could be underground. They'll never hunt us out. It's up to you and me, Jazz. Remember to treat me as your pet.'

He folds his wings in and gently kisses my cheek. I smile and nod before searching our new room.

The room is three times the size of Nogard Hollow's bedrooms. Its decor is modern, with a large bed at one end next to a bathroom and a small kitchenette. It's a layout you'd see in a city apartment, not a vampire lair.

There are two large curtains opposite the bed. Ash opens them to confirm our prediction. Rock walls!

A knock on the door makes me jump. Ash indicates with his hands for him to open it. I nod. He rolls his eyes and frowns at me, pulling an angry face. He wants me to order him to open the door.

'Ash, door!'

He bows, giving me a cheeky smile and a flick of his brow.

'We have food for the queen.' A male vampire stands in the doorway holding a large tray of food.

'Ash will take it!' I snap.

'Yes, Queen.' The vampire eyes me before passing the tray of food over.

'And where can my pet feed? Do you hunt close by?'

'Your pet does not feed, my queen. No gargoyles feed. It's easier to control them.'

'Mine needs feeding as he is my protector. I'll speak to King about this.'

'It was King's orders not to feed him.' He smiles as if he won the conversation, then bows and leaves, closing the door.

Ash turns and frowns at me again. I'm no good at this acting game.

'Put my meal on the table then resume your position at the door.' I shrug my shoulders, apologising.

Ash places the tray on the table then moves to the door without a word. I grab a smoothie from the tray and the roast beef meal. I tiptoe over to Ash and lay the meal before him. I nod for him to eat and he shakes his head. Ignoring him, I move back to the tray and show him I have a bottle of water, toast and biscuits. I rub my belly and smile. He mimes the words 'thank you' and eats the meal before him.

He needs his strength as much as I do, especially if we're planning on taking on this leech.

'Relax, gargoyle!' A loud voice wakes me.

I sit upright, pulling the covers up to my chin. 'What the hell?'

Ash his on his toes, his wings spread wide and his claws out.

'I will say it once more, gargoyle, relax,' King snarls.

Ash folds his wings to his side and drops to his heels but no lower. King flicks his hand out, pointing to Ash's knees, making him drop to the ground. 'When I say relax, you will relax and bow down to me immediately.'

'How dare you enter my room unannounced!' I draw his attention away from Ash.

'Don't mistake me for a gentleman because I've put you in a bedroom and not a cage, my queen. I can change my mind very quickly.'

'As can I!' I jump out of bed, dragging the bed sheet with me. 'I have the power to leave here if I choose.'

He bellows a boisterous laugh. 'Do you think you're powerful enough to just walk out of here?'

'I have brought down a storm of dragons and sorcerers. You leeches will be a walk in the park!'

I feel his cool breath on my face before realising King is standing in front of me, his movements too quick to see. Out the corner of my eye, I spot Ash, his wings vibrating against his sides, forcing himself not to attack. I need to defuse the situation to keep our plan on track.

'Oh, I know what you did to my dragons. Don't play me for a fool because you will soon realise the devil himself is me.'

'Are you threatening me, my king?' I keep my heartbeat steady, but my hands sweat with the threat of my white energy.

'Yes. If you'd prefer to join Emily on her journey to hell, I'm happy to accommodate.'

'Is this how vampires romance their women?'

'Get dressed. I have bought clothes for you.'

'Where are we going?'

'I want to parade you around. I need to see if I have any unfaithful men or women. I can't have anyone taking a bite out of you.' He cups my face in his cool hands then kisses my cheeks one at a time.

'Speaking of being someone's meal, when do I get fed?'

'Forgive me. I forget you are human first. I will take you to the kitchen as I parade you.'

'And my protector needs to be fed. He can't do his job if he's undernourished.'

'He is a gargoyle and will protect you even if he is not fed. I will not waste food on a pet.' He speaks through gritted teeth, his breath becoming cold as ice.

'I hope you're correct. It would be a shame if it is some mere vamp who takes the first bite.'

He pulls my hair away from my neck and tilts my head to the side. He stares at my neck and I can see the pulsing vein mirrored in his red eyes. He leans in. I hold my breath, waiting for his teeth to pierce me. Instead, he licks the length of the artery in my neck. I keep calm; the only sign of being disgusted is my skin lifting in goosebumps.

'I will turn you when we are wed, my queen, even though a small taste is tempting.'

'I can't marry a man I barely know, plus, I need my father's permission to marry.'

'Your father is a sorcerer?'

'No.' I laugh while King frowns. 'I don't mean to laugh at you, but he knows nothing of this life, my king.'

'Mm, I like how you say my name.' He licks my neck again. Ick! He makes me sick to the stomach! 'If your father isn't one with powers, you must have gained it from your mother. Am I correct?'

'My mother and her father were both sorcerers. They have both passed away. I added to my powers from the kills and death of loved ones.'

'I will contact your father and ask for his permission.'

'Excuse the interruption, my king. But my queen means for you to meet her father in person,' Ash says, making King step back from me. 'It's an Australian tradition.'

I reach forward and clasp both King's hands in mine, stopping him from hurting Ash.

'He speaks the truth. I refuse to marry any man without seeing my father's face and hearing his words of approval.' I give a sharp nod, trying to make my words final.

'I am not any man. It is said you are the strongest sorceress in your country, but I know of another—Aldore. A visit to your country may be beneficial for both of us. If I kill Aldore, his powers will be an added bonus to me. Do you know this sorcerer?'

'I've heard of him and that he is in hiding, but I've never met him.'

'Hmm, I'm yet to decide if you tell the truth or whether you're a very good liar. Get dressed.'

King spins and heads straight out the door, flinging it shut behind him.

I draw my silencing spell with Ash moving beside me. I dress as we speak to save time and so as not to make King suspicious. 'Why the hell do you want King in Australia and near my father?'

'If we get him on our turf it will be an advantage for us. I don't know how many elite creatures support King here. We could be outnumbered. But our clan will fight with us. Your father was once a strong sorcerer. I pray he's still in touch with his powers. Together we have a better chance of killing him.'

'I fear he will attempt to turn me before we get there.'

'We need to become better actors.'

'Did he hurt you?'

'No, I'm made of stone, remember? Now let's put on the best performance we can.' He leans forward and kisses the top of my head. 'I love you, Jasmine. We will get through this together.'

King does as he said and parades me around the castle,

letting his vampires sniff my blood. Fangs drop down from several sets of mouths with King's henchmen disciplining a few and killing one.

It gives Ash and me the chance to see our surroundings, which are dark and gloomy. No daylight shines through, confirming our suspicion that we are underground.

'The place could do with a skylight,' I say.

'Are you not warm enough, my queen?' He says, showing me the kitchen. It's industrial size, with several vampires preparing food.

'It's cool but I was referring to the light in here. It's so dreary.'

'You must be hungry?'

'I was but seeing someone's head ripped off has turned my stomach.'

'Any vampire that steps towards you with their fangs dropped will receive the same punishment. Maybe it would be wiser for you to spend most of your time in your room.'

'I can handle myself, plus I have my gargoyle as protection. Why do you have chefs? I thought vampires drank only blood,' I whisper, seeing if he can hear my low voice.

'Most vampires here are human first. They consume blood for survival but enjoy food out of habit. My sorcery side allows me to enjoy both worlds.' He picks up an apple and drops his fangs into it. He sucks and drains the juice through his fangs, leaving it shrivelled. 'I will join you every morning for breakfast and lunch. You will eat your main meal in your room, as I will eat downstairs.'

'Downstairs?'

'Come, my queen. I will show you downstairs.' He holds his long skinny fingers out to me. I force a smile onto my lips and place my hand in his. 'Hmm, I enjoy your warmth. It will be a shame when I take it from you.'

He leads me down a winding stairwell lit by the glow of the golden souls of the gargoyles he's killed. Each one cries out as I pass them, asking to be returned to their clan's vault. It tears at my soul, but I don't answer them. I must be careful not to reveal my powers to King.

The temperature drops the lower we go with the walls becoming too cold to touch. A gargoyle stands guarding a door at the end of the stairs. He snaps to attention when he spots King and unlocks the door. He opens it and steps back, scanning me with a questioning brow as I approach. I hold eye contact and give him a questionable frown. The corner of his mouth lifts slightly to a smile; he sees hope in me, as do the souls.

'My queen,' says King.

The gargoyle shoots his eyes away from mine and again snaps to attention, his hope fading. Two small words from King and the gargoyle's faith is shattered.

There's a bright glow coming from the room and, as I approach, I recognise it to be from more golden souls. As I step into the room a disgusting smell hits me, so vile it makes me stagger backwards. There must be forty people in this room, amongst them are gargoyles in stone sleep. The people are in a foetal position, curled up and shaking.

'This is what happens to disloyal members of my clan,' King whispers in my ear. 'They are our blood bank.'

'You drink from them?'

'What is the difference between me eating and a creature killing a cow to survive? You kill to eat and so must I.'

I glance around the room. Everyone keeps their eyes on the ground, too scared to look at me or in King's hypnotic eyes.

There are metal plates and cups scattered on the ground, empty. He must feed them enough to survive and nothing more. The colour of their skin is pale and sagging from their bones.

'You're a monster!' Tears instantly fill my eyes.

In a blink, King is at my side, inflicting pain by squeezing my arm and digging his long nails into my flesh.

'That is the second time you've called me a monster. There will not be a third. Do you understand?' He spits his words into my face. 'You live in my world now, Jasmine. If you'd prefer to join them, I can always find another bride.'

Without thinking I release an electric shock, feeling it leave my body before I can control it. King jolts but it doesn't deter him. Instead, he applies pressure on my arm, piercing my skin with his nails.

'Is that all my queen has for me? I'm disappointed, I was hoping for so much more.' He smiles, then lets my arm go and licks his fingernail. He groans, sucking on his fingers like an ice cream. 'Hmm, you are the finest wine I've tasted. I'm going to enjoy draining you.'

'Excuse the interruption, but the queen is getting cold,' Ash says, drawing King's attention away from me.

Keeping his finger in his mouth, King whips his free hand towards Ash, throwing a small black anoric into his stomach. He crashes to the ground, buckling over in pain.

'What are you doing?' I run to Ash's side.

'You seem very attached to your pet. Maybe I should find you another who doesn't know what temperature my queen runs at. Maybe the gargoyle is more than your protector. Maybe he's your lover?'

'How dare you make that accusation?' I jump up and quickly move so I'm standing in front of King.

'If you care nothing for your pet, I will leave him down here.'

'He protects me against your leeches. If he stays, then so do I. At least I know he's loyal to me.' I can see the thought ticking over in King's mind. I need to get the focus off Ash.

'But if you distrust him then let me have him until I train another. Unless you wish your queen to be taste-tested by your vamps?'

'I know and you know you can overpower any of my men.'

'Maybe one or two but my powers seem to be limited here in your castle.'

'I too have my secrets. One is controlling what powers you can use.'

King walks a small circle around the room. The people pull their limbs in, shrinking away from him. He stops when he is face-to-face with me. 'My patience is wearing thin. I can drain you, take your powers and find another to wed.'

'It will be one hell of a fight if you try to drain me.'

'Oh, I am hoping so. It's something I look forward to.'

'In regards to my powers, they die along with me. I made sure of it before I left Australia.' I keep my eyes locked on his, giving strength to my voice.

'No creature has the power to do that.'

'I'm not a creature or an ordinary sorceress.'

'Oh, I know you hide many things from me but what baffles me is why you haven't tried to escape. I doubt your feelings have grown towards me.'

Two people behind King slowly lift their heads. Their faces are stricken with fear, but hope is etched in their eyes. I'm their last chance to survive. I wish I could give them a signal that I will free them somehow.

'A queen would never speak her feelings, but she would show them in her actions, as should a mighty king.'

He breaks eye contact to glance at Ash. 'I will allow you the small pleasure of keeping your pet. But I will ask for a small pleasure in return.'

'And what might that be?'

'All in good time.'

He nods to the door, indicating for me to exit. I walk past Ash, refraining from looking down at him, pretending to not care.

King's hand presses against the small of my back as he guides me upstairs. He returns me to my room and within a few short minutes, Ash comes in, locking the door behind him. He falls to the floor, still grasping his stomach.

I quickly throw a silencing spell over us. 'Change form, Ash. I can handle anyone who tries to enter.'

'We need to play his game until we can get him to Australia. He's mad enough to kill us both.'

'I'm trying.'

'Well, try harder.' He opens his hands, pulling them back from his stomach. He has a large burn which is blistered and bleeding. 'You can't push his buttons like you do Lazarus.'

'I'm sorry. I should have protected you and put up a shield to prevent this.'

'You can't reveal what you can do to King. He will use it against you in a fight. And you are mine to protect. I can't return home with your dead body. My soul would be no good to anyone.'

'Your soul will be fine. I promise not to use any powers in front of him.' I race to the bathroom, returning with a wet towel to gently clean his wound. 'Speaking of souls, I had to block out the pleas for help from the golden souls.'

'Imagine how hard it is for me to walk past as if not hearing them. It's in my blood to protect them and return them to the vault.'

'I'm sorry I got you into this.'

He takes the towel from my hands and presses it firmly against his wound.

Closing my eyes, I place both my hands on his arm and draw from within myself the colours I saw when the

Aboriginal family cared for me. They used bush medicine to heal my wounds so if I draw on those colours from the earth it may help Ash.

'What are you doing?' I ignore him and keep going. 'Jasmine?'

I flick open my eyes to see Ash staring wide-eyed. 'I was trying something out.'

Ash removes the towel. His wounds have partially healed.

'It worked! I drew on the Aboriginal healing colours and it worked.'

'I felt it leave your hands and surge through my body until it hit my stomach. A warm heat circled there, which must have been it healing.' He frowns. 'I've never heard of a sorcerer healing. Maybe you are a witch. Is this the first time you've used this power?'

'Yes, and it makes me wonder how long I've had it and whether I could have prevented my mother, Sky and Drake from dying.'

'You healed a superficial wound, not a life-threatening gash.'

'Glad you're here to keep my ego in check.' I smile and kiss him on the cheek.

'What are mates for?' Ash stands, the pain still evident. He wraps his large frame around me, including his webbed wings, hugging me. 'We will get out of this but for now, let's play his game. I need to heal so be a good girl and behave.' He kisses the top of my head before releasing me.

'I miss Lazarus.'

'I know you do, beautiful. And no doubt he will think I've had something to do with this.'

'No, he trusts you as I do. He may blame you.'

'Being a dragon, he will be jealous that we got kidnapped together.'

'I'm starting to wonder if King has quashed the powers he thinks I have. How can I draw on this healing power and succeed but when I try to draw on my dragon form I'm hindered?'

'He knows you've killed dragons and that you've probably gained their powers.' Ash rubs his chin and narrows his eyes. 'I reckon you're right. Make sure you don't slip up and reveal any more.'

'I won't. I promise.'

He squats down in his resting position. 'Later, beautiful.'

Dinner arrives, delivered by the same vampire as before. I keep the smoothie for Ash and the main meal. He needs more food than I do. I can survive on the breakfast and lunch I ate earlier.

'Can you lie beside me tonight, Ash? I miss Lazarus so much.' I move over in the bed and pat behind me. 'Just hold me.'

'It's tough being your friend with all these demands.' He winks at me before changing into human form.

He gives a cheeky smile then jumps over me to lie behind me. He draws me back into his chest. 'I knew you couldn't resist me.' He sniggers for a short second before his tone turns serious. 'We'll get out of this and when we do, I'll have so much pleasure telling your jealous dragon how we cuddled at night.'

'Do you value your life at all?'

We laugh but soon silence falls between us. 'I'll protect you and get you home to him. Trust me, Jazz.'

He pulls me in tight as Lazarus does. I picture Lazarus' smiling face before drifting off to sleep.

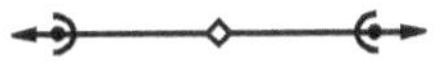

Chapter Five

It's been two weeks since King imprisoned us. The daily routine has been the same. I eat breakfast and lunch with King then return to my room with Ash and wait for our dinner to come so I can feed him.

I sneak food when I can, sticking it under my jumper. There is one chef who knows I'm stealing food, but he looks too scared to say a word. He turns his back when I reach for a bread roll and I now find he leaves leftover food out for me.

We have, on the odd occasion, roamed the castle but it usually ends up with someone dying. Ash has ripped off two vampires' heads who found my blood tempting. Lucky for me, none have come close to piercing my skin.

King questions me daily about my past life and fishes for information on the elite creatures who live in Australia. He usually becomes frustrated with my limited answers and inflicts pain on Ash. Once he ripped a soul from a gargoyle in a threat to take Ash away from me. All because I continue to admit to never meeting the greatest sorcerer, Aldore.

King demanded me to remove my dragon engagement ring, which I reluctantly did. I hid it safely behind a loose rock in the wall, telling King I had lost it.

The days are long and the nights longer. I miss Lazarus and know he will be beside himself with the fear of what has happened to me.

I mentioned to King that we were on our way to see the city when he kidnapped me. I say regularly I'd love to see it in the hope he will take us above ground.

I've flirted with his ego, giving him the impression I'm trustworthy and faithful to him. I should get an Oscar for all the acting I've done.

King often asks me if I still have feelings for Lazarus. I lie, saying the thought of a dragon repulses me. I tell him all my markings are due to untrustworthy dragons. Ash believes King is falling for my lies and for me, but up until now, I fear I failed.

Out of the blue, King decides to take me to see the city's highlights before we head over to see my father. The day, the hour, the minute can't come quick enough. We need to get our bearings and I need to show King I won't run. I need his trust to make our trip to Australia concrete.

'You do realise King is testing you so behave and stick to the plan even if we have a chance to escape. The goal is to kill him,' whispers Ash.

'I won't let you down.'

'We didn't go through all this to stuff it up now. We're so close to getting him back home. Just a few more days of playing the game, Jasmine, and you'll be back with Lazarus.'

'You have my word as a friend and as Australia's sorceress.'

After walking up a million sets of stairs we arrive at another grand house. His underground castle sits beneath it. We walk out the front door and the first thing that hits me is the warmth from the sun. I close my eyes and let my skin soak up its rays.

After a few seconds, I scan the area. The house is situated on a busy road at the edge of the city. 'You live next to the city?'

'Yes, there's no threat to our kind here.' King smiles.

'What if someone sees you or another creature?'

'I can fix that with one look.'

'You hypnotise them?' He nods. 'As you have hypnotised me.' The words leave my mouth but my skin crawls. I will never be hypnotised by him. Lazarus holds my heart now and will forever.

King turns and smiles at me. 'Don't confuse me with some-one who has a heart, my queen. You will be very disappointed.'

'I disagree, my king. I believe you do have a heart. You just have to remember how to use it.'

He stops dead still and holds eye contact. It's an eerie and unnerving feeling. I may be finding a softer side to the leech, one I can plunge a stake through.

A black van with tinted windows pulls up, interrupting our staring contest. The driver promptly gets out and slides open the side door.

'I thought you'd drive a Batmobile,' I joke, trying to break the ice.

King moves quickly to my side and leans to my ear. 'Please don't dissatisfy me today. I enjoy your wit and would hate to kill you.'

'I will prove I can be the queen you require. I may not kill for no reason, but I will stand by my king.'

'As soon as I get permission from your father I will wed, bed and turn you.' His fangs drop down, which makes my skin crawl.

'Until then.' I force a smile to my lips before climbing into the van. The fear of being wed, bed and turned flows cold through my veins.

'Maybe my queen can show me the location of the clans in Australia, as a show of trust and the favour you promised.'

'I only know of two but when in Australia I will show them to you if it will make you happy.'

'It will.'

Ash is the last to climb in, sliding the door closed before we take off. It's a short drive which doesn't give me enough time to get my bearings. Ash's head is on a swivel, but his face is blank. I wish he is telepathic so I can hear what's going on in that rock head of his.

The streets are littered with people, making my heart skip with excitement. If I can cause a commotion, we may be able to escape. King can't hypnotise everyone.

I glance over to Ash. His eyes are locked on mine. He shakes his head slowly. He must be reading my mind and knows I want to run.

King pulls out a pair of sunglasses and places them over his eyes. 'Shall we, my queen?'

'Yes, I'm excited to see the city.'

The door opens, and we step out onto a large area in front of a cathedral. The massive old church is covered with gargoyles. I glance at Ash and he nods. They are true gargoyles that we hope will help notify Hudson of our whereabouts. Ash is quick to be by my side.

'Stick to the plan. We don't know whose side these gargoyles are on. I doubt King would bring us here if they're in Hudson's clan,' Ash whispers under the noise of the crowd. 'And remember King is telepathic.'

Darn it. That was my next move. I need to stick to the plan or jeopardise our lives. King wouldn't be stupid enough to bring us here if there was a chance I'd overrun him.

King moves to my side, taking my hand in his cold one. My skin lifts but I glance up and fake a smile. He gives me a small squeeze of my hand, something a lover would do.

King shows us Big Ben, the London Eye and the Tower of London before heading into a shopping area. The whole time we've been walking I've noticed at least twenty people following. To make sure I wasn't paranoid, I walked backwards, pretending to get a better look at Big Ben. The people followed. Ash also notices and gives me a discreet nod. I thought it funny how King allowed me to leave his side.

King opens the door to an upmarket clothes and beauty store, ushering me in. The saleswomen race over to us. They bow their heads and cup their hands in front of them.

'Our king, your presence is unexpected. Please forgive our tardiness.'

'This is your queen.' King points his open hand in my direction.

The women bow further, 'How can we serve you, Queen?'

'Firstly, call me Jasmine.'

King has my face cupped in his cold hands. 'Never contradict me, especially in public. I have killed for less.' He leans in and for the first time, kisses my lips. A cool rush floods my body and I know it's not a spell but the sick feeling I get when he touches me.

He spins and speaks to the women. 'She is my queen and you will address her as such or pay the consequences. Now, please find some warmer clothes for her. Our home is a little chilly.'

'My queen, please follow us,' the women say in unison, obviously under King's hypnotic spell.

They dress me in clothes and jewels, none of which I will wear but I shut my mouth and play the game. I try to speak to the women, but they keep their eyes down, avoiding any conversation except to tell me how great I look.

I ask King for a little extra time to be pampered in the beauty salon. He agrees, leaving Ash and several henchmen in the store to guard me.

I ask the beautician if she can put a tattoo over my heart. She smiles, still not looking me in the eye, and says yes. I quickly scribble the design on a scrap piece of paper. She removes my t-shirt and cleans the area with alcohol. She holds the vibrating needle near my skin but stops when her hand starts shaking. 'For some reason, I find it hard to pierce your skin. It's like someone is holding my hand back.'

'Look at me in the eye,' I say, and she tries. 'I order you, as queen, to look at me in the eye.'

She does with wide, scared eyes. I smile and her eyes relax a little. 'I order you to give me the tattoo I desire.'

'Yes, my queen.' She places the vibrating needle onto my skin. She's not hypnotised, she's scared.

I watch as she starts, then an unbelievable transformation occurs. She stops and stares, her jaw gaping wide open in amazement. My tattoo completes itself. The design is slightly different from the one I drew but it is a yin-yang symbol with Lazarus' name scrolling through it. Maybe I do have dragon blood in me?

'My queen, I don't know what to say.'

'There is nothing to say. You will not repeat what you have seen here today. I came in and you helped me buy clothes and nothing more. Now I'd like one more jumper before I leave.'

I need to see if she will say something to the henchmen or the other sales assistant. But she does what she is told, obviously too scared of King to do anything different.

I'm relieved when we leave but unfortunately for Ash, his arms are full of shopping bags.

The day is ending and so is our outing. I'm disappointed there wasn't a chance to run or attack, but it would have been a death sentence for Ash, me and any humans close by.

Stopping me in my tracks is the scent I wish to never lose. Lazarus!

Ash is by my side pushing me forward. 'Keep going, stick to the plan or you'll kill all of us, including Lazarus.'

'Is there something wrong, my queen?' King says in a loud voice.

'An old scent I wish to remove,' I say with a quivering tone.

'I'm sure I can help you with that but let's see how you plan on doing that.' King smiles but narrows his eyes to something behind me.

'Jasmine!'

Lazarus! My heart jumps in my chest when I hear his voice. I hear Ash growl beside me, bringing me back to why we are here—to gain King's confidence. But all I want to do is wrap my arms around him and smother him with kisses.

'Hello, Lazarus.' I keep my tone flat, and with every fibre of my body, control my heartbeat.

'I've gone mad trying to find you. Hudson has every creature in England looking for you. Oh, babe, it's so good to see you.'

Lazarus takes several quick steps towards me. King steps in front, blocking him.

'Am I doing your job for you, gargoyle?' King spits and looks directly at Ash.

'Forgive me, my king.' Ash bows before dropping the shopping and moving in front of us. It allows King to move beside me.

King wraps an arm around my shoulders, draping it the same way Lazarus would do. The chill from his body cools me which is a firm reminder of why we are here—to kill him and save the humans and gargoyles he has captured. I'd be selfish if I ran now.

'Jasmine?'

'She has moved on, dragon, and so should you,' says Ash, his tone firm.

'With him? A cold-blooded vampire! I doubt that.'

'Does your blood bubble under that leather skin, knowing she now lies with me, dragon?' King speaks in a condescending manner.

'You're a venomous snake. Jasmine would never be with you.'

King drops a fang down from the roof of his mouth and runs his tongue along it.

'My venom is more powerful than a mere snake.' King pulls my hair away from my neck and runs his finger up and down the length of my artery. In an aggressive movement,

Lazarus steps forward but is stopped by Ash's large frame. 'Please, take that step you're anticipating and you'll feel for yourself how quickly my venom can work. This woman stands by me as my queen and me her king. Together we will rule the mystic world, eventually taking control of the pitiful human one. Together we are an unbeatable god!'

'You're deluded if you think any elite creature that isn't drugged by your venom will follow you.'

'I already have the majority of the gargoyle clans in England at my mercy.'

'As I said, drugged by your venom! None follow you voluntarily. No creature bows to another as it is known that all creatures are equal.'

'They are all equal, under me, their king. They are all equal servants to obey and praise me and once Jasmine is united with me in blood and marriage they will bow or crumble to her or she will break their legs so bowing will be easier.'

'Jasmine will never stand by you!' Lazarus spits through his sharpening teeth. 'Tell him, babe.'

'My king speaks the truth!' I say. I need to stop Lazarus from losing it and transforming on the streets of England. 'You need to walk away, dragon, before I blow a hole in you.' I slip my arm around King's waist and draw him in tight to my side.

'Jasmine?'

'You heard our queen. Move on, dragon.' Ash leans into Lazarus and puffs his chest.

'Ash, I will break your neck if you ever chest me again,' growls Lazarus.

'Give it your best shot, leather-guts. Give me the excuse I've been waiting for. I've been praying for this day.'

'Ash, step down, he's not worth it,' I say.

'It would be a great shame if you broke the queen's favourite toy,' snarls King.

'Toy?'

'As I said, dragon, the gargoyles bow down to me. Ash does the same for his queen.'

Lazarus laughs, 'You can't be serious?' His eyes lock with mine. 'Jazz, come with me. We can leave as soon as you want and go back home to Australia.'

'Enough, dragon!' King's loud tone makes me jump. 'I need to take my queen back to her castle.'

'She's not going with you!' growls Lazarus.

'I will devour you in public if need be, dragon. Then I will hypnotise any onlooker.'

'Jasmine?' Lazarus pleads my name, but I hold firm, hoping he will forgive the words that are about to come out of my mouth. I dig deep and draw on the issues Lazarus and I fear most.

'You were a phase in my life, dragon. I could never risk being with a creature who has little or no control. How could I trust you with any child I conceived? Not that I can conceive with a dragon. Malachi didn't show you as the father of my child. It's King who can give me the child I desire.'

My heart is being strangled by the harsh words, but I need Lazarus to go before King kills him. The memory of him killing innocent creatures is still fresh in my mind. I love Lazarus too much to see him hurt and if it means he hates me, so be it.

Ash steps with purpose toward Lazarus and blocks my view. He's trying to make it easier for me.

'Move on, dragon, this is my last warning before I crush your human body. The queen is now inked to the king.'

'She'll never be inked to anyone but me. Tell him, Jasmine.'

I take a deep breath to control my beat before I speak. 'Do you see a marking on my chest, dragon? No, I am not yours as I don't and will never trust you. I'm scarred from head to toe from burns and the talons of dragons. I despise all of them and will take great pleasure in bringing down your kind.' I take another breath and hit him with the words I know will tear at his heart. 'I wanted to be with Drake, but he died, so out of boredom I chose to be with you. But now I have met a better man. King is my fiancé.'

He exhales a defeated breath. I need him to leave and now.

'Drake?'

'Yes, we were in love and together we planned on leaving the clan to live a life far from you. You were my third choice.'

'Third?'

'There was another.'

'Who?'

'Enough! I've moved on!' I draw on a small anoric and hold it in the open palm of my hand. 'I care not for you or this boring conversation. Do you need more persuasion to move on?'

I keep my heartbeat ticking over at a controlled pace, catching my breath as it tries to take off. Lazarus will be listening for anything irregular. He tilts his head and falls back a few steps as if my words have punched him in the gut. I suppose they have.

My heart is breaking silently into a hundred pieces. He is the last person in the world I want to hurt.

'Good choice, dragon. Move on and I'll spare your life only because my queen reassures me, on a regular basis, you mean nothing to her. She is giving me her ultimate sacrifice. She will give up her human life and become like me. I will turn her myself on our wedding night.'

Lazarus locks his fiery eyes with mine in desperate hope. I lift my hand and his eyes widen. I know a threat like this will boil his blood. He has warned me many times to never raise my hand to him. I pray he will forgive me.

'Quench your threat, my queen. I have the situation covered.' King smirks.

I scan the area. There are at least twenty vampires moving in and circling us. Lazarus also notices and grows another foot taller. I pray my words have hurt him and he decides to walk away.

From out of the dark, Keira moves to Lazarus' side. I know my eyes widen with anger and my breath hitches.

'My queen, I sense your dislike for this creature. As a gift, I can snap her delicious but fine neck,' purrs King.

'She is another insignificant dragon.'

Keira wraps her hand over Lazarus' arm, tugging him gently away. 'We're out-numbered.'

'But a gift to show your gratitude would be nice,' I say, sarcastically grinning at Keira.

Ash flicks me with a soft finger before stepping towards King.

'Excuse the interruption, King, but we seem to be attracting several sets of human eyes. Maybe the queen would enjoy a gift that doesn't attract so much attention.'

With a movement quicker than the eye can see, King slaps Ash's face, making him stumble away. The force had to be hard to move a man like Ash. It would have concussed a mere human.

'Don't ever stand between me and my queen, gargoyle. But I agree, I now have her scent and can hunt her down, kill her, and offer her head as a gift.'

'There will be no need. I have obviously made a mistake in thinking Jasmine was someone with a heart. You have darkened it, King. Congratulations,' growls Lazarus, holding his fiery red eyes to mine. His body is trembling; he's forcing himself to stay in human form.

He turns and walks away with Keira clinging to his arm. She turns her head and smirks, whispering low, 'I should have taken a bite out of you when I had the chance. You're a disgrace to your family.'

'Bring it on, anytime, any day, you slithering snake,' I whisper.

'Is everything all right?' asks King, grasping my hand in his. He must have heard her.

'Yes, my dearest King. Everything is as it should be.' I smile through gritted teeth.

'I love hearing you say my name with your cute Australian accent.' He stops and grasps both my hands in his cold ones. He drops to one knee and holds up a ring. 'Since you are so old-fashioned I wanted to ask you to marry me whilst on bended knee.'

'Oh!' I'm totally shocked and drawn back to Malachi's vision of my future. There's a dark-headed man who is down on his knee proposing to me. I always thought it was Lazarus. I blink away the vision.

'You have proven today you are loyal to me. Will you marry me without force?'

I flick my eyes to Ash who nods and frowns as if telling me to agree. 'No force needed. I accept your proposal but only on the blessing of my father.'

He lifts the ring higher allowing me to see the sharp teeth underneath.

'Its teeth bite into your flesh so it's held in one spot for eternity. Once on your finger, it can never be removed.'

'Please keep this ring until we receive the blessing. It is proper etiquette to do so,' I say, knowing what I said is a load of frog-pooh. He smiles and kisses the back of my hand, making my skin crawl.

We arrive back at the castle with King going straight down to the blood bank for his evening drink. I quickly head to my room with Ash in tow. I turn on the shower then cover us with a silencing dome before bursting into tears.

'You did well, Jazz,' says Ash. 'King believes you're standing by him.'

'It felt like sticking a knife into Laz's heart.'

'He looked devastated if that's any consolation.'

'He didn't fight very hard for me.'

'You were very convincing. Your words were stinging like salt in an open wound.'

'And then there's Keira! Ugh! You should have let King snap her neck. She's probably all over him right this second!'

'Laz wouldn't stand by and let any dragon be killed. King would have killed Laz as well. Remember who we're dealing with. He's not just a vampire. He has sorcery powers.'

'He didn't fight for me, Ash.'

Tears well up in my eyes again and before long I'm bawling. Ash embraces me, pulling me into his firm chest. He kisses the top of my head and rocks me gently.

'We need to stick to the plan, especially now King thinks you like him. Laz will forgive you when he knows why you said those things.'

'I fear it won't be that easy to get his trust back. I'm sure Keira is consoling him as we speak.'

'I don't believe I'm saying this, but Laz loves you and hopefully, he saw through your charade. He may be brewing up his own plan of attack.'

I look up into Ash's blue eyes. He smiles warmly down at me.

'I don't believe you, but thanks for being my friend. And I'm sorry King hit you. I felt helpless standing by and doing nothing.'

'As I said, beautiful, it's all a charade. You're giving up more than I am. King's day will come and when the mighty dark sorcerer dies, we will party like no other.'

'I love you, Ash.'

'I know you do. What's not to love?' He smiles before kissing me on the forehead. 'It will be all over soon enough. Now turn the shower off as King may become suspicious.'

As usual, I am brought my evening meal before bed. True

to form, Ash waits until the vampire leaves before jumping up from his designated position to devour the main meal and smoothie. I didn't get a chance to steal food for him today and feel guilty when he swallows it down in one mouthful.

Ash sleeps beside me, trying to comfort me but I'm beyond gutted. I fall asleep with a broken heart and a soggy pillow from the continual flood of tears running down my face.

CHAPTER SIX

KING'S PRIVATE PLANE has enough fuel to get us to Australia without stopping. I've anticipated today—the day King meets my father. I pray my plan works and my father uses his power to overcome and help kill the dark sorcerer.

The last few days have been torturous. Remembering the look on Lazarus' face when I spat hateful words at him, together with the thought of Keira's warm arms comforting him.

I've stolen enough food to give Ash the strength he needs. For some reason, he's finding it quicker to change form, and his strength is becoming more powerful. He swears there's something in the water that is making him stronger.

Last week, King lifted the spell covering my room, allowing me to use my powers within it. He wants my sorcery strong for when he changes me.

I've practised all my powers, much to Ash's anguish, as he's been at the end of all my anorics and shocks.

I calm my heartbeat as we approach my house. My father is outside, tending to the garden. which would have to be the first time he has ever done that. He lifts his head as we drive in. He is shocked to see us. This is not a good sign. I was hoping the 'Aussie grapevine' would have notified him of our arrival.

I pray he reads my signals and destroys this dark monster before King works out that my father was once a sorcerer.

I open the car door and race towards him. His arms spread open as I throw myself at him. I feel King behind me, moving like a lightning bolt. I pray my father recognises him as a vampire and not a dragon.

'My baby girl.'

'Dad, I've missed you so much.'

'Let me look at you. You've grown.'

'I'm exactly the same size.'

'What brings you here? Don't get me wrong, I'm happy to see you.'

'I came to introduce you to my… fiancé. I am to be married to King.' I force a fake smile on my face. I flick my eyebrows and hope King doesn't catch me.

'I see. This is happening very quickly.'

'Let me introduce myself.' King steps up to my father with his hand held out to shake. 'I am King, and together Jasmine and I have come to ask for your blessing.'

'I see.' My father shoots his eyes towards Ash. 'And what brings you here Ash? Again, I mean no disrespect. It's always nice to see my daughter's friends.'

Ash opens his mouth to speak but King interrupts, 'He is our chaperone, of course. Jasmine is very old-fashioned and will not be alone with a man until she is married.'

'I see.' My father shakes King's hand. 'I sense an accent, King.'

'I am from England, but we will be living here for several months of the year. Jasmine has a house she wants to show me. One we hope to acquire. We will be negotiating with the present occupants in the next week as to when we can move in. I have several family members who will be joining us.'

'It sounds like you have everything covered.'

'I do. All we need is your blessing.'

'I see. You're very quiet, Ash,' my father says, eyeing him.

'Yes, sir. I'm excited to help plan the wedding.' Ash keeps his distance from King, as ordered.

'Where's this house you love so much, Jasmine?' asks my father.

'I don't think you know of it but it's near the forest area and a hollow pass.' I try to give Dad the message I'm heading for Nogard Hollow.

'You're right, I don't. But if this is what you want who am I to interfere? You have my blessing, sweetheart, as do you, King. But I ask that Ash continue to be her guardian until you're married.'

'Thank you and I agree that Ash will stay around to be her servant.'

'Servant? I said guardian.'

'That is what I meant. I'm sorry, I was distracted for a moment,' says King, his head high and tilted.

I know what distracted King because I felt and smelt Xandria as well.

'Can you men excuse me for a moment? I need to use the bathroom.'

'Of course, my queen. Ash will accompany you.' King smiles.

'To the toilet?' my father says.

'I value your daughter's safety, sir.'

'As do I but this is and will always be her home and she is safe here.'

'Humour me.' King stands closer to my father. I see his eyes start to swirl, locking with my father's. If he doesn't play along, this could be over quickly.

'It makes me happy that you protect my daughter. Ash should always be by her side,' my father says in a flat monotone.

'I knew you'd see it my way.'

King has either hypnotised my father or my dad is one great actor. I'm hoping for the latter.

I walk casually into the house and sniff out Xandria.

'Hello human traitor,' she whispers.

'Xandria, I don't have time for your games. I need you to listen carefully. Warn the creatures King is here and I'm taking him to Nogard Hollow. I need help to bring him down.'

'Why should I help you? You are a traitor to everyone, even to the angel, Malachi. You stole five years from him and never offered to give them back. Plus, Paul went to England to find you and now he's missing.'

'What do you mean give them back?'

'When an angel gives you lives you can give them back to him in a ceremony. But you, human, are a traitor and never offered. He will die young because of you.'

'Listen, fairy, we don't have much time,' Ash spits, grabbing her petite arm.

'Let go or I'll scream!'

'Keep your voice down or you'll be King's dinner,' I snarl.

'You put me under a glass jar when all Xandria wanted was to be your friend.'

'Are you kidding me? I'm asking for help.'

'Jasmine!' yells King from outside.

'I've got to go. Do as I ask, please Xandria.'

'Xandria will think about it if you return Paul to me.' She pulls invisible lint from her dress.

'I don't know where Paul is.'

'Do it, fairy, or I will hunt you down myself and de-wing you,' says Ash.

We're quick to move out of the house and away from Xandria. I wipe my hands on my pants, pretending I had just washed them.

'Better, my queen?'

'Yes, thank you, King. But we need to get going if I'm to show you the house before dark.'

'You can't leave. You only just arrived,' my father says.

King steps up to my father and stares directly into his eyes.

'We've been here for the last week getting to know each other. You're happy with our union and you look forward to when we return one day with our children,' dictates King.

'It was fantastic seeing you all. Can't wait for the grandkids to start arriving.' My father shakes hands with King while patting him on the back like they're long-lost mates.

I clench my teeth at the thought of ever being with this dark man.

As we drive away, my father waves and smiles. His face looks oblivious to what has just occurred. Maybe he has lost his powers since he hasn't used them for so long.

'You didn't have to hypnotise my father. He is no threat to us.'

'We needed to move on. So when you entered the house did you see anyone?' I take a deep breath to speak but he interrupts. 'Be careful how you answer because if I don't like your answer, Ash will receive our punishment, as you know.'

'No one was inside but I did sense someone watching us while we were outside.' I keep my tone level.

I feel his eyes boring into me. I flick my head to catch his eyes swirling. 'How dare you question me, King!' I try to sound hurt, hoping it will convince him I'm loyal.

'Pull the car over,' he demands.

I fear Ash is about to be punished for my lie. I do as he asks, turning off the ignition. I face King and huff as if I'm annoyed.

'Don't look at me like that, even though your tight pout is cute.'

'You hypnotised my father and accuse me of lying, so excuse me if I'm a little ticked off!'

He leans over and tries to kiss me. I pull back and turn my head.

'You may be "ticked off" but I smelt fairy. It's a taste I quite enjoy, similar to how humans like chocolate.'

'I've smelt fairy and that's not what I sensed.'

He grabs hold of my wrist and squeezes it, his long nail piercing the skin. He lifts my wrist and sucks on the small hole he pierced. He closes his eyes as if enjoying the taste then suddenly flicks them open, alarmed.

'Have you been drinking and eating your nightly meals?'

'Sometimes.' I'm curious to why he asks such an odd question.

'The smoothie you have been drinking every night has my blood in it.'

'What the hell?'

'If you decided to leave me, you will still turn into a vampire. You would also be attracted and linked to me and only me. I had to be sure the dragon was out of your system.'

'Does my word not mean anything to you?'

'You mistake me as an angel. I'm King, a vampire who takes whatever the hell he wants!'

'Including me?'

'You never wanted to be with me at the start or have you forgotten?'

'Maybe so but I fell in love with you. Maybe that was a mistake.'

He swirls his dark blood-filled eyes and I frown at his attempt to still control me.

'Excuse my behaviour, my queen.'

'I didn't know vampires were jealous.'

'We aren't. If we don't get what we want, we kill it!'

'Threatening me will not make me love you more. It will do the opposite.'

'Jasmine,' he whispers in a low tone. I give him my full attention, fearing his next move. 'I will never threaten you. If I choose to kill you, you won't see it coming.'

'I take that as a threat.'

'As you wish, my queen.'

He leans forward and this time I let his foul lips touch mine. It's a cold and chilling kiss. He punctures my bottom lip with his fang and I pull away.

'Since you're not drinking my blood, I may have to inject it slowly into you. If I do it in one large bite, I may accidentally kill you.'

'Don't underestimate my strength.'

'Oh, I know you're strong and hiding your powers. I am King for a reason. I didn't get here by being naive and trusting anyone, even someone as sweet as you. You don't think I came all this was without backup?'

'I'd be disappointed if you haven't brought back up. I hope you'd have me protected from any unexpected attacks.' I silently kick myself for not keeping my senses open. I should have known he wouldn't come alone. How stupid am I?

'I plan on the unexpected.'

'As do I, King. Now can I continue driving?'

'Yes. I will have you alone soon enough, without your guardian gargoyle. Then I will teach you how to obey me fully.'

'You have enough lap-dogs. Surely you want your queen to be someone with substance and a strong backbone,' I say before switching on the car.

'You will need both of those things but defy me once and you will quickly learn what pain is.'

I decide not to push him further, instead, I use my senses to work out who he has brought here. I need to know what I'm up against.

I flick my eyes to the revision mirror, catching Ash's blue eyes. He winks at me and slightly nods his head. I wish he was telepathic. That's it! When we approach Nogard Hollow I'll try to contact one of the dragons. I'll need to be grounded and start to transform into the dragon form using their telepathic wave. I pray Falcon or Corbin is around to hear me.

'Since we have your father's consent, I think it now proper to place the ring on your finger.' King turns in his seat and surprises me by grabbing my hand. He holds it tight and slips on the ring. He abruptly lets my hand go when it's firmly on my ring finger. 'Try pulling it off and the metal teeth will rip your finger off.'

In shock, I glance down at the black metal ring circling my finger. I try to move it, but the teeth bite down into my flesh. Blood trickles down my finger. King grabs my hand and with his tongue, licks around my finger, cleaning the blood away.

'Hmm, delicious! It will stop bleeding soon enough. Drive on, my queen.'

I'm too shocked to say anything. My only fear is getting it off.

We drive through the night with Ash taking the wheel, giving me time to pretend I'm asleep.

I sense four other vampires nearby; I lose their scent now and then. King has placed a cloaking spell on them, but it drops intermittently. I've noticed when he is using one power, such as the cloaking spell, his other senses lessen. He can't seem to use two powers at once. This may be an advantage.

As dawn breaks, we arrive at the forest between Nogard Hollow and Elyograg Castle.

'I need to use the ladies' room,' I say from the back seat of the car.

'We are in the middle of nowhere, Jasmine,' states King.

'Your queen has squatted behind a tree before, she can do it again.'

'You're full of surprises.' He chuckles.

'I wouldn't want to bore you.'

'That you will never do.' He laughs as if we are friends.

Ash pulls the car over next to the trees' edge and jumps out to open my door.

'The queen can relieve herself by herself, gargoyle.'

'Of course, my mistake,' says Ash, bowing his head but not before giving me a quick look.

With a brisk stride, I head into the trees and move behind a clump of thick bushes. My head tells me to run for the castle but in my heart, I know Ash will die before I reach it. With my feet firmly planted on the ground, I draw a silencing spell over me before drawing on my dragon telepathic powers. I pray King doesn't penetrate my cloaking spell as I did his.

'Lazarus? Falcon? Corbin? Kite?' I echo, but nothing. *Jet?'*

'I hear you, Jasmine. I knew you'd come back home. Where are you? What happened?' echoes Jet. How can he hear the telepathic waves of a dragon?

'My queen, you're taking a long time. Is everything going according to plan?' yells King from the other side of the bush.

'Please, King, give me some privacy,' I say in an annoyed tone.

'Which I am giving you, for now!'

I hear him move away and return my focus to Jet.

'I can't explain everything now. I explained it all to Xandria.'

'She was here earlier but never mentioned you. Please tell me King hasn't turned you?'

'He plans to soon. I don't have long but in short, I have brought King here in the hope, that together with my father, I can kill him.'

'I will kill him,' echoes Jet.

'He's too strong for you or me but with my father, I can do it. I'm heading to Nogard Hollow. Can you reach my father and the dragons? There are another four vampires following us.'

'The dragons won't help. To them and to most of the elite creatures you are a traitor.'

'He would have killed Ash, Laz and me if I didn't obey.'

'I won't let that happen!'

All of a sudden, I feel a tightening grip on my throat. King is strangling me.

'What were you doing?' he says.

He loosens his grip allowing me to answer.

'I was breathing in the smell of the forest and the creatures that roam it.'

'I don't believe you.'

'Am I not showing you where the dragons and gargoyles live?'

'Yes,' he hisses.

'Let's go, my king. I'm sure our presence is being spread across the land. We need to slip by them before they get wind of us.'

'If this is a trap your pet gargoyle will be the first to die.'

I nod and pull my neck from his grasp. While walking to the car I contact Jet again.

'Jet?'

'We're on our way but the dragons are still calling you a traitor. Laz is wild so keep your distance.'

'My father?'

'He's with them. Let us deal with King and his goons.'

'No, he's too strong for you.' Our conversation is interrupted as King lifts me into the car.

Ash is behind the wheel and slowly drives towards Nogard Hollow. I sense the four vampires closing in. My heart is starting to race in fear that King knows of my plan. I try my best to calm down, but my palms start to sweat.

Ash pulls the car over, giving us a good ten-minute walk. As soon as I am out of the car the four vampires land beside me. I fear I may have made the wrong decision and have brought the devil and his henchmen to the people I love.

'We will have to walk from here,' I say as confidently as I can. Ash shoots me a look in the rear vision mirror, concern etched in his eyes.

'Gargoyle, change form now. My queen will need protecting and you're useless in human form.'

'As you wish, King.' Ash has a glint of a smile that reaches his eyes. He has hope. I wish I had the same confidence.

Ash doesn't waste time. I follow suit and King is soon behind me. He reaches for my arm and grips it firmly as the four vampires surround us.

King turns to the vampires. 'Have we been followed?'

'There are dragons, kangaroos and large dogs,' one replies, making me laugh.

'Excuse the snigger but I once thought every animal could change form. The dogs are dingoes. Both dingoes and kangaroos and even koalas do not change form or work with the elite creatures.' King stares an unimpressed glare. 'You're hurting me.'

He smiles and loosens his grip. 'I'm reminding you of who is in charge.'

'Of course, my king. Let's move quickly to stay undetected. My cloak spell does have its limits.'

He steps away and whispers to his head vampire, 'What of the dragons you saw?'

'There are two dragons, both feeding and unaware of our presence. The queen's cloaking spell works well.'

'Huh, you doubt me!'

I turn my back on them and see a snide look on Ash's gargoyle face. The dragons and dingoes know exactly who and where we are. The stage is set.

Ash and I lead the way through the forest, making as much noise as we can. Covering myself in a cloaking spell, I send out a message to Jet letting him know we are minutes away from ground zero. He tells me they're ready and waiting.

In my last battle, I lost my mother. I think about drawing on hers, Grandfather's and Sky's energy to help me fight. But last time they drew from my powers and sharing them may weaken me too much and be my undoing.

'I feel the welcome mat has been rolled out, Jasmine,' says King, close to my ear. I hadn't realised he had moved so close to me.

'Your senses are stronger than mine.'

'Oh, I doubt that,' he snarls.

We step out from the trees with King on one side of me, Ash on the other and the four vampires behind us.

My Father is standing in front of Nogard Hollow with five dragons behind him. I sense Jet and the heartbeats from several other dragons hidden in the forest on the far side. The dingoes are also close by—their howling gives their presence and location away.

'I presume your Father has hidden talents. He must be a powerful man or have the dragons brought him here as a pawn? I will remind you I will not be persuaded by the likes of him. He means nothing to me,' says King.

'But he does to me. We came all this way to get his approval.'

'That is what I wanted you to think. I came to see if you would be a traitor to your clan and that, my queen, is yet to be determined.'

Ash interrupts. 'Shall we proceed? I believe we are expected.'

'Lead the way, gargoyle, as it will be your head that falls first.'

I step towards Ash so I can protect him when the fight starts.

'My queen, you will remain by my side and under the protection of me and my men.'

'As you wish.' I move beside him with Ash dropping back as well.

We walk the clearing, the distance becoming closer to the moment I've prayed for.

My father slowly moves towards us with two dragons

flanking him. It's Falcon and Corbin. I can't see Lazarus and presume he is one of the dragons-in-waiting. I don't want to waste my energy or lose focus to work out where he is.

Out the corner of my eye, I see the two angels, Malachi and Gabby, standing in the doorway of Nogard House. I didn't sense them, so I presume someone has covered them in a cloaking spell. I wonder who else is hidden under the spell. My heart thuds hard, rushing the adrenaline that fuels my veins.

We stop with a fifty-metre gap between us and my father. King bursts into a boisterous laugh. 'Do I sense angels? Mm, delicious,' he slurs, dragging the 's' through his teeth. 'I may keep them alive until I turn you, my queen, as they are the ultimate drop to taste.'

'I'll pass.'

'Is that all you Australians bring to a fight? I can sense your gargoyles-in-waiting. Show yourselves!'

Six gargoyles step out from the treeline, wings expanded in attack mode. I gasp when I spot Jet who is being flanked by Jarius and Lysander.

'Ah, yes, my queen. Your white heart gives you away. Which one is your nephew or shall I kill them one by one until I get a reaction from you?'

'I don't know what you mean.' But my voice quivers, betraying me.

He raises his eyebrow as if to question me. 'You have a spy amongst the Australian clan. One who has told me of your nephew, Jet. The powers he holds are like none other. He will join me or die.'

'No!'

He turns to nod to his head-vampire who does the same to the treed area. I'm confused until six gargoyles step out, wings held out in defence mode, mimicking the Australian clan. Another two vampires follow and stand behind them.

'I also have the power to cloak. Did you think I'd come all this way unprepared? I knew you would alert your old clan to our arrival. I anticipated this outcome. But the difference between your gargoyles and mine is that mine will fight on my command, not like your peaceful bunch.

'My vampires will take care of the dragons, leaving Jet and you for me. You will be my bride after this fight, where I will turn you, and together with you controlling your nephew, we will be unstoppable.'

Out the corner of my eye, I spot Ash scanning the gargoyles who support King. He indicates by holding four fingers together that four of them will side with us. During our time at King's lair, he had searched out gargoyles who would support us in battle in return for sanctuary in Australia.

I let Jet and any other dragon who can hear me know telepathically not to attack those four gargoyles. I pray my silence spell is still holding over King and he doesn't catch wind of my message.

'Is it me you're looking for?' Jet stands in front of my father, his large gargoyle arms perched on his hips.

'And what a fine specimen you are, Jet,' says King snidely. 'Lower your guard, young gargoyle, or your precious Jasmine will feel the pain.'

'Touch one hair on her head and you will be the one feeling the pain,' he snarls.

Without warning, my head feels an extraordinary agony, as if stuck in a tightening vice. I scream, grabbing both sides of my head, dropping to the ground.

Use your cloaking spell but draw it from the earth not the air, my father echoes.

I summon up the strength to push away the pain and force a cloaking spell over me by drawing it from the earth. The pain subsides slowly.

Ash pulls me to my feet in a slow but sure sweep. I feel King's eyes bore into me, but I keep my focus on my Father and Jet.

The dragons in the background snort smoke and spit small warning flames. The tension between the two groups is bubbling to a quick boil. The fangs on the vampires have dropped to indicate they're ready to kill.

'I offer all gargoyles sanctuary if you stand down,' yells King.

'Huh! You mean to become a slave to the vamps,' replies Jet, crossing his clenched fists across his chest.

King smiles. 'I believe it's better than death.'

'You'd know about that, leech!'

'Ah, I see you get your wit from your Aunt Jasmine.'

'I've inherited more than you can handle, bat.' Jet drops his hands, opens them and displays bright white anorics in each hand.

'Jet, control! This is what he wants,' says my father.

'No, Aldore, this is what I want!' growls Jet.

'Aldore?' I say under my breath.

The mighty mystical wizard of all wizards is my father.

King bursts out laughing. 'I should have recognised you. It has been a long time since our last meeting and you were in a different form then. I must congratulate you on hiding for so long. I was starting to presume you were dead. Or maybe it was my wishful thinking.' King bows slowly but keeps his eyes up. 'Your cloaking spell is one of the strongest I've known. I didn't sense your sorcery when I shook your hand.' He smiles wide and rolls his shoulders back. 'The handshake blessing your daughter's union to me.'

'Aldore?' I find myself repeating in disbelief.

'Don't tell me that you've never told your daughter who you are?'

'I didn't want her to be a part of this world.' My father holds my eye contact.

King faces me. 'You just became even more valuable to me, my queen. Your powers are unlimited and you kept them hidden.'

He nods to the vampires beside me.

'If anything unexpected happens, I want both of you to bite your venom into her. Make them small but deep bites and don't either of you dare drink from her. That will be my pleasure. I'd prefer to turn her myself, but my circumstances have changed, and I now need to kill my greatest rival. Her father, Aldore.'

'No, He's not Aldore. He's my father!'

'I've wasted enough time.'

King waves his hands in the air, pointing towards my father and the clan. Lightning bolts fire from his fingers, heading for them. The bolts crack and ricochet off an invisible shield. Jet retaliates with half-a-dozen anorics, hitting three vampires and one gargoyle. King moves forward but I'm caged in by his vampires.

'Bite me and I'll rip your fangs out!' I say.

A deafening band of roaring dragons, growling gargoyles and howling dingoes vibrates my eardrums. Four of the gargoyles behind me move beside Ash, who orders them to get me released. I keep my eyes on my father, drawing up an electric shock, mixing it with the draw of an anoric while keeping the cloaking spell over me. I explode, shooting the shocked vampires away from me. The gargoyles attack them on Ash's command, with him darting to my side.

King is metres in front of my father, penetrating the force-field. My father stands tall and looks ready to attack. I spin around and the gargoyles rip apart the two closest vampires.

'Jazz, light them on fire,' yells Ash.

I stand stunned at how easily the gargoyles killed them.

'Now, damn it!' He opens his wings wide, covering me from King's sight. In a breath, I do as he orders, and blue flames fire from my fingertips, hitting both torn vampires. They burst into glorious black and red flames.

Two vampires are closing in on the gargoyles while the others back up King. Several dragons stomp out from the tree line behind me.

King turns his head around and smiles at me. 'I told you I came prepared, my queen.'

'I will never be your queen.'

I throw a lightning shock towards him. It bounces off a shield that encases him. My attempt amuses him and infuriates me.

King throws both his hand towards the earth, then holds them up as if scooping up an invisible force. He's breaking my father's shield! He smiles at me.

'That was too easy.'

'Drop dead, leech!'

'Oh, how I'm going to enjoy disciplining that mouth of yours.'

King's dragons are quick to move, eager to attack Falcon and Corbin, who are behind my father.

Several dragons appear from behind Nogard Hollow. It's Lazarus! He's angry, loud and in full attack mode, as are the dragons beside him. I'm awestruck at the sight of the man I love and distracted until I feel a set of vampire teeth enter my neck.

I scream, shooting an electric volt through my body. It shoots the vampire several metres away. Jet pounces on top of him, biting a chunk out of his neck before ripping his head off. He holds his body between his strong gargoyle hands and rips him apart.

'No one bites my girl,' he growls, winking at me. 'Go to the angels. They'll draw the venom out!'

'Not now, Jet, we need to kill King. My father needs my help!'

I glance over at Ash, who is fighting King's dragons and the remainder of the vampires with the help of the gargoyles.

Jet takes off towards my father who stands square-shouldered to King. I chase after Jet, stopping when I stand in front of my father, Jet to the side.

'Look at all the bloodshed that could have been avoided. You should have stayed away, Aldore. Now I'll have to kill you and do it in front of your daughter.'

I quickly scan the area and every creature is in combat with King's clan. Blood and bodies litter the ground and I can't work out who is winning.

'You're mistaken, as it is me that will kill you before my daughter's eyes,' says Father in a calm tone.

'With Jet on my side and Jasmine as my bride, we will take over Australia, England and then the world. All creatures will bow down to me or they too will die.' I spot the red swirls circle in King's eyes as he locks them to Jet. 'Will you stand by me, Jet?'

Jet's features calm before he replies, 'Yes, my King.'

'No! You're hypnotising him!'

'Come stand by me, my son.' Jet moves to King's side and folds his wings behind his back. Jet is the strongest amongst the elite creatures. He has sorcery, dragon and gargoyle strength. It's a mixture made for an unbeatable king. If he's under King's spell we are all doomed.

'Dad?'

'Go to Malachi,' says my father.

'No, we do this together.' I glare at King.

'One out of three. I'd hope you'd join me voluntarily, Jasmine. But Jet here is more than adequate to help me reign and rule. With my blood running through him he will be unbeatable.'

Before King can utter another word, my father ignites his hands with a magnificent blue anoric. Lightning sparks within them as he fires at King. They hit him hard but fade away to nothing. It's like water off a duck's back.

King throws back the same ammunition, except his are as black as coal. Father drops to the ground and rolls to the side before sending a large boulder torpedoing toward King.

King flicks them to the side with a point of his hand, hitting and injuring a group of dragons fighting close by, one being Falcon.

'Falcon!' I yell. He slowly staggers to his feet; blood draining from the fresh wound gaping on his side.

'*I'll be fine. Concentrate on King,*' he says telepathically.

I spin around in time to see Jet pounce onto King's back, digging his sharp claws and teeth into his back. He was acting! By the look on his face, he is set on killing King. His growl echoes louder than the dragons behind me. He's trying to tear him apart.

King shoots out an almightily blast, flinging Jet violently from his back. When he lands it sounds like the crack of a whip. I pray he has not broken anything. He releases an ear-splitting roar and tries to get to his feet. He collapses. He tries again but fails, screeching out in pain.

Anger automatically fills my veins.

My body jolts into a mixture of dragon and gargoyle, firing an electric bolt toward King. It hits him in the chest, blistering him.

My father counter attacks with his blue electric anorics, striking him several times. I attack again, my bolts darkening in colour with each throw. Each attack throws him back several metres but seconds after he's hit, he starts to heal. I've never seen anything like it.

I draw from below the earth, digging deeper than I have before. I feel the vampire's venom surge and run through my veins, which fuels my anger further. I'm not spending another day without Lazarus. The only thing keeping me away from him is King. So today I will kill him and take back my life and my fiance!

King lifts his hand and points at my father. My father drops to his knees, his hands grabbing at his throat. King is strangling him.

'Dad, your cloaking spell,' I remind him.

'It seems like the great Aldore has lost his powers. That's what happens when you go into hiding.' King laughs.

My father's face is turning blue. I draw deeper, shaking hands with the devil himself, and lunge at King, hurling every bit of anger and hatred I have. Black electricity surrounds my giant anorics as they hit him.

'Now that's the queen I want to stand beside me. You're so beautiful when you go dark. Draw deeper, draw darker,' he growls, trying to gain his stance.

'As you wish, my beloved king!'

I lift rocks, boulders and trees, filling them with an electric current before launching them at him. They illuminate the darkening sky before hitting their target, catching him off-guard. My father gains his strength and fires a few of his own anorics.

King staggers backwards. I fill my anorics with all the electric current I can draw and hurl them at him. My father does the same, all hitting him head-on.

King loses his balance. He shakes his head, trying to compose himself. He's disorientated. I fill my hands ready to fire but stop as Jet clambers to his feet and surprises him, jumping onto King's back. Jet's large teeth bite a chunk out of his neck. He spits it to the ground before cracking his neck, roaring like an attacking lion. With the strength of twenty gargoyles, he twists his neck before pulling his head clear off his shoulders.

Jet staggers before dropping King's head at my father's feet. 'Burn the bastard, Jazz.'

I fire a dragon flame over King, igniting his heartless body.

Jet races over to me, clearly in pain. He throws open his wings, forcing me into his chest.

'I won't let you inhale any of that leech's powers. Leave them for the devil to have.' His large wings encase me, blocking out the noise of growling and screaming creatures.

After a few minutes, his hold loosens and he releases me. My father's face is the first thing I see. He wraps his arms around me and kisses me on my forehead. 'I kept it a secret to avoid this very day. I promised your mother I'd protect you.'

I scan the field which is littered with injured and dead creatures. There's a vampire heading for the tree line trying to escape. I throw an anoric, hitting and ripping off one of his legs. Rhys and Ellie appear in dingo form just in time to pounce onto him; sinking their poisonous teeth into the vampire's neck and back. They clamp down, dragging him to the ground. After a few violent shakes, he lies motionless. Corbin walks over and waits for the two dingoes to move aside before igniting the leech with his hot flame.

I scan the area for more escapees. My heart thuds to a stop when I spot Lazarus. He has several bite marks on his back but other than that he looks fine.

'Go to the angels. They can help with the venom before it settles permanently in your system. I need to help clean up the dead and help heal our injured,' says my father. Before stepping away he adds, 'I'm proud of you, but we need to work on your anger issues. You are drawing from a dark place.'

'It only happens when I'm not connected to Lazarus.'

'You don't need anyone but yourself when it comes to powers.' He kisses my head again before walking over to Falcon and Corbin who look like they've been tossed in a washing machine full of sharp rocks.

Gabby is tending to Jet, for which I'm grateful.

I walk over to the charred remains of King and stare down

at them. 'You will never wed, bed or turn me, leech. I win!'

I spot Lazarus, in dragon form, staring his red fiery eyes my way.

'We need to talk,' I whisper, knowing he can hear me loud and clear.

I head in his direction, but his posture becomes defensive. I slow when he forces his wings out in a defensive manner.

'Lazarus?' I question telepathically.

'You brought King here! To our home!'

'I can explain.'

With my guard down, Lazarus pounces on top of me, pinning me down with his large clawed talon. I force my power to calm due to the raging fire brewing in his eyes. His sphere tail curls over his back and descends towards me. He lowers it so the tip is pointing directly at my heart.

'I brought King here so together with my father we could kill him.'

'You lie, just like you lied about caring for me. Drake is the one you loved!'

He presses his sphere further, tearing my t-shirt and piercing my skin. I see blood forming over the tip of his sphere.

'Move a millimetre, dragon, and I will rip your heart out,' snarls Ash. 'I haven't gone through all this to lose her now.'

'No, Ash! No one is to interfere. This is between Lazarus and me.'

'If he moves his tail a millimetre you will be dead.'

'If I'm to die I want it to be by his hand. Then when he takes my powers, he will see how much I love him and how I said those things to keep him safe.'

Lazarus growls and puffs smoke over my face. *'You made it very clear you could never be with a dragon.'*

'I was acting because King was going to kill you, Ash and me.'

Lazarus presses his sphere a small millimetre further into my chest. With all my effort I control my heartbeat as his razor-sharp teeth come closer to my face. *'You made yourself very clear, witch!'*

'Ash and I made a plan when King kidnapped me. I was—'

'Of course Ash was involved!'

'He kept me sane, telling me you'd forgive me when you heard the truth. He protected—'

'He was wrong!' A large line of saliva drips from the tip of his largest tooth and hits me on my cheek. I don't blink and keep deathly still as it slides down my face. I take a deep breath and feel the tip of his sphere deepen.

'I love you, Laz. I always have and always will.'

With a steady hand, I pull down the top of my t-shirt to show him my marking. A tattoo showing two dragons in a yin-yang symbol with his name laced through it. *'It appeared by itself. We're inked for life, Lazarus.'*

His eyes cool as they scan my tattoo which his sphere is piercing. Slowly he removes his tail and releases the pressure from his clawed foot.

I sense another dragon nearby.

'She brought death to our clan. She's not worth it, Laz. Let's go,' says Keira telepathically.

Lazarus gives me one long look before walking away.

Ash helps me to my feet. I stand stunned as I watch the man I love walk away.

Keira turns her head and, even though in dragon form, I recognise her snide smirk. In a dazed blink, my hand fills with an anoric.

I raise my hand to throw it, but Ash jumps in front of me, grasping my hand mid-throw. 'Not now, Jazz.'

Lazarus and Keira spin around and fire a warning breath of flames that falls just short of us. They turn and fly away together. Tears fill my eyes, spilling over to run down my cheeks.

'He'll come around. He's just finished fighting for his home and his clan,' says Ash.

'You said he'd forgive me. He hates me!' I thump my clenched fists onto his rock-solid chest.

'Give him time to work it out.'

'He's with her now! Where's the great celebration we were going to have when we killed King? You lied!'

I storm off heading towards the yards that hold the horses. I pray Blue Boy is here.

'You need Malachi to help remove the venom,' yells Ash.

'You're the one who was drinking his blood, remember? A few bites won't kill me.'

'King bit you as well. It will darken you. We don't know what else could happen.'

I ignore him and continue towards the corrals, finding Blue Boy in the yard. I grab a bridle and swing up onto his back.

Nogard Hollow is covered in blood, creatures and fire. Lazarus is right—I brought death here, to my family.

I kick him into a canter and head towards Elyograg Castle. With every step Blue Boy takes it thumps through my body to my broken heart.

Once away from everybody I pull back to a walk and sob hysterically.

I've lost the man I love. Everything I did was for us and now I have nothing.

I cry all the way to the castle, arriving weak and drained.

I collapse onto a large rock and close my eyes. Breathing deeply, I draw on the spirit of my dear cousin, Sky.

I feel a warm sensation spread down my arm. Opening my eyes, I see Sky's spirit sitting beside me with her hand in mine. Tears fill my eyes and my heart tightens.

Hello, Jazzle Dazzle, she says, making me hiccup a smile.

'Hey, cuz.'

'You did well. King is dead because of you.'

'I fear I may have started a war against any remaining vamps.'

'You can deal with them. You're a strong sorceress. They don't have a leader anymore and will be hesitant to attack the one who killed King.'

'It was a team effort.'

'Even so, you should be proud of your achievements amongst the elite creatures.'

'My achievements? I brought death to so many.'

'You brought back peace between the gargoyles and dragons.'

'I killed you and Mother. Should I be proud of that?'

'That's not my Jazzle talking. That is the venom. Don't let King take any more of your life. You can beat him. You've done it physically, now do it mentally and internally.'

'I miss you so much, Sky.'

'I'm always here, Jazzy. Granddad, your mother and I are always a breath away. And if you look hard enough, we are always inside of you—in your heart.'

I smile at my cousin's fading face. She's leaving me with a smile that warms my soul.

'I love you, Sky.'

'I love you more, Jazzle,' she murmurs before fading away.

CHAPTER SEVEN

THE CASTLE IS eerily quiet as I climb the stairs to my old room. I lock the door with a key and a spell. I don't want to speak, see or hear anyone.

I rip off my protective pendant and throw it onto the side table. I don't want to be sheltered from the truth anymore. I want to see and feel the pain I've caused.

It doesn't take long, with memories of my grandfather's death taking over my dreams. I wake sweating and scared, firing of an electric bolt through the roof.

As days go by and when my eyelids close, I'm reminded of Sky's and Drake's deaths. My dreams are like a recorder—stop, start, shuffle and repeat with the same nightmares over and over. By the end of the week, I'm exhausted, haven't heard from Lazarus and my room looks like a battlefield.

'Jasmine, open this door! You need to eat,' my father yells.

'Go away. I'm a grown woman and will do as I wish.'

'Damn it! I didn't want to do this,' he spits before my bedroom door flies off its hinges.

My father stands with his hands plastered on his hips and Ash beside him. I fly out of bed and instantly fill my hand with an electric bolt.

'Don't you dare raise your hand to me!' he yells, glancing around the room. He points to the floor, 'Put your pendant around your neck now.'

I close my fist and extinguish my threat before picking up my pendant and slipping it on.

'That's better. Locking yourself away won't help things. Eat, or Ash will force-feed you.'

I raise an eyebrow to Ash—asking him if he's game enough to force-feed me. He answers by frowning and giving me a determined nod.

'Not hungry and Ash, you don't need to guard my door anymore.'

'Some habits are hard to break.' He winks.

'So I'm a habit?' I snap.

'Stop with the attitude. I'm still your father!'

'Who has lied to me all my life, Aldore.'

'I'm not your issue and you know it. So stop with the dramatics.' My father's tone is the harshest I've ever heard. 'You're in a dark place and that's not good for someone as powerful as you.'

'I'm fine.'

'I can see that.' He points his finger up and down the length of my body. I'm still in the same clothes I was wearing during the battle. 'Life goes on with or without Lazarus.'

'Get out. Leave me alone or I will disappear forever!'

'Respect your father and yell at me all you want, Jasmine,' says Ash. 'I took King's abuse and he's as tough as you can get. I can easily handle yours.'

I stagger backwards. His words punch me hard in the stomach. Memories flash before me of Ash being punished by King because of me; because of my stupid mouth. Maybe I am full of evil. Maybe King's venom is inside me. Maybe running away will protect everyone from me.

'Get the thought out of your head,' Father says, interrupting the flood of escape routes my mind is conjuring up. 'Running away will not help. You need to deal with your issues head-on. You chose the elite life, now live it.'

'Like you did, Aldore?

'Jasmine!' says Ash.

'It's all right, Ash. Malachi is on his way up to see her.' My father moves slowly towards me and kisses me on top of my head. 'Things will become clearer after you get the venom out.' He smiles but it's not one that reaches his heart. 'It's time to stop being selfish. Have you spared a thought for Jet?'

'Jet?'

'He broke his back while in gargoyle form. The healing has taken longer than usual with vampire venom and bites from other creatures.'

'Why didn't someone tell me?'

'If you opened your door someone may have,' says Ash.

'I need to see him!'

'Gabby refuses to let anyone interrupt his healing.'

'I'll get past her!'

'Stop thinking about what you want and start to think about what's good for Jet. Your mother taught you to always think of others first. Don't let King's venom change your character.' My father nods before leaving.

Ash turns to leave and stops at the broken door with his back to me. 'I miss sleeping in your room. I feel a little empty not hearing you breathe and snore.'

My lips curve into a smile, the first genuine smile I've had in months. 'I don't snore.'

He keeps his back to me and pretends to shut the door before leaving. My smile drops when Malachi enters.

'Hello, Jasmine.'

'Malachi,' I say with a nod.

'I need to scan your blood to see how much venom is in your system,'

'Ash drank most of it. I just got bitten.'

'I have had one session with him. He needs more but refuses to leave your side.'

'I didn't ask him to sit at my door,' I spit, then instantly regret it.

'We all do things for each other because we care, Jasmine.'

'I stood by while King punished Ash. I stood and did nothing! My heart is already blackened.'

'No, Jasmine. You did what you had to, to keep everyone alive. Ash knows that.'

'Lazarus doesn't!'

'He knows.'

I flick my eyes to the angels. 'He knows? Why doesn't he come to me?'

'That I don't know.'

'What good are you, then?'

He ignores my tone and moves so he's standing in front of me. 'May I?' He raises his hands above my head, his eyes locked with mine, awaiting my answer.

'Do I have a choice?' I snarl, which makes him raise an eyebrow. I sigh. 'On one condition.'

'Yes?'

'When I asked you to look into my future and I took, well stole, five years of your life, you never told me I could give those years back to you.'

'Who told you that?'

'It doesn't matter. I want to give you the five years I stole and the five years you gave me willingly.'

'It will take ten years off your life.'

'If I don't have Lazarus, I don't care. Do we have a deal?'

'As you wish. May I now proceed?'

'As you wish, Malachi.'

He raises another eyebrow. I've never seen an angry angel and I'm not sure I want to. He closes his eyes and slowly trails his fingers over the top of my head all the way down my body. 'I can withdraw the venom one of two ways, but both are painful.'

'Do it. But then I give you back your ten years.'

'You do understand it may kill you. You may not have ten years left.'

'Then I leave this Earth owing nothing to anyone.'

Malachi nods, accepting my reason. 'We need to do the transfer away from the castle. It can be interrupted, and the years given lost.

'But first I need to draw out the venom. The quickest way is to use leeches, placing them over your lymph nodes. It's painful when the venom is being withdrawn.'

'Fine, do it. I've been living with leeches for several weeks. A few more sucking on me makes no difference.'

'If I don't do it now, I may lock you back in here myself and throw away the key. You are not the Jasmine I love dearly.'

'Whatever!' I roll my eyes and sigh. 'Make sure Ash has another session.'

Malachi leaves and returns with Ash and a large cardboard box.

Ash nods. 'I'll do this with you, Jazz. If it gets too much, I'll rip those suckers straight off.' He strips out of his clothes and stands comfortably naked before me.

Malachi opens the box and pulls out the largest leech I have ever seen.

I remember, when I was younger, camping with my father and getting a leech on my leg. He laughed, telling me it was nothing compared with what he'd seen. I now know what he found amusing. These critters are as big and thick as a gargoyle's thumb.

Malachi laughs. 'We breed them for this and other medical reasons.'

I close my mouth, unaware it was gaping wide open, obviously amusing him.

Malachi places the leeches over Ash's human body. When

he's finished, there are twenty little suckers digging into his flesh.

I remove my clothes, stopping at my underwear. Ash winks at me for support when Malachi places them on my skin. The leeches are cold and feel like snails sliding over my skin.

As a child, I was fascinated with snails and how they could disappear into their shells then slither out and pop up their tentacle eyes. I'd have them slipping and sliding all over my arms, much to my mother's disgust.

I feel no pain but it's like someone running ice blocks over me.

Suddenly the pain hits. One, then two, then three leeches bite in. 'Ouch!'

'They travel to a point where they can taste the venom. They will draw it from your system until it's clean, that is if you can handle the pain,' says Malachi, running his hands over my skin.

Ash jolts; his face shows no pain, but I can see past his charade. He has twenty leeches crawling over him and I only have ten of the filthy critters. I feel the venom being drawn out of the three that have bedded down. The fourth, fifth, sixth and seventh do the same.

I keep my face rock hard, showing no pain. I owe Ash the support more than he owes me.

The eighth, ninth and tenth leech bite down. I clench my teeth and concentrate on my facial expressions. I can tell Ash is doing the same for my sake. The silence between us is deafening with neither of us willing to admit to the pain.

Ash laughs. 'Nice undies, Jazz.'

I glance down to my granny undies, which are hitched up over my hips and belly button. 'Never know when I'm going riding.'

We all laugh, including Malachi.

'Okay I'm admitting this is painful,' I say.

Ash sighs. 'Thank goodness you said it!'

'Not long now, guys,' says Malachi. 'You're doing great.' He moves next to me with a mechanical tool in his hand. 'I can remove King's ring from your finger. But I can guarantee it will hurt more than the leeches. The teeth in the ring are already embedded into your finger.'

'Do it! It's a constant reminder of that big bat.'

I hold my finger out and close my eyes. Ash holds my other hand as Malachi clamps onto the ring, breaking it. I jump at the sound of it breaking and then feel the pain as he removes it from my finger. It hurts like hell and I force myself to not pass out.

He clasps his warm hand over my finger, which slightly soothes it, before wrapping it in a small bandage.

For the next hour, the three of us talk about everything and anything, trying to take our minds off the leeches sucking on our blood. Malachi then removes the leeches, one by one, heightening the pain.

We look like a vampire has gone crazy on us. I feel lighter within myself, within my heart. I feel whole as a person, but not totally complete.

Ash and I take turns bathing in a concoction Malachi brewed to help heal the leeches bite marks.

'I've never apologised for what happened,' I say to Ash who's now soaking in the tub of goo.

'There's nothing to apologise for. It was my job and my pleasure to protect you.'

I hold my hand up to stop him talking. 'You went beyond your job, Ash. I can never repay you.'

'Your friendship is all I ask for but if you want to kiss me, I won't stop you.'

'You had my friendship the day I met you. I love you like

a brother, Ash. I trust you with my life.'

'Your love is thanks enough. I love you too, Jasmine.'

It's been several days since my cleansing and I plan to meet Malachi at the foot of the forest to transfer the ten lives I owe him. He wants to do it alone and without any interference.

I use all my strength to lie to everyone in the castle, saying I'm heading out for a ride to visit the dingoes. No one is suspicious when I head off towards the creek.

As soon as I feel Jet's presence fade, I cover myself with the silencing dome and turn towards Malachi's and my meeting place.

He is a vision of beauty in such a harsh and unforgiving outback. He sits, smiling, on a large rock which protrudes out and into the river. He is a true vision of an angel; an angel I stole ten years from.

'Hello, Jasmine. Are you sure you want to proceed? You seem anxious.'

'I've never stolen anything in my life. I went carelessly ahead and stole from you, someone who gave without question. I'm sorry, Malachi. I want to make things right between us.'

'Even though the transfer may cost you your life?'

'If this is where my life ends, so be it.'

'We need to start, as I sense elite creatures close by. I don't have the power to cover myself in a cloaking spell so my trail can be followed.'

'I sense them too.'

Malachi moves close, similar to how Lazarus would just before kissing me. I close my eyes and open my mouth; the same position I was in when I stole the ten years.

'Good girl. Relax and keep your breathing calm. I don't want any fireworks.'

I try not to chuckle. 'Don't we all want to feel fireworks?'

Malachi's lips press a kiss on my cheek, 'Thank you, Jasmine.'

His action shocks me. It's the first time I've heard emotion from him, from an angel.

'I'm repaying my debt… and you are my family.'

'I'll take the first five years and see how you cope.'

Closing my eyes, I open my mouth again, feeling his body closing in. There's an enormous pull from deep within me, within my soul.

The sound of the running creek disappears. The singing of the birds dissipates. I am calm, silenced and at peace. Is my time over? Have I arrived in heaven?

Breaking the calm, I wake with an almighty jolt, thrown to the ground with a painful thud.

'Malachi?' I gasp, not being able to focus on what is happening. 'Am I dying? Is this heaven or hell?'

'It will be hell if you ever do that again,' yells a voice I know to be Jet.

'Jet?'

'Yes, it's me! What the hell do you think you are doing?'

'This is none of your business,' I yell back, slowly regaining my vision.

Jet is standing over me, glaring. His hands are folded across his chest.

'You threw me to the ground?'

'No, that would have been me,' says a voice my heart longs to hear.

I spin around and behind me stands Lazarus, who is in human form, towering over Malachi, who is also flat on the ground. Keira stands in the background, much to my dismay.

'This is none of your business. It's between Malachi and me!'

'You are my business. Drake made you my business. Sky made you my business,' snarls Jet.

'Don't make me feel any worse than I do for their deaths.

There's not a day that goes by when I think of them and miss them. Don't you get it—death follows me! You're better off without me in your life.' I tilt my head pointing toward Lazarus, my stomach a tight knot. 'He has moved on and so should you.'

'Is that what you think, Jasmine? That I've moved on?' says Lazarus, his tone hurt.

'Actions speak louder than words, dragon.'

Jet faces Malachi. 'You are so lucky you're an angel, mate. If it was anyone else, I'd rip their bloody head off!'

Silence falls over everyone, the creek becoming the deafening voice.

'You need to head back to the castle. Hudson has arrived with news,' says Jet to Malachi.

Malachi nods then surprises me by telepathically telling me he has gained five years. I still owe another five.

'I understand,' I say aloud.

'Get out of her head,' yells Jet, stalking the angel.

'Jet, stop it. He only did what I asked.' I jump in between them both. 'Malachi, I will see you back at the castle.'

He smiles and nods before leaving. Jet paces the ground in front of me.

'Do you know he could have killed you?'

'I have nothing to live for. Plus, I owe him. Even though the future he showed me was false and a waste of five years.' I flick my eyes to Keira, who is staying in the background and out of this argument.

'I should snap your neck right now and save me the worry of protecting you,' growls Jet.

'You won't have to worry much longer.'

'What's that supposed to mean?'

'I've decided if Malachi didn't kill me, I'd go back to England and help Hudson eradicate the vamps. One way or another, I'll eventually end up dead. May as well do it helping to kill those bastards I despise so much.'

Lazarus joins Jet pacing the ground in front of me, but he is a little quicker. I watch the two men strut back and forth. 'Would you two stop?'

'She's not going anywhere, Jet,' says Lazarus.

'Oh, I can guarantee she's not going anywhere,' says Jet. 'We can lock her in her room and place a spell on the door, hindering her from leaving, or even better, in your cave.'

'Um, hello. I'm standing right here and if I remember correctly, I'm a hell of a lot stronger than you both. I can also transform into any creature and climb or fly out of his stupid cave.'

They stop pacing and look at each other.

'Lazarus, let's go,' whispers Keira.

With anger fuelling my veins, I fire a small but hot anoric at her feet. She jumps back quicker than the eye can see. Her eyes start to swirl red.

'Jasmine!' yells Jet, shocked.

'What have I got to lose? Laz hates me and thinks I'm a traitor just like everyone else does. If I didn't do what I did I would have watched King kill my friends and the only man I love.' Silence falls, with the two men's eyes on me. 'So who gives a frog's arse if I offend the little dragon? She drools all over the man I love?' I glare at Keira.

'I don't hear him complaining,' she whispers, knowing I would hear her.

'Give me a reason to retaliate!' I snarl.

'I know the truth,' says Lazarus.

'You know and you're still with her?'

'Is that what you think?'

I point my index finger at him then at her. It's obvious he's left me for her. She follows him like a little lap dog. 'I tried to explain to you that King had all the control until I could take it back. Hell, my body is inked with your name!'

I pull the top of my t-shirt down, showing the tattoo marking over my heart. Lazarus' eyes lock onto my marking. His eyes blister a colour I've never seen before—a glowing red with a green outline.

'This isn't a backyard tattoo. It formed by itself. We're linked whether you like it or not!'

'I've heard enough,' says Keira.

'Of course you have, little red dragon.' I move in her direction.

'Jasmine,' cautions Jet.

'Did you know, Jet, we have a traitor amongst the elite creatures. And it's not me.' I stop several feet away from Keira, locking my eyes with hers.

'Make your move, witch,' she snarls.

'Oh, little traitor, I don't have to. Your time is coming.'

I step back and purposely turn my back on her. There's a small commotion behind me and I presume Jet or Lazarus has stopped her attempt to hurt me. I spin and find Lazarus staring at me, his words lost. Our eyes connect and my heart tightens.

'Know this, Lazarus, I love you and I always did.' I move away from the creatures. 'I have a debt to pay and I will kill anyone who gets in my way.'

Jet takes off quicker than a bullet, leaving me in an awkward position.

'Head back to Nogard Hollow,' Lazarus says to Keira.

'You can't be serious!'

'Leave, Keira.'

With a dramatic huff and a glare that would kill an angel, Keira changes form and takes to the air. Billows of smoke and flames exude from her.

'Ash dragged Xandria over to Nogard Hollow and made her explain what happened. He broke her wing in the process.'

'Good. She's a little brat.'

'What were you thinking, taking on King and giving five years of your life away?'

'What do you care?'

In the blink of an eye, Lazarus has me pinned against a solid rock, my hands behind my back. I can't blame him since I've been throwing anorics at everyone lately.

'Don't push an already irate dragon.'

'I won't as I can still feel your sphere piercing my chest,' I say curtly.

He loosens his grip but not enough for me to slip free.

'You know what state I was in, especially after fighting,' he says. 'You purposely pressed my buttons.'

'It looked like Keira was pressing your buttons.'

'Do you think I'd move on from you that quickly?'

I shrug my shoulders in response.

'Mature answer. Really mature.'

'Drop dead, lizard!'

'If I did would you care?'

I stop and look hard into his eyes. Of course I'd care. I'd die for him and for his love. I have been dying for his love for the past few weeks.

'Your last breath would be my last breath. That is why I'm giving ten years back to Malachi. Knowing you are with Keira made the decision easy. You were my one and only. I don't want anyone else and if those years together where my best years, so be it. I'm happy to leave this Earth knowing I loved and was once loved.'

'I'm not with Keira.'

'What?'

'You heard, witch. How could I ever get over loving someone like you?'

'What? But you and she…'

'She and I are friends. I've already told you she will never be anything but a friend and a part of our clan. When a creature is inked to another, it's unbreakable.'

'That's not true. What about Falcon? He moved on from Sky.'

'Falcon never moved on until her death, when she released him. That's the only time it can happen. She wasn't a dragon, hence she wasn't inked to him and could love another.'

'When I give Malachi the remaining years and I die, I will release you.'

His grip tightens on my wrist, his breath and body temperature heating. 'Don't you get it? I don't want anyone else. If I don't have you, I'd rather be alone.'

'You don't look very alone.'

'Stop it, Jasmine. I thought the venom was withdrawn from your system. Your spiteful tongue should be gone.'

I have no comeback so I keep my mouth shut. His eyes search mine, a slight victory flashing in them. I don't want to fight with him. I love him.

For several minutes we stare into each other's eyes. So many things are being said in just one look.

His gaze drops to my chest. Releasing my hands, he cautiously pulls my t-shirt to the side, revealing the marking over my heart. His eyes instantly change colour from green to a warm red, then they widen, giving them a green tinge. His heart beats faster, his temperature rises. 'You said it just appeared?'

'King took me into a salon and left me with the store assistant. I drew what I wanted but as soon as the needle touched my skin, it appeared. Shocked the hell out of the tattooist.' I chuckle.

'Is this the design you drew?'

'Not identical but similar. I shortened your name to Laz, but it came out in full.'

'Lucky for you it did come out in full.'

I frown, confused.

'I have a relative in London called Laz. I'd have to kill him if you were inked to him. But I'd say his wife may beat me to it.'

'I showed you this the day we battled King. Why did you leave me?'

He runs his finger over the area where he pierced my skin; a small scar has formed since.

'I had just finished killing dragons, gargoyles and vampires. I was all creature and no human.'

'You are a creature foremost.'

'You knew approaching a dragon after being at war is a death sentence. Plus, you were with a vampire! You ripped my heart apart saying I'd never be the father of your children and how you couldn't trust me with them. Two issues we'd struggled with.'

'It was an act to protect you and my family.'

'You said I was your second choice; that you wanted to be with Drake. Then you said there was a third. Who is that? Jet? Ash?'

'There is no third. I needed you to leave so we could continue with the plan to get King to Australia. It was a lie and an act to win King's trust. I was disappointed you didn't fight harder for me.'

'I had to use every bit of self-control not to burst out of my human skin in the middle of London. We'd searched everywhere for you. Contacted every elite creature within Europe only to hear you'd joined King's clan. I didn't believe them and kept searching.

'Then Hudson got word from a gargoyle loyal to him, but under King's law, that he'd spotted you in the city.'

'Why didn't you bring more creatures or organise an ambush?'

'We had many false sightings. Dragging creatures out of hiding risks revealing their location to King. I was pretty much on my own in the end.'

'You had Keira.'

Lazarus frowns and shakes his head.

'I was disappointed you walked away without even a puff of smoke. I cried myself to sleep. Poor Ash had to console a blubbering mess that night.'

'You played a very convincing role.'

'Would you have killed me if I'd pushed you further the day of the battle?'

'No, I have control over who or what I kill, Jasmine. It was my jealousy that did this to you.' He places his finger over the scar, covering it from view. 'I was jealous of you loving someone else. Jealous you were to be married and that you would lie down with someone else.' His eyes heat to a fiery red.

'I never laid with King!' I snap.

'I smelt him all over you, mixed with Ash's scent. You still smell of Ash.'

'I allowed King to kiss me but not the way you kiss me. I did it to keep Ash and me alive. Not one day did I enjoy his company. He made my stomach churn and my skin crawl.'

Lazarus pushes away from me and paces the ground. His temperature and heartbeat rise.

'Ash's scent is over me for a good and an explainable reason.'

Lazarus stops in his tracks and in a second is towering over me. 'He was protecting me.' I know Lazarus is firing up and could take off any second to hunt Ash down. 'He took my punishments and they were painful.'

'That doesn't explain why his scent is all over you.'

'He slept in my room every night because he was my guardian.'

'What? Ash, who can't keep his hands off you slept in your room?'

'Calm down, dragon. You know perfectly well nothing happened!'

'Do I?'

'Just as I trust you when you say nothing is going on between you and Keira.'

'Ugh! I'm a dragon, Jasmine. I kill for less than that.'

'You're jealous and nothing more. When I shifted into a dragon, I saw how many triggers your brain has and how easily they can be pressed.' He frowns as if evaluating what I've said. 'Ash would be dead if I hadn't pretended he was my servant. It was his idea to take my punishment and that he should be my guardian until I'm married so I didn't have to lie with King. His clever thinking saved me from King's hand in more ways than one.'

'But he lay with you?'

'He slept in stone form beside my bed to protect me, as he still does.'

'No man should be in your room except me!'

'You weren't around. He's not just a man, he's my friend and I owe him so much. He took every punishment King gave and never once complained. King's treatment was cruel and painful.'

'I expect, with your smart mouth, he copped a lot of punishment.'

'He did, so back off a little.'

'He never mentioned anything of this when explaining what happened.'

'Pride, I suppose. He kept reassuring me you loved me and would forgive me when you heard the truth. He probably also likes his head attached to his body. Telling a jealous dragon that he has been sleeping beside his fiancée is not a good move.'

'I see your point.' Lazarus' lips curve into a smile. 'I may thank him one day when I can't smell him on you.'

'Do I smell that bad?'

Lazarus inhales my scent, drawing it down deep into his lungs. 'You smell delicious.'

'So do you,' I purr.

'I missed you, Jazz. But if I ever catch you giving away lives, I will do more than push you to the ground. What the hell were you thinking?'

'You wouldn't talk to me. If I don't have you in my life, I have nothing to live for.'

'Promise me you'll never do something so careless again.'

'I can't promise you, as I owe him another five years.'

'No, you don't. He was willing to give you five, so take it. I will kill you myself if I hear about another trade.' He pulls me into his heated arms. 'I won't lose you. I love you too much.'

My heart flutters. 'Do you know how desperate I am to hear you say those words?'

'I can tell.' He taps his ear. 'I. Am. In. Love. With. You.'

My heart somersaults in my chest.

'Control, babe. I am still a dragon.' He chuckles.

He leans closer so our lips are centimetres apart. His body instantly heats mine. I close the distance by slipping my hands around his waist. He pulls back slightly with a cheeky grin. 'Will you marry me, witch?'

'Definitely, dragon.'

He presses his lips to mine and kisses me passionately. A lustful groan rolls in my chest and he growls in response. His grip tightens to near suffocation. Our bodies are reaching a dangerous temperature. I pull back, smiling.

'Do I need to ask your father's permission, again?'

'No, but Jet mentioned Hudson had arrived with news. I'm curious as to why he's here.'

'The very same thought crossed my mind. Let's get to the castle to see what's up.'

I step back and give a cheeky grin, making Lazarus cock his head with curiosity. I draw on my dragon powers, pulling deep from the earth below my feet. My vision alters but clears enough to see Lazarus' eyes widen with adoration. My eyes pop and my vision magnifies everything around me.

Lazarus steps back, his jaw dropping, as my dragon form pulls from the colour of the earth. Swirls of nature break down and form particles around me. My temperature spikes and my limbs stretch as I would after a good massage.

In a few quick seconds, I stand in a glorious golden dragon form. I make sure my tail is down and to the back of me, as he is still in human form.

His eyes scan me, his heartbeat is erratic. Without thinking, I lick my lips at the sound of his healthy heartbeat. He grins and instantly calms his beat.

He walks my length, running his hands along my scales. It's a soothing and sensual feeling and gives me some idea of how he feels when I slide down from his back. No wonder he needs to kiss me passionately afterwards.

It makes me laugh and a lungful of smoke puffs out my mouth, which is not very lady-like. *Finished your appraisal?* I echo.

'Never! You're amazing and bigger than I thought you'd be.'

'I'll take that as a compliment. Change form and let's go flying.'

In a heartbeat, Lazarus is in dragon form, larger than me, rubbing his scales against mine. It's a warm ticklish feeling; one I enjoy.

He takes off in a glorious gust of wind. It's a sight I will never get tired of.

LAZARUS AND I walk into the castle through the back entrance. People are speaking in raised voices.

'She needs to return with me,' demands Hudson.

'She's not leaving Australia,' yells Jet.

'She's better off without the dragon in her life.'

'That's not our decision,' my father says. 'The discussion is closed.'

'No, it's not,' growls Hudson.

'Yes, it is,' I say, entering the room.

'Jasmine!' Hudson smiles. 'We need to talk.'

His smile drops when Lazarus moves beside me, but he still embraces me and kisses my cheek.

'It's good to see you. What needs discussing?'

'Can we talk in private?'

I look around the room. Apart from Lazarus, my father, Ash and Jet are the only other creatures here. 'I have no secrets amongst these elites. I have gone into battle with them, each putting their lives on the line for me as I did for them.'

'Very well. Word of your betrayal of King has reached England's shores and we thought the remainder vamps would disperse and release any surviving gargoyles. They haven't and are still attacking anyone who approaches the city. They have too many golden souls inside and we need to collect them and place them in the vault as it is written.'

'I saw too many to count. They used them as an electricity source, lighting their underground castle.'

'Underground?'

'The castle on the surface is superficial. The one that houses the vamps is underneath. There's a whole world under there.'

'I know it was a traumatic experience and one you don't ever want to relive, but I'm asking you to come back to England. You know the layout and whereabouts of King's lair.'

'No way in hell!' growls Lazarus.

'No!' yells Jet.

'I'll go,' says Ash, moving beside me. 'I won't leave my relatives to fade out and die in the hands of those leeches.'

'I'll go with you, Ash.' I smile.

'Like hell you will,' says Lazarus. 'You're a traitor to them and will be killed on sight.'

'Every night I closed my eyes, I'd hear the plea for help from golden souls. It haunted me the whole time I was there, and it still does. They are my relatives too and I promised so many that one day I'd set them free.' I hold eye contact with Lazarus.

'Thank you, Jasmine,' says Hudson, moving in my direction.

Jet steps in front of Hudson and pushes him back several metres with two strong hands. 'You are not taking her anywhere. She was punished and pumped with venom. She could have died!'

'It was Ash who received most of the punishment and he still wants to return,' says Hudson.

'My punishment was nothing compared with what Jazz had to endure. I only got knocked to the ground, burnt, shocked and broken, but if I had to deal with that slimy slug kissing me as she did, I'd keel over and die,' says Ash.

Lazarus growls a deafening roar making Ash step sideways and out of his way.

'Ash, think before you speak,' I whisper.

'She is not going! I will kill any creature that tries to take her out of this country or out of this area.' Lazarus growls, aiming his anger towards Hudson.

'Laz, I want to do this. If it was your family in trouble, I'd do the same. It's not just the golden souls and gargoyles in the lair, there are humans being used as blood banks.'

'I don't like it and, as you say, there's a traitor amongst us creatures.' He folds his arms across his chest, narrowing his eyes at Hudson.

'It may flush him or her out.' I reach over and unfold his arms before standing on my tippy-toes and kiss his cheek. 'I need to do this for them and for me. Please support me.'

'If you're determined to go, I will go with you. I'm not letting you out of my sight. And you've spent enough time with Ash.' He slips his arm around my waist and pulls me in tight. His focus is drawn away from Hudson and now on me. He kisses my temple, letting me know he's calming.

'Trust me, Lazarus, if I kissed your girl you'd know about it. One kiss from me and she'd never look at you again.' Ash turns to face the door, ready for a quick escape, in case Lazarus doesn't find him funny.

Lazarus flicks his head and narrows his eyes at Ash. 'In your dreams, mate.'

The rest of the day is taken up with our plan of attack. We discuss how we can enter the castle unannounced, with the layout of the underground castle our main topic.

Jet complains the entire time about wanting to come, but he is too valuable to be found out or hurt. Everyone knows I am a sorceress, but we don't know how much they know. King may have kept the knowledge of Jet and my powers to himself. Time will tell.

Hudson has arranged for my father, Ash, Lazarus and me to fly out tomorrow night. For now, Hudson is enjoying the company of his wife, Demona, and his sons.

Falcon and Corbin will bring their clan over to Elyograg Castle in case there's a counter-attack. It's good to see all the elite creatures unite as one.

As everyone heads to bed, I corner Malachi. 'I need to give you the remaining five years.'

'There is no need to repay me, Jasmine.'

'I want to do it now before I leave tomorrow in case I don't return.'

Interrupting us is a crashing thunder rolling down the staircase as Lazarus and Jet fight to reach me.

'Did you not hear me!' growls Lazarus, rattling the castle

walls. 'I warned you not to do this!'

'There is no need to repay me,' repeats Malachi.

'Darn right she has no need!' Lazarus spits, a puff of smoke escaping his mouth.

'There's no need because I gave him five of my lives,' says Jet.

'You did what?' I ask.

'Ash was in the process of offering himself and I interjected and offered my life instead. Ash had already given you protection when I couldn't. This is a way I can contribute. Ash needs to be strong and by your side in England.'

'You shouldn't put your life in jeopardy for me. Too many have died for me!'

'A simple "thank you" would do, Aunt Jazz.' Jet smiles.

'Thank you, Jet. I owe you.'

He embraces me, ignoring Lazarus' huffing and puffing.

'I owe you?' he questions, staring his bright blue eyes into mine. He wants to hear more.

'I love you.' I kiss his cheek.

'That's better.'

'I'm right here, guys!' growls Lazarus. 'You seriously don't understand how hard it is to control myself.'

We laugh before bidding everyone goodnight.

Lazarus closes and locks the door.

'Come to bed.' I pat the mattress beside me.

'Do you think I've forgotten what you were about to do with Malachi? Flirting and fluttering your eyelashes at me won't calm the dragon within me. I warned you there would be consequences if you offered any more lives.'

I stand up next to the bed and slip off my t-shirt. His heart skips a loud beat. I wiggle out of my jeans and flick them to the side and hear his heart skip several beats.

'I'm ready for the consequences.' I give him a sassy smile.

'You don't fight fair.' He pins me down on the bed. 'I'm so close to locking you away in a cave to keep you from doing stupid things and so only I can have you.'

'You have me now, dragon.'

'I don't just have you now. I have you forever!' He breathes me in, deep and long. 'I can't lose you again. My heart couldn't take it and nor could my brothers. They were sick of me moping around the cave.'

'If you weren't so pig-headed and listened to me, you would've been in my arms weeks ago instead of—'

'Jassmmmine, don't go there.'

'Hers.'

'You went there. How many times do I have to tell you?'

'No more. Just kiss me and show me how much you missed me.'

I run my hand through his hair and cup his cheek. His eyes search mine back and forth as they heat to a radiant red. His body warms, as does mine, and he hasn't even kissed me yet. What is he waiting for? 'Have you forgotten how to kiss me?'

He chuckles and vibrates through his chest to mine. He releases my pinned hands and pulls back a few loose strands of my hair that are sitting on my face.

He closes his eyes and inhales a lung full of my scent before pressing his lips to mine. His kiss is soft and gentle, sending shivers through me. His hands race over my body, reacquainting themselves with my curves.

I let mine do the same, seeking out every rolling muscle he has. Our kiss deepens to the most passionate kiss we've shared.

My mind lost in the passion, as is my body. As we join as one, a bed-shaking jolt shoots out from our bodies, sparking a small fire on the pillow beside me. Lazarus is quick to pat it out with his hand before returning to kiss my latest tattoo.

'Does it feel like I've forgotten how to kiss you?' he murmurs against my skin.

I wiggle underneath him, suddenly feeling shy. 'No, you definitely haven't forgotten.'

I WAKE TO an empty bed and presume Lazarus is feeding before our trip to England. I head for the shower but am swiftly snapped up in a pair of webbed wings.

I'm lifted off the floor and silenced in the cocoon made of wings. I thrash my arms and legs, trying to escape. Maybe this is the traitor coming to finish me off.

I still have control over my senses and take in the scent of the creature. 'Jet!'

'I'm not letting you go. I can't protect you from here and it's obvious none of them can protect you. It rips my gut out when you're not close by.'

'Put me down so we can talk.'

'I know how you work, Aunt Jazz. As soon as your feet hit the ground, you'll blast me. I'm doing this for your own good. Ash can show them the way. They don't need you.'

'Jet, if you lock me up somewhere, I will never forgive you, just as I have never forgiven those who have done it before. I killed them all, remember?'

'You won't kill me even though your threat hurts my feelings. It's for the best.'

In a sudden gush, I fly across the room, hitting the wall with my back. Lazarus stands in front of Jet, still transforming down from dragon to human. I keep still when I spot the colour of his fiery eyes.

'She's not leaving!' growls Jet.

'You were taking her away from me and against her will. I will kill you!' Lazarus' words barely scrape through his teeth.

I move slowly to stand in front of the two angry creatures.

'Jasmine, back away,' says Lazarus.

'We're inked forever, Lazarus,' I say. His eyes blink and look my way. 'Jet, I hear your pain, but if you had heard all those screaming souls and seen those scared and dying humans, you would understand my reasons for going. Please support me and let me leave knowing I have your blessing.'

'I don't want you going. I will not give my blessing. You should be here where it's safe!' He storms out of the bedroom, banging his large wings against the door as he exits.

'If another man, creature or angel kisses, cuddles or even touches you, blood will be spilt,' says Lazarus, puffing smoke.

'It's in Jet's blood to protect me. I'm not angry, just frustrated, as he probably is.' I move to stand in front of his tense frame. 'I only want one set of lips and arms holding me.'

He blows a mouthful of smoke over my face.

'Maybe I should call you Puff the Magic Dragon.'

He steps forward, closing the distance between us. He grabs my hands with his and pulls them behind me to rest on my bottom.

'If you do you will lose both your hands. I will bite them off.' He nuzzles me with his nose, his lips skimming mine. He is teasing me even though he is still red hot with anger.

I hold eye contact and with an ever-so-small smirk I say, 'Puff...'

Before I can say another word, he has my lips pressed against his. Before long he has me back on the bed, kissing me with an angered passion.

CHAPTER EIGHT

WE ARRIVE IN England unhindered due to my father's and my cloaking powers. We spend the night at Hudson's castle, allowing the creatures to feed and reboot their systems.

Waking early, we head into the city as both Ash and I were knocked out when we first went to King's lair so we can only remember the direction from the city.

We leave the vehicles several miles out from King's lair and head in by foot. As it's daylight, all the elite creatures need to stay in human form to avoid attracting attention.

Our rescue party is small. I'm sure we'll enter undetected but between us, we're strong enough to fight King's men. Hudson, my father, Ash, Lazarus and I hike to the castle in no time.

Ash cups my hand in his, giving it a gentle reassuring squeeze. He lifts my hand to his warm lips and softly kisses it. 'Here we go again. But this time we're going in voluntarily.'

'I've got your back, Ash.'

'I know you do, just like I have yours, beautiful.'

'Can you two stop reminiscing?' hushes Hudson. 'Be on alert! They'll be expecting an attack at some point and will have guards watching.'

I nod and release Ash's hand. Lazarus moves in front of me and Ash drops back with my father and Hudson either side. They are so transparent—obviously, they have made a pact to protect me.

As soon as I see the castle my heart ricochets around my chest, my palms sweat and I feel light-headed. I didn't realise returning here would have such an effect on me.

I pinpoint the rear entry and it's guarded by two creatures in human form.

'They're gargoyles.' Ash nods his head towards the roof. 'There are two more in stone sleep on the roof. They are two of the original owners of the castle before King ambushed it.'

'Our plan is to casually walk up like a group of tourists looking at the castle. Being so close to the city I expect they get people approaching all the time,' my father says. I frown at him. 'Sometimes the most obvious and boring approach is the best.'

'Boring or stupid?' whispers Ash.

'And your idea of an approach would be with guns blazing? My father flicks his eyes to Ash.

'Yep!' Ash smiles, rubbing his hands together.

'Yep!' Lazarus adds before Hudson turns and growls low in his chest, disciplining them both. 'Or your idea sounds good.'

We start a conversation about the enormity and gothic design as we approach the creatures.

'I wonder if we ask the guy at the door if we can have a look through,' says Ash, loud enough for any deaf creature to hear.

'What a great idea,' says Hudson.

The closer we get the harder it is to walk. My legs are shaky, as is my entire body. I don't know if I can go back inside the underground cave. Goosebumps run over my skin and I gasp in fear.

Lazarus drops back and wraps his arm around me. 'I've got you, babe.' He kisses the top of my head. Then louder he adds, 'Maybe there's a souvenir shop inside and we can buy you a jumper, babe. You're freezing!'

My father spins his head and, with a frown, gives me a nod. He's telling me to toughen up and stick to the plan.

'You know me. If there's a shop inside I need to go through it.' My voice is quivering.

Hudson is the first to approach the two men. Ash drops back in case he is recognised.

There is a loud cracking sound from above. Hudson keeps his focus on the two men at the door, ignoring the commotion above.

I step back and see two sets of bright blue eyes glaring down at me. The two gargoyles that were in stone sleep have moved along the roof and are standing above us.

Ash acknowledges them with a quick wave and I see one nod and nudge the other. They are no threat to us.

Hudson tries to convince the guards he is a tourist and wishes to visit the castle.

'We know who you are, Hudson, so you can stop with the charade.'

'Then you know why I am here. Will you step aside or do we need to kill you?'

'You'd kill one of your own?' the guard asks.

'To save fifty more, yes.'

'If you don't succeed, we will be killed by the vamps.'

'If you join us you will have a better chance of survival,' I say.

'I recognise you. You were King's wife.'

'She was never his wife,' says Lazarus. 'Enough talking. Move or I'll move you.' His teeth sharpen and his eyes fire red.

'We killed him, as we will the rest of the vamps if they attack us,' I say.

The two guards look at each other before stepping aside.

'Remember the vamps use humans as blood banks. There are a few humans who are turning due to over-feeding and are harmless,' one guard says. 'I'm happy to point out who these ones are.'

Hudson nods. 'Thanks for your help.'

'I won't fight the vamps. I fear them. I watched them kill my family and listen to the cry of golden souls every hour. But

I will help collect the souls of our dead,' the other guard says.

'We understand you and your clan have been through a lot. Any help is appreciated,' my father says, placing his hand on the gargoyle's shoulder.

'The vamps spend most of the day terrorising what humans and gargoyles are left. When news of King's death came, they took it upon themselves to become rulers. The fight for supremacy preoccupies them. Do you remember the layout, Queen Jasmine?'

'I'm not a queen and yes, I remember only too well.'

'I pray you kill 'em all.'

They open the door and lead us into the main house. They both stop and indicate with their heads there are vampires and gargoyles in the next room.

'Let's do it,' Lazarus says before storming into the room. 'Hello, boys!'

With no time to become anxious, we follow him. Three men stare at us in shock.

'I can make this easy or hard. Which do you prefer?' Ash smiles. 'Please make it hard, as I need some payback.'

Two sets of fangs drop. The third man holds his hands up in surrender.

'Bring it on, baby.' Ash quickly transforms into his large gargoyle form. 'I had twenty leeches sucking your venom out so today I'm gonna kill twenty vamps. And you, my friend, are number one.'

He runs towards a vampire while Hudson, who has also transformed, runs at the other.

'Stay behind me, Jasmine,' my father orders. I disobey. I want to fight beside Lazarus, but his fast movements are hard to keep up with.

By the time Ash reaches the vampire Lazarus has already snapped his neck. Ash rips his head off and tosses to the ground.

'Nineteen to go! Light him up, Laz,' he snarls.

A flame bursts out from Lazarus, igniting the vampire. How can he use his dragon power in human form? He locks eyes with me for a few seconds; a frown crowding his brow. He seems confused.

He speeds over to Hudson and ignites the decapitated vampire, the flame firing from his mouth.

He has partly transformed into his dragon form. His teeth are vicious and his hands are now dangerous talons. He glances at me and shrugs. He doesn't know how he's doing it either. I notice Hudson running his eyes over Lazarus with a look of confusion over his face.

'Don't breathe the vapours.' Hudson says.

'Use your cloaking spell to protect you. The same one you used when King was inflicting pain,' says my father.

I do it just as the vapours float my way and hold my breath.

'Let's keep moving. They know we're here now,' yells Hudson.

'This way,' says Ash, pointing to the stairs leading to the underground castle.

We run to the stairs, with me at the rear. My legs shake as we descend and I pray they hold me up.

There is a commotion up ahead.

'Oh, my goodness! Look at all the souls,' gasps my dad.

'Shall I start collecting them?' I ask.

'Good idea. It keeps you behind us and out of harm's way.' He throws me the backpack.

I head back upstairs and grab the few souls we had already passed. Each one wants to know who I am, blocking my tele-pathic passage to Lazarus.

'I'm sorry to be blunt, souls, but you need to shut it until the rescue is over.'

The deafening noise of growling and clashing bodies fills

the dim hallways. I keep my senses on alert, ready for any unexpected surprises the vampires may have.

I come to a T-intersection and decide to move away from the noise to avoid tripping over dead bodies. I collect another ten souls, placing them in the backpack.

I follow the hallway down several steps, arriving at a familiar door. It's locked so I draw on my gargoyle form. When my hand begins to turn grey I stop drawing and turn the door handle, which disintegrates. I push the door open and realise why it seemed so familiar. The blood bank!

There are at least fifteen gargoyles in stone sleep and eight humans crumpled on the ground. They try to shrink their bodies and move away.

'I'm here to rescue you. Gargoyles, can you change from stone sleep but stay in gargoyle form? I'll need a hand carrying the humans out.'

'Jasmine?' croaks a broken voice.

'Yes?'

'Over here.' A dirty blackened hand waves at me.

I hesitate to enter. The fear of being locked in here permanently still haunts me. But I take a deep breath and push on. I bend down beside the voice and pull open my backpack, giving me enough light to see the human's face.

'Jasmine?'

'Is that you, Paul?' It sounds like him.

'Yes.'

'Xandria said you came here looking for me, but you never returned. How long have you been here? Are you OK?' I squint my eyes trying to get a better look at him, but he's huddled in a dark corner.

'Please tell me you've killed King and his blood-sucking ticks!'

'King is dead and we are in the process of rounding up the other vamps.'

'Please, miss, are we free to go?' a young woman asks, her voice full of hope.

'It will be safer for you to stay here until my clan come. You're safe with me. I won't let anyone touch you again.'

I want to keep them calm and together. We will need to erase these humans' memories before freeing them back into society.

Loud cracking echoes around the room as the gargoyles break out of stone sleep.

'Is anyone injured, apart from the obvious?' I direct my question at Paul.

'There is a young man in the corner who needs help. He stood up against two vamps who took a shine to one of the women. They bashed him while draining his blood. He may not be alive.'

'And you?'

'See to him first, please.'

I'm about to stand when Paul crawls on the ground and grabs my hand. It's filthy and dehydrated and his nails are broken and blackened. 'Thank you.'

The young man in the corner is alive but laced with vampire bites, bruises and has skin greyer than a gargoyle.

'My name is Jasmine. I'm here to help. Can you tell me what your injuries are?'

'I can't feel anything. I don't know if anything is broken or if they just sucked me dry. If I'm dying and you're my angel, please make it quick. But on the way to heaven can we pass over my wife and children so I can say goodbye?'

Half of his face is swollen with one eye barely open and his lips are cracked and dry.

'I am no angel and you are not going to die if I have anything to say about it. You will be home with your family soon, my friend.'

I lift his t-shirt to find more bruises and several blistering bubbles of blood. Closing my eyes, I place my hands on his stomach and draw from the earth the colours of Aboriginal bush medicine. Brown and dark blue colours flood my mind, small red berries mixed amongst it.

The young man's body jolts and squirms beneath my hands, trying to move away from me. I hold firm, pressing my legs against him to keep him still. He screams out, begging me to stop, but I continue, not taking my mind away from the colours spinning in my head. He grabs my hands with his and tries to pull me away, but he is too weak to make an impact.

After a few minutes, he stills. I flick open my eyes to find he's passed out. To my amazement, his wounds have partially healed, and his skin colour is now more pink than grey.

'What have you done?' asks Paul, who has crawled over. 'How can you heal someone? Did King turn you?'

'He tried but failed. I'm unsure how I gained this power and right now all I care about is using it.' I force a small smile. 'Who else is hurt?'

'The man you're talking to got most of the punishment. King smelt his queen's scent on him and used him as his personal blood bank, draining him daily,' a gargoyle says, squatting down beside me.

I flick my eyes to Paul. He shrugs. 'He smelt your scent and when I denied any connection to you, he punished me.'

'King drank from you so that means you may be full of his venom.'

'He pumped me full of it! He didn't want any of his clan feeding from me. I was his and only his because I smelt of you.'

'Holy hell, Paul! I'm so sorry. If I had known you were down here, I would have struck a bargain with King to free you.'

'I came here looking for you and several relatives. He hyp- notised me several times to learn about what elite creatures are in the Australian clan. I wasn't strong enough to keep you a secret and everyone else. Something had to give, and I revealed information on our clan. I told him of Jet and your powers, well, what I knew of them. I'm a traitor to our kind.' Tears fill his eyes.

'You're not a traitor. You are my family. Let me heal you as much as I can. Hopefully, it will give you enough strength to get home where the angels can remove the venom.'

'I don't think they can do that.' He lifts his top lip up to reveal a set of fangs.

'Oh, shit.' I lean away from him.

'I won't hurt you or anyone, for that matter.'

'I know. It's a shock, that's all. Let me transfer what I can and let your body take what it needs.'

I lay one hand on each of Paul's arms. I pray before I begin that he doesn't heal and get full vampire powers and take a bite out of me. I draw on the same earthly powers and force them through my body to his.

He screams and I shoot my eyes open in fear of his vampire side. His fangs have dropped, droplets of blood sitting on the tips.

'Keep going!' he yells.

I crease my eyes closed and draw hard and fast. He growls a blood-boiling noise before passing out. His superficial wounds have healed but I fear the internal ones have not.

The gargoyles have stayed in true form and have gathered around to watch my powers.

'Who of you is strong enough to follow me out and fight if need be? I need to collect the golden souls before the vamps destroy them.'

'We will all follow and protect you but none of us has eaten in months. Our stone sleep barely repairs our bite wounds.'

'I need two. The rest must stay here and protect the humans.

The vamps aren't as strong as King, so you'll have more of a chance of killing them together.'

'We haven't done a very good job of protecting anyone. We're a disgrace to our race,' one of the gargoyles says, dropping his head.

'You will never be a disgrace. When you're this malnourished and with your blood being drained daily, your strength would be similar to a human child. No one is questioning your loyalty, my friend.'

He lifts his head and nods with a sad smile.

'Stand with me and we'll get through this. I promise.'

I walk over to an old fireplace that has kindling and wood stacked inside it. I throw my hand at it, sending a flame to the kindling.

'Remember, don't look a vamp in the eye and if anyone touches Paul, you'll have me raining down on your backside. He's not a threat to anyone, even if his fangs drop.'

'We're the strongest,' says a gargoyle, pointing to himself and another beside him. 'We'll follow you.'

They look the strongest out of the dozen, but I could overpower them in human form. They are too weak to fight but can help collect souls.

'Thank you.' I nod to my volunteers and tell the others to keep the humans here. The less they witness the easier it will be to cleanse their memories.

We head back up the stairs, collecting souls as we pass them. We arrive at the T-intersection and head towards the area I first avoided. It's quiet now and I pray my clan have killed King's men.

At the end of the long hallway is a large lounge room with spotted fires all over the floor. My clan have killed and left the remains to burn. I redo my cloaking spell to keep out any vampire powers before walking through the room.

There are several corridors leading off from it, so I take the one closest to us. It's dark and I wonder if someone has already gathered the souls or if a vampire has crushed them.

'This is King's room,' whispers a gargoyle.

I open the door and a cool breeze blows over me. My skin crawls and when his scent hits my nose I feel my blood freeze.

His room is bigger than the one I was locked in. There is a massive round bed in the middle of the room.

The gargoyles walk around collecting the golden souls that illuminate it and give a small fraction of life to the dreary room.

I walk over and touch the bed. If we had lost the fight I would be lying here. My heartbeat races at the thought of King kissing me, touching me and making love to me.

'Jasmine!' yells Lazarus. 'I heard you a mile away. Are you all right?'

I nod and quickly pull my hand away. Lazarus tilts his head as he walks quickly over to me.

'I'm fine.'

'That's not what I heard.' He frowns, tapping his finger over his heart. 'I know when you're happy, sad, angry and scared.' He glances around the room. 'Was this King's room?'

'I found the vampires' blood bank, including Paul,' I blurt, not wanting to discuss King.

'Paul?'

'He's in a bad way. He was the one giving information about the elite in Australia. King tortured him daily. He eventually gave in. I'll snap anyone who calls him a traitor or questions his loyalty to us. I've seen how cruel King can be.'

A chill floods through me, making the hairs on my arms lift. I shake the memory of him out of my head and concentrate on killing more vampires. 'These two gargoyles are here to help but they won't be any good in a fight.'

Lazarus acknowledges the men with a nod. 'Welcome to our clan, guys.'

'Is anyone hurt?'

'Not when I left them. Sadly, we had to take out a few gargoyles that were brainwashed past repair. I sense at least six vamps left to track down.'

I smile. 'These two can finish collecting the souls, so let's go hunting.'

'Stay behind me, babe.' He points behind him as we head out and down the corridor.

We come to an area I know well; too well. The door is open and I catch the scent of Ash in there.

Lazarus walks in and gives him a friendly smack on the back, making him jump. 'Wow, what's got you nervous?'

'Memories,' murmurs Ash.

'This was our room,' I say in a sombre tone.

Lazarus' head spins, his eyes wide as he glances around the room. I stand beside Ash and rub his back before clasping his hand in mine.

'Xandria can erase this experience from your memories, if you want, Ash. But for now, we need to grab the golden souls and eliminate the last few vamps,' says Lazarus.

Ash inhales deeply as if the air in his lungs gives him strength. He smiles down at me and kisses the top of my head.

'Not everything that happened in here was bad.' He smirks while looking directly at Lazarus. He drops his head so his lips are next to my ear. 'Lucky he didn't sniff the bed and pick up our mixed scent.'

'The backpack is big enough to carry your golden soul, boulder brains. Keep pushing my buttons and I'll give you free entry,' growls Lazarus, who runs his hand over the bed, gathering its scent.

The banter between the two creatures reminds me of Drake and Lazarus' friendship.

I walk over to the wall where I hid my dragon engagement ring and pull it out from behind the loose stone. I'm about to put it on when I realise my ring finger is still scabby and healing from King's ring.

'I'll keep it safe until you heal,' says Lazarus, who slips it onto his little finger.

We leave our room and head to the end of the corridor where there's a solid door with bars on it.

'Step back.' With one fierce tug, Ash pulls the bars off. He squashes the door handle and opens it.

Inside are four people—three men and one woman. They are barely alive and are covered head-to-toe in bites.

'Jasmine, go back to the last room and wait for me there,' orders Lazarus.

'No.'

'For once in your life do what you are told.'

'No!'

'Do as he asks.' Ash blocks the door with his puffed-up chest.

'I'll come with you, miss,' says one of the gargoyles, clearly intimidated by them.

'Fine!' I huff as I turn and head down the hallway. Halfway, I head back, walking straight into the room. 'They're hurt. I can help them.'

'Jasmine,' says Lazarus. 'Get out!'

'No. I can heal them, especially the woman. Her wounds look fresh.' I walk past them and squat beside her. 'My name is Jasmine. I can help heal your wounds.' I smile, and she forces her eyes to blink.

Her legs and arms are cut and bleeding and need stitching. I don't know how much my powers will help but I'm eager to try. I place one hand on her leg and one on her arm.

'What are you doing?' asks Lazarus.

'She's healing them. Jasmine healed me when King launched an anoric at my stomach. It seemed like a small miracle,' explains Ash.

'You never told me of this power.' Lazarus sounds offended.

'I was her first.' Ash smiles, bumping him.

'You will never be her first, mate. Open that backpack up, I've got another soul on its way.'

'Quiet, you two. I need to concentrate.'

'I don't want you anywhere near these people, Jasmine. Ash and I can take care of them.'

'Shut it or get out!'

Closing my eyes, I draw on the Aboriginal healing colours, pulling them up and through my body then into the woman's. Her body jolts. I keep a firm grip, waiting for her to struggle against me, but she doesn't.

A vision flashes before me, mixing with the colours and particles circling around. There is a woman's face, which slowly transforms into a dog, or is it a wolf? Behind her is a black smoke similar to the smoke a burning vampire exudes. It floats around her then shoots towards me and into my hands.

In a sudden movement, her hands grip my arms. I flick my eyes open and she is staring wide-eyed. 'I'm sorry.'

Lazarus pulls me away, 'Darn it, Jasmine!'

'What are you?' I ask.

'I am what you saw. A wolf, as are my two brothers and husband.' She nods towards the three men comatose on the floor.

'The black smoke?'

'King wanted to make an indestructible creature and was using us as guinea pigs. He would bite his venom into us when we were in human form so when we changed to our true form his poison would travel straight into our souls.'

'The black smoke?' I'm anxious to know what she has passed into me.

'I'm sorry. I don't know how it happened.'

'Don't know how what happened?' snaps Lazarus.

'It represents his venom or the devil, whichever you believe. Once in your soul, it takes over, altering your perception of everything, making you do things you wouldn't normally do. I'm so sorry.'

'Such as?'

'You hate, attack and murder for no reason. It makes you draw on your dark side. I'm so sorry.'

'Why do you keep apologising?' asks Ash.

'Because somehow I drew it out of her and into me.' I flop back onto my bottom.

'Hell!' Lazarus growls, his teeth sharpening.

'We need angels! Where are the castle's angels?' I ask.

'There is only one pair in England and they won't help. Too many of their relatives have died helping creatures like us.'

'They have to. It's their job!'

'No, they don't. We need to get you all back to Elyograg Castle. Malachi and Gabby may know of a way to pull it out of your soul. If it was in your blood, I'd willingly suck it out myself,' says Ash.

'There's nothing we can do now. Let's finish what we started and get back to Australia.' I force myself to stand and be strong. These people have been through much more than I have.

'I'll round up a few gargoyles to help me carry these guys to the car. You go with Lazarus and find the others. Let's hope they've eliminated the remainder of the vamps,' says Ash.

I nod and head out and down the corridor. Halfway down I'm stopped by Lazarus' angry frame. 'If you didn't want to marry me, you could have just told me.'

'What? I do want to marry you.'

'Well, why are you so hell-bent on killing yourself?'

'I…'

'Exactly! Do as you're told and stay behind me.'

He slowly turns and heads down the corridor. I childishly poke my tongue out.

'God help you if that was your tongue sticking out at me, Jasmine!'

'I was scratching my nose.'

He shakes his head in frustration.

I jog to catch up with him, walking two steps behind as he ordered. He slows and moves in a predatory way. I do the same so as not to bump into him. I use my senses and smell and hear vampires in the next room. I sense my father nearby and pray he's captured the last of the vamps.

We peer around the corner and I'm glad my senses are working correctly. My father's body is bound by rope and hanging from the ceiling. He spots us but is quick to look away. I follow his eyes and catch a glimpse of Hudson slumped on the ground behind a couch.

Lazarus holds up four fingers, one for each vampire in the room. He is about to step into the room when I'm shunted past him, falling onto the floor.

Lazarus falls to the floor beside me, knocking his head on a concrete table. He's out cold. A vampire towers over me, glaring his blood-filled eyes at me. I force myself not to smile as his eyes start to swirl, knowing he can't hypnotise me. But it's in my favour, he doesn't know it.

'Well, what do we have here? I sense a witch,' says the leech, standing over me.

'I am a sorceress.'

'What is this creature to you?'

'My fiancé.'

'Let's have some fun,' he says, bending down to hold my chin in his cold hand. 'I want you to kill the dragon.' He nods towards Lazarus.

'As you command, my king.' I nod, pulling out my acting card.

'Ooh, she called me king. Look out, boys. This one is going to be a cracker! I've got dibs on her afterwards.'

I crawl beside Lazarus and flick my eyes to my father. He winks, letting me know he's on board with whatever plan I have up my sleeve. He starts to swing in the rope, getting some momentum up. Hudson is still motionless and, for now, safe behind the couch.

'Wait, my little sorceress, I want your fiancé to see this coming,' says the vampire.

'Be careful not to wake the dragon up too much. I'd let her kill him while he's out cold,' says another vampire.

'Where's the fun in that? You surprised him and knocked him out so I'm sure I can handle him.'

'Suit yourself, but I think you're playing with fire. No pun intended.'

He grabs Lazarus from the ground and holds him up. He slaps his face several times, making my blood boil. I will rip that particular hand off when I get the chance.

Lazarus rolls his head before focusing on me.

'Continue to kill the dragon, my little sorceress.'

I move to stand in front of Lazarus and place my hands around his neck. We lock eyes before another vampire walks into the room. I draw the earth's energy up through my body and hold it tightly in my stomach.

'What's happening?'

'We stumbled across a little sorceress who I've hypnotised to kill the dragon. Just a bit of fun,' answers the vampire holding Lazarus.

I whisper to him while they're in conversation, 'Together we can do this.'

'You fool! She's King's sorceress, the queen. She can't be hypnotised!'

Lazarus' eyes swirl red. I force the built-up energy into his. Our bodies ignite internally, exploding in an electric blast. It shoots out from our bodies, hitting everything in the room. My father swings his body up and out of the way.

The ferocity of the blast bursts four vampires into flames. The newest arrival is knocked to the ground, landing beside Hudson. I'm glad our blast didn't reach Hudson but I'm disappointed there's one vampire left to kill.

He shoots to his feet and pierces his fangs into my father, who tries to kick him but misses each time.

Lazarus is about to launch on him, but I hold him firm.

'Stay back. He's mine.' I throw out my hand and a ghostly white steel spear protrudes and points at the vampire. Before he has time to withdraw his fangs, I lunge forward and stab the dark monster in his heart.

He withdraws his fangs, grasping the steel spear that is staking him in his chest. He gurgles and spits blood from his mouth. 'No one bites my father,' I growl, before twisting the spear, deepening the wound. With my free hand, I draw on a smaller blade, slicing off his hand. 'That's for slapping my fiancé.'

Lazarus pushes the vampire away and sets him alight. I withdraw the spear and use it to cut the rope holding my father.

He drops to the ground with an ungraceful thud. 'Geez, Jasmine, you're bruising your old man.'

'Would you prefer I left you hanging around?'

He shakes his head, 'It was good to see you draw on positive energy but seeing your two powers combined was truly amazing.'

'We're a good team,' says Lazarus, helping my father to his feet.

'I see that now. I'm glad you found each other.' He smiles at Lazarus and pats him on the back before heading towards Hudson. 'Also, I didn't think much of her last fiancé.'

'Speaking of which, Jasmine drew out venom from a wolf,' says Lazarus, following my father.

'Wolf! I don't want her anywhere near them. Do you understand?'

'Too late, Dad. They're coming back to Elyograg Castle with us. They're filled with venom which needs to be withdrawn.'

'Then you will stay at Nogard Hollow. You are not to mix with those creatures.' My father's tone is raw.

The two of them pick up Hudson's limp body.

'I don't see a problem—' I start to say but the dark glare my dad gives stops me.

'I am ordering you to stay away, as your father and as Aldore! End of conversation.'

I huff loudly and screw my face up, making him stop and glare at me. It's a look I've never seen before and it makes me cower slightly. 'Fine. Anyhow, how did you and Hudson get caught out by these vamps?'

'By not listening and doing what we've been told!'

I knew by his tone it was the end of our conversation.

We catch up with Ash, who has the drained and traumatised humans in one car. The wolves are in another and are already on the way to the airport where we will use King's private jet to fly us back to Australia.

Hudson eventually comes to; embarrassed he was taken out by a group of vampires.

'They snuck up on Laz and me as well. Quiet little leeches.' I smile.

'The stench of burnt vampires covered the scent of the

living ones,' says Hudson, rubbing his nose.

'I wouldn't call them "living".' I giggle.

'We all got a little cocky and let our guard down. Something no elite creature should do,' my father says.

'I've decided to stay here to protect the gargoyles as they heal and rebuild their home. Demona has arrived from Australia and I'm eager to return to my castle and our clan,' says Hudson. His eyes light up when he mentions his wife. 'Ash, this castle needs a strong leader who is level-headed. I can't lead this castle and my own. You'd be a great candidate for the job.'

'You don't know him very well if you think he's level-headed,' stirs Lazarus, making us all laugh.

'I'd have to agree with Laz. I've done some stupid stuff in the past,' Ash says humbly.

'You've shown to be loyal, powerful and a productive leader over the last few months. You kept me under control and made me stick to your plan, which paid off, as we killed King. You'd be great as the head of this castle,' I say.

'Is that the same plan where my fiancée pretended to be in love with the king of vampires?' Lazarus raises his eyebrows.

'You didn't like it?' Ash teases.

'It was a great idea, mate. Remind me to thank you personally when I'm in my natural dragon form.'

Hudson interrupts the boys' banter. 'The position is yours, Ash. There are a good bunch of elites here. They're disheartened and humiliated after what they've been through. They need to draw and rely on the strength of their leader.'

'Can I have some time to think about it?'

'I understand it's a big decision to leave the sanctuary of Australia and your clan. Take your time, as I'll be here cleaning up for several months. I have a bunch of gargoyles full of venom and pray they won't turn before I can get them cleansed. The angels in England haven't been cooperative in the past and I'm praying they will help this time.'

'You can always send them to Australia. Our angels will help. I hate to cut this short, but we need to get a move on. I don't like the idea of mixed elites, full of venom, altogether in one aeroplane,' says my father.

We bid Hudson goodbye and head out to King's private airstrip and our newly acquired plane. The mixed scent of the elite creatures stings my nose, forcing me to switch off my sense of smell.

We've taken half the golden souls with us to place them in our Australian vault. Their voices are a deafening hum against the aeroplane's engine.

'They are beautiful to look at. I remember stealing two from Nogard Hollow cave. I stuck them in my bra, hiding them from Laz.' I lift one out of the backpack, letting it illuminate the room.

Laz shakes his head at me. 'That was a very risky thing to do. I was in my natural form and may have bitten your arm off for stealing them.'

'Didn't you steal them first?' Ash asks with Lazarus shrugging it off and grabbing a soul from the backpack. 'Is that when Falcon kidnapped you and Demona?' He directs this question to me.

'Yes,' I reply, examining the soul in my hand.

'I can see the attraction.' Lazarus smiles, licking his lips while gazing lustfully at a soul.

'Do need to take you down, leather guts?' sniggers Ash.

'You can always try, boulder brains.'

Paul wakes and joins us in the lounge area of King's fancy jet. He smiles and nods at us in greeting, showing us his newly acquired teeth. I smile and point to my small human-sized fang. Paul lifts his hand to his mouth with a shocked look when he touches his long large fang.

'The fangs drop down at the most inappropriate moments,' he says, shrugging.

'Like now.' I laugh. 'I'm laughing with you, not at you. I learnt very quickly to not laugh at a vampire.'

'Can you control your hunger, mate?' asks Ash.

'I'm fine at the moment, but I fear it's a long flight.'

'If you need to feed you can come and suck on me. I don't want the plane landing without any survivors.' Ash smiles, standing up with the backpack.

He takes the soul from my hands then holds his hand out to Lazarus, who jokingly hesitates to give back the golden soul. 'I've done a headcount on these little beauties. If any go missing, I know who to hunt down.'

CHAPTER NINE

THE TRIP HOME is long, with my father sitting in the middle of the plane, separating me from the wolves. I don't see why he has an issue with the creatures.

We land on a dusty red dirt airstrip with several waiting trucks. I never knew there was a landing strip close to our clan's land. The fewer eyes on these dishevelled humans the better.

We arrive at Elyograg Castle with Falcon, Jet and Corbin our welcoming committee.

'Hello, Aunt Jazz.' Jet wraps his muscular arms around me, lifting me several feet off the ground.

'Hello, handsome. Hope you've been behaving.'

'Who are all the extras?' He inhales their scent then screws his nose up.

'There's a group of humans who need to heal before we can erase their memories. We also have four creatures that need healing. They've all have been injected with vampire venom. Paul was bitten on a regular basis and is now showing signs of vampirism.'

'You bought a vampire here?'

'No, I brought Paul home.'

'If I find him sucking on you or any of our clan, I will rip his head clean off his blood-sucking shoulders.'

'Nobody is sucking on anyone, Jet. Now give me a kiss and help carry the humans inside.'

He kisses my cheek and breathes me in, long and deep. 'It was pure torture not having you close by. You must stop leaving me.'

'I love you too, Jet.'

His shoulders roll back, happy hearing my words of love. He releases his hold and heads over to Ash, who helps the humans into the castle.

MY FATHER HAS remained and seems to be making Elyograg Castle his home. The creatures regard him as Aldore, so I do the same. They look up to him and his rational way of thinking. He spends most of his days with Lysander and the many golden souls, documenting which clans they were originally from. Returning them to their original clan is a high propriety, as a newborn may need a soul.

I haven't seen the wolves—Erin and her husband, Nate, her two brothers Tyson and Luke. Every time I enquire about them, everyone changes the subject or holds their breath. I pray they are alive and ready to return to their homeland, England.

Lazarus has the two clans preparing for a vampire attack. I spot Kite amongst the group and whisper to her to sneak away from training. 'I'm desperate for some girl time. Meet me by the creek in five.'

She acknowledges me by nodding her large dragon head. Lazarus turns his head and winks at me. *'You can have her for ten minutes then I need her back here.*

'What can I say in ten minutes? Make it half an hour. Please, babe.'

'I know you can say and do a lot in ten minutes, Jazz. I need her in training.'

I bow to him. *'Your wish is my command, oh great one.'*

'About time you realised who was in charge of this relationship.' He bellows a puff of smoke.

'Lucky you're in dragon form otherwise I'd punch you for that comment. But since I like my arm attached to my shoulder, you can win this one.'

'Remember babe, when speaking telepathically make sure you

connect directly to me, as every other dragon can hear you.'

I look around the training ground and all eyes are on me. *'Oops, sorry guys.'*

When I reach the creek, Kite is already there with two glasses of homemade lemonade. 'Compliments of the angels.' She hands me a glass while sipping from the other one. 'Hmm, delicious! Tastes better than a human.' She smiles and flicks her eyebrows. 'How are you coping with Keira still being here?'

'She's an old friend of Lazarus. He has asked me to respect her so that's what I'm doing.' Kite raises an eyebrow. 'I'm green with jealousy.'

'I find her quite nice, but she does turn bitchy when you enter the room. I think she's jealous of your relationship with Laz.'

'I hate knowing she is with him every day, training. Anyhow, changing the subject, how are things with Falcon and you?'

'We're going good, not that we have much time together. Laz has us training nonstop. He has us search the one-thousand-kilometre radius surrounding both castles on a daily basis, even though the dingoes assure us no creature has entered Australia.'

'He's lost faith and trust in all elite creatures since I hurt him in England. He believes I'm hiding powers from him, even though I'm not. I've broken his trust and I'm trying desperately to repair it.'

She swallows the last mouthful of her lemonade, looking into the glass as if there should be more. 'He is wound tight and it's starting to rub off onto Ash.'

'He has Ash heading up the gargoyles, which is a tough job, teaching them to attack without reason or warning. It's not in a gargoyle's nature to attack unless attacked first.'

Kite stares at my full glass of lemonade, licking her lips. I offer it to her. She doesn't hesitate to take it and hands me her empty glass. 'I heard he continually drags them down to the vaults, where they can hear the horrid stories the golden souls have, stories of how their lives were taken so callously and without warning by the vamps.'

'I snuck down to the vaults and heard his lecture, it's true. And the stories told by the souls are terrifying.'

Kite finishes the lemonade and hands me the glass. 'You need to go get yourself some lemonade. Whoever created it was a genius. I better get back to training as my coach is a real tyrant.' She kisses me on the cheek before stepping away.

The earth swirls at her feet as it collects what it needs to return her to her natural form. When her transition is complete, she nudges me with her damp nose. '*Forget Keira, go get some lemonade and good luck with the elder.*' I watch her walk away before getting ready to visit the dingoes.

Malachi and Gabby have had trouble removing the venom from my system. They have never come across someone who withdrew it from another the way I did. It's usually injected by a pair of sharp fangs and floats through the bloodstream. The venom in me floats deeper.

The dingoes suggest I meet with a healer who has an alternative way of cleansing my system.

'Hi, Ellie. It's been a long time.' I wave, sliding down from my truck.

'It has been way too long. I presume you're having trouble dealing with the dark venom floating around in your system.'

'It's playing havoc with my head, but luckily for me, I have Aldore, Ash and Laz to keep me in order.'

'I bet they do.' She laughs, rolling her eyes. 'Kanangra is expecting you. She is an Aboriginal elder who is known for healing elite creatures of all kinds. I told her you were human with venom from the darkest snake inside your soul. It's not my place to mention the vampire. She's done many miracles and I pray she can help you.

'I worry the venom is breeding inside you and will eventually take over your soul.'

'I haven't mentioned it to anyone, but I feel the venom bedding down inside me. If I draw on an anoric it's automatically black. And while sleeping, I have visions of the murders King committed. It's as though I am committing them.'

'Tell Kanangra every little detail, even if it seems irrelevant. She has dealt with many creatures whose souls and bodies were being taken over. She knows how to eradicate the devil.'

'I will. Thank you for organising this.'

'How are the humans bearing up?'

'They are healing well physically and some mentally. I'm picking up Xandria on the way back, so she can erase their memories prior to me taking them back to civilisation.'

'Has her wing not yet healed from Ash ripping it off?'

'She says not but Gabby insists it's fine.'

'Maybe she fears Ash or Laz?'

'I doubt it. I'll get to the bottom of her issue when I see her.'

'You better get moving. You need to follow the creek bed for five kilometres, then cross the river at a cluster of palm trees. It's shallow so you'll drive through easily. The wolves train close by so keep your windows up so not to distract them.'

'The wolves?'

'Yes.'

'They're healed?'

'Malachi had them covered head to toe in leeches. It took ten painful days to eradicate the venom, killing most of the leeches.'

'Every time I mention them, everyone goes silent. I was starting to think they'd died.'

'Why would they keep you away for your cousins? They're used to a human's scent, plus you smell nothing like a human.'

'Did you say my cousins?'

'It is said that you saved them in England and brought them back here. I presumed you knew who they were.'

'How can they be related to me?'

'I've obviously said too much. Aldore should be the one to explain. Please don't ask me to.'

'I understand the creature code but when I see Aldore he's gonna have one angry sorceress before him.'

'Let's hope the venom is extracted prior to you seeing him.'

I give Ellie a warm embrace before I leave and arrive at the cluster of palms minutes later. The palms are easy to spot, standing out amongst the Australian native flora.

I wind my window down and try to inhale the wolves' scent. Their scent hits me, but their heartbeats are silent. Using my x-ray vision, I scan the area. There's nothing but a few timid critters.

Shaking my head to remove my dragon vision, I continue towards what I hope is my saviour and healer.

Coming to a small clearing, there's an Aboriginal woman who I presume is Kanangra. It looks as though she's waiting for a bus except there is nothing but bush for miles.

She stands beside an enclosed humpy. It's made from branches that are standing upright, giving it height. There are leaves and dried mud covering it. It would only cover several metres inside. Maybe she uses it to shelter from the blistering heat and the storms in the wet season.

She flicks her hand in front of her. I'm unsure if she is shooing flies or if she's indicating for me to get out of the truck. Her face is a blank canvas, which doesn't help.

'Hello, Kanangra. I'm—'

'No name. No one cares,' she grumps.

'Oh.'

'You got venom from dark snake, but I see in your eyes you got it from King.'

'It's more than just in my eyes.'

'I know that. I'm not stupid.'

'Of course,' I say, bowing my head, embarrassed.

'Sit and tell me what happened and what symptoms you have.'

She plops to the ground looking out to the landscape. It's as if I don't exist.

I join her and start to relay my story. She doesn't interrupt but nods now and then to indicate she is listening.

When I finish, she checks me over in a rough manner by lifting my hands and firmly pushing back my cuticles with her chipped nails. She opens my mouth, tugging at my teeth, then pulls my toes apart to see between them. If I wasn't so desperate for help, I'd find her actions comical.

She leaves me to go and work on something inside her hut. After what seems hours, she ushers me inside. The entry is so small I have to crawl on my hands and knees to get in.

The humpy is full of white smoke which takes my breath away.

'Lie down,' she orders, which I do.

I cough and cover my mouth with my t-shirt, trying to avoid the smoke, but she's quick to slap my hand away. 'Breathe in smoke. It will draw out the venom.'

I do as she orders and breathe in a lung full of the smoke only to cough until I vomit. 'Allow it to enter your body. Venom is making you cough it away.' She flicks my face with her fingers. 'Look at me and not cough!'

I try again but this time I inhale through my nose and exhale out of my mouth. I muffle a small cough. The smoke has a familiar scent—a mix of lavender and eucalyptus which is quite pleasant.

'Not good enough! Breathe in through your nose, drawing in the Earth's positive energy. Breathe out mouth, blow away dark energy.' She taps my nose firmly. 'Do now!'

As instructed, I inhale through my nose, drawing on the Earth's good energy, concentrating on the colours that help me shift and create. While exhaling, I pull deep within me and feel the cold colours that are bedded into me—the colours of King.

With my eyes closed, my concentration heightens, as does my senses. My body starts to heat. I fear I may ignite and hurt Kanangra.

'Push that thought away. Concentrate on good Earth energy. In good and out bad.'

Breathing in and out, I force my mind to seek out the devil and draw him out. It puts me into a trance state. I hear nothing except the air being circulated around my body, pumping my blood forwards and backwards, cleansing me of King.

My body starts to drip with sweat. I shiver when my temperature drops and my teeth begin to chatter. Then I heat up again.

The rise and fall of my temperature happens more times than I can count. But with each breath, I feel lighter and at peace.

The sting of Kanangra's hand, slapping my leg, brings me back to the smoky hut. 'Open eyes.'

Slowly, I blink my eyes open to find the hut full of dark green smoke. 'You need to get out. Smoke got all your venom. You don't want to draw it back in.'

I scamper out of the small opening into the cool evening air. We must have been inside for hours. I take a deep breath and feel lighter within myself, within my soul.

'You need to keep away from vampires. If you get bitten

again it will change you. No magic will erase that.'

'I don't plan on going back to England.'

'There is one living with you. Your blood sings to him, as do the fairies'.'

'Paul would never hurt me or Xandria.'

'He is human first and that makes him weak. Your blood is a drug and he is an addict.'

'I trust him.'

'Huh! Trust will get you killed.'

'I'll take my chances. Thank you for healing me, Kanangra.'

'Not totally healed. Can't remove the dark you already had. Not good for a sorceress. Keep breathing good energy in and keep away from bad. It will manifest inside of you.'

'I will.'

By the time I get to the river crossing it's pitch black. There's no moon to lighten my path and I fear I might hit a boulder and roll the truck. I pull over and search the back of the truck for any dry clothes or blankets. There's one small blanket which I wrap around myself.

The temperature is dropping dramatically. So many people die in the outback due to the freezing night air. My wet clothes are making my temperature drop quicker than normal. I wish Lazarus had come with me, but Kanangra didn't want anyone with me. His body temperature would have heated me up in seconds.

That's it! I'll change to dragon form and sleep beside the truck until morning.

Moving a safe distance away from the truck, I draw on the earthly colours, but as I do, there's a noise from behind me with several heartbeats attached. I inhale and catch their scent. It's the wolves.

'Show yourselves.'

'We mean no harm, Jasmine,' says a man, walking in

front of the truck with his arms and hands open wide.

'You're Nate,' I state, but it's more of a question.

'Yes.'

'You're my cousin.'

'Yes, but not by blood.'

'That explains a lot. The wolf blood must have been married into our family.'

'I married Erin. She, Tyson and Luke are your cousins.'

'I don't understand.'

Erin walks around the front of the truck with her brothers following. 'My father is Aldore's brother.'

'Uncle Bill?'

'Yes. You remember him?'

'He's a wolf?'

'He was a sorcerer, the same as Aldore. He was bitten while in Canada and was banished from Australia because of it.'

'Banished? Who has the right to banish a creature?'

'Aldore has the right.'

'My father sent his own brother away?'

'There are no other wolves in Australia, so my father couldn't form his own clan. Aldore, together with Grandfather, had peace amongst the Australian clans. The creatures here fear wolves and were becoming anxious and unsettled.'

'Why would they fear wolves?'

'Because they are naive and fear the unknown,' she says with a sad tone. 'My father met my mother in a wolf clan in Scotland. We were born and recently captured by King. The rest you know.'

'So you're human first or wolf?'

'Because of the way my father got his wolf blood, we have human traits that are stronger than the normal wolf. We can live as either for long lengths of time without having to change back to reboot. It allows us to live amongst wolves and humans unnoticed.'

I shiver, feeling the temperature drop further.

'You're cold,' says Tyson; the first words he's spoken.

'I was about to change form when you interrupted me. I can't navigate the bush at night. It's too dangerous and I can easily flip the truck.'

'We can change form and sleep beside you,' says Nate. 'The luxury of having human blood run through our veins means we don't want to attack you.'

'That's a luxury some dragons wish they had.' I chuckle through chattering teeth. 'One thing that baffles me is why my father would keep this a secret.'

'It wasn't until our father's death that our mother told us our history,' says Erin.

'Uncle Bill died? I mean, we never spoke of him, only that he was on a never-ending holiday. I never thought to question it.'

'Why don't you change into a wolf form? We can continue to talk, and you'll be warmer,' says Tyson.

'Sounds like a good idea.'

I move closer to Tyson and notice Luke moving awkwardly away from me.

'If I inhale on your scent it helps me to see what I need to draw on to transform,' I explain.

'Luke is nervous around any creature that has been in contact with King. We know how powerful you are and it's intimidating,' says Nate, slapping Luke on his back. 'The memory of the leeches sucking on us for days is still very fresh.'

'I can only imagine the pain. I had a few sucking on me and whinged about it. But I can assure you, Luke, I would never hurt you.'

'You were to become queen. We were locked in a cold cell and fed from.'

'It was an act to get King's confidence so I could bring him undone. In regard to you been held hostage, the first I knew about it was when I found you.' I say through chattering teeth.

'You'll catch pneumonia. Let's transform then finish our conversation,' says Erin.

I watch with great intent as the four of them change form. They look scary as hell.

I quickly join them just in case they change their minds and take a bite out of me. Halfway through transforming I panic and stop the process. The four wolves burst into laughter, which sounds ridiculous coming from these scary-looking creatures.

Nate chuckles. *'Sorry to laugh, but you changed into a half-wolf, half-dingo.'*

I glance down at my four paws which look manicured compared with theirs. *'Well at least I'm warm and I can hear you loud and clear—laughing at me!'*

I curl up on the ground after walking around in circles trying to find the right spot. Who knew it took this much effort to just sit down and tuck four feet and a tail underneath your bottom?

The other four move slowly towards me and, after circling me several times, curl up beside me.

It doesn't take long before Lazarus contacts me telepathically. After thirty minutes of arguing, he accepts it is safer for me to be off the road and with my cousins. I neglect to tell him I've transformed into wolf form.

For added warmth, I wriggle in closer to my cousins. We talk all night about our lives, past and present until, the sun pokes its head above the horizon.

But the peaceful horizon is soon interrupted with the outline of a distraught dragon. I change form, as do my cousins. Explaining the situation to Lazarus will be easier in human form than wolf form.

AFTER CALMING LAZARUS down and saying goodbye to the wolves, I reach Nogard Hollow by mid-morning. It gives me enough time to drive Xandria back to erase the humans' memories before dark. Lazarus is already annoyed with me and no doubt Aldore will be too.

'Xandria!'

'I'm here, Jasmine.'

I spin around to find her sitting stiffly on the sofa in human form.

'What's going on with you? You called me Jasmine and not human?'

'Mellowing with age, I suppose.' I like it when she's in human form, as she doesn't speak in the third person.

'Is your wing still broken?'

'No.'

'Then why did I drive all the way out here to pick you up?'

'I can't help erase the humans' memories unless you bring them here.'

'I don't understand.'

'A fairy as strong as me doesn't need to explain to a mere sorceress.' She turns her back.

'Cut the charade. I thought we got past all this and decided to play nice.'

'I don't need anyone being nice.'

'Stop it right now! Paul tells me you haven't even visited him since he got back. Are you scared of Ash breaking your wing again?'

'No!'

'I thought you wanted to be friends. I can't help if you don't talk to me.'

She sighs and turns to face me, her eyes welling up with tears. 'I'm scared to be near Paul.'

'Because of his vampirism?'

'Fairy blood is so attractive to vamps. It would be unfair to him and unsafe for me.'

'I've been around him every day since our return and not once has he lost control or shown any sign of not coping. He hunts with the gargoyles and dragons and feeds on animal blood. Since he's human first he only needs a small amount to satisfy his hunger.'

'Fairy blood is like gold to him. I'm too scared.' Tears start to roll down her cheeks.

'We need to return the humans and we can only do that with your help. What if I stay with you the whole time?'

'Why should I trust you?'

'You need to trust someone. Do you love Paul?'

'With my whole heart. That's why this is so painful.'

'He loves you too. Give him a little credit, Xandria.'

'What if he can't keep his fangs in his mouth?'

'If I need to, I can use my powers to cripple him so he can't hurt you.'

'If you promise to stay with me, I will come and help and, in return, you will help me and Paul.'

I study her. She is scared and heartbroken. 'You don't need to blackmail me or demand terms. I stand by my friends and do what I can to help them.'

'Am I your friend?'

'Yes, of course.'

'Even when you needed me the most and I let you down?'

'Yes, yes and yes! Now stand up give me a hug and let's get going. If I'm home after dark you can explain it to Lazarus who is already seeing red.' I smile and open my arms wide as an invitation.

'Ha! You have that dragon wrapped around your little finger.'

'As you have Paul. Just wait and see.'

It's a long drive back to Elyograg Castle, even longer with Xandria sitting beside me chatting nonstop. I may have to rethink our new-found friendship.

True to form, Lazarus is pacing around the top of the castle, awaiting my arrival even though he asked me telepathically where I was every five minutes. I told him to keep Paul in his room as Xandria is nervous about seeing him.

When we enter the castle, everyone is sitting together discussing the clean-up of rogue vampires within Australia. Paul is amongst them. He is engrossed in the conversation and arguing about the elimination of all vampires. He believes they can be civilised amongst other creatures as he is and learn how to feed as he does. It sounds as though he's losing the argument.

'Does that mean you eliminate me? Not once have I threatened anyone within these walls or when I was captive at King's lair. They are elite creatures who need a chance to survive amongst us. Just as the wolves do,' says Paul, frustrated.

'I've never met a vamp I can trust. Present company excluded,' says Aldore.

'I don't expect you to open your castle doors but let them live in Australia under the elite law.'

'Who's to say they'll abide by our law?' Jet growls. 'I'm not jeopardising any member of my clan on your hearsay.'

'Oh no! He's here,' whispers Xandria, drawing attention to us, even though they would have smelt us miles away.

'You're fine. Look how many creatures are here to protect you.'

'Hi, babe. You still smell like wet dog,' says Lazarus, kissing my cheek. 'You taste like one too.'

My father's eyes shoot to me and narrow. I presume he will discuss my association with the wolves sooner rather than later.

I asked you to keep Paul away. I snap telepathically at Lazarus.

He's harmless.

'That's not the point.'

'Xandria!' Paul jumps up off the sofa and moves quickly in our direction.

I put my hand up, indicating that he should slow down. Paul frowns when Xandria steps behind me.

'Slowly, Paul. We've had more time than she has to get acquainted with your new teeth.'

'I'd never… is that why you've avoided me, Xandria?' The hurt in Paul's voice makes it quiver.

The room falls into an uncomfortable silence with pairs of eyes ticking back and forth, unsure of what to do.

'Maybe we should move into the kitchen, guys, and give them some private space,' says Aldore.

'No! Stay and keep me safe,' says Xandria.

'What are you saying, babe? You don't need protection from me. I'd never hurt you.' Paul frowns, moving closer. Sadly, his fangs drop, making her squeal.

Aldore and the creatures abruptly remove themselves from the scene, leaving Lazarus and me to deal with Paul and Xandria.

'My fangs drop when I'm happy, sad, angry, hungry or just plain bored. It means nothing.' Paul puts his thumb and index finger over their tips.

'It's the hungry side I'm worried about,' she says.

'It's still me inside. I have the same heart and soul I had prior. I've no urge to bite or drink from anyone, especially you.'

I speak to Lazarus telepathically, *Maybe you should suggest that Paul and you go feed and give her time to relax.*

'Why don't we go feed and leave the girls to do girl stuff?' says Lazarus, patting Paul on the back.

'Great idea. I wanted to go through my wedding plans with Xandria and that will bore you two silly.' I smile, but Paul's face is distraught and locked on the fairy.

She places her hand on my back, sending a swirling, tingling current over my body. My mind becomes fuzzy and my vision blurs.

'Xandria whatever you are doing stop it before I zap you!'

'Oh! Sorry, I wasn't thinking about you.'

'Are you okay, babe?' Lazarus asks.

I reply telepathically, *'Go before the stupid fairy erases my memory and I forget who you are.'*

'Let's go feed, mate,' he says to Paul.

Paul shakes his head and breaks eye contact, leaving the castle, with Lazarus sprinting after him.

Xandria instantly relaxes, sighing loudly.

'I understand you're nervous, but Paul cares for you. He has this under control. My blood sings to him just as yours does and not once did he even sniff me.'

'One bite and I'm dead!'

'As am I. I can't be bitten ever again but I trust him. It's Paul.'

'It shocked me. I've never been close to one before.'

'It's Paul!'

She drops her head and flops back into the sofa. 'His feelings were hurt.'

'Yes, they were. Trust amongst any creature, be it human or animal, is how we survive. But you can repair it if you want and if you don't leave straight after erasing the humans' memories.'

She looks down at her twiddling fingers. 'I've made a real mess of it.'

'Nothing you can't fix. Maybe if you stay here awhile you'll find your feet with him. It will make you more comfortable when you're alone. I'd also love your opinion on the wedding. I presume you've been to a creature's wedding before, unlike me.'

Her eyes light up. 'You really want my opinion?'

'Yes.' Actually no, but for Paul's sake, I force a smile. 'And tomorrow you can erase the humans' memories.'

Within minutes, she has called all the females in the castle to discuss the wedding, taking over as my bridesmaid. She says that each creature has its own ritual, and dragons usually rub scales and fly off.

It's not long before Lazarus and Paul return.

Xandria was so focused on the wedding plans she didn't realise Paul had sat beside her but when she does, she freezes.

I quickly move from sitting on Lazarus' lap to sit on the other side of Paul, touching his hand and arm whenever I can. He is warmer than King but colder than a gargoyle in stone sleep.

Xandria notices and slowly reaches over to touch him. This is my cue to leave.

Once in my room alone with Lazarus, I question him on our wedding plans. 'I was told a dragon wedding is very quick. Apparently, we rustle our scales then fly off.'

'Some are done that way,' he says with a cautious eye. 'The fun happens afterwards.'

'So why are we doing it differently?'

'Because you are human first and it has been your dream from a young age to be married at the altar.'

'How would you know what I dreamt as a child?'

He taps his ear and his heart.

'That's not an answer.'

'Drake told Jet who told me. I want to marry you the human way and the creature way.'

'Now you're being greedy.'

'You're marrying a dragon, babe.'

Xandria spends many exhausting hours cleansing the minds of the humans, placing a memory of an exhilarating Outback tour they have all just completed.

Jet and I pack them into my truck and an old army truck

Lazarus had acquired many years before. Lazarus demands that Kite comes along for security, as Aldore and Lysander need him to discuss the elite law since he is the clan leader of Nogard Hollow. Kite flies the whole two days above us, keeping an eagle, or dragon-eye, out for the rogue vampires.

'Well, folks, this is the end of your one-year trip. I know you'll have many fond memories of the Aussie Outback,' I say, smiling, pulling them out of the trucks and pushing them towards the train station. 'Your tickets are paid for so all aboard!'

'Excuse me? Um, sorry. I've forgotten your name,' says a lady who is looking one-hundred-percent better than when I met her crumpled on the floor of King's cave.

'My name is Kelly.' I smile sweetly.

'Where is my luggage?'

'Oh!'

'It's all of a taken care of,' interrupts Jet. 'I've already got it on board the train.'

'You're so efficient. You have been a terrific help on the whole tour. I will give you a fantastic online review, Leonardo.'

I try not to laugh before quickly jumping back into my truck to disappear from these poor humans' lives.

Jet is driving the other truck, so I echo to him. *'Leonardo. What are you, a turtle?'*

'I like the turtles. And I needed a name that is nothing like ours.'

'You definitely did that.'

We drive through the night, trying to get as far away as we can from the humans we've left behind.

'Jasmine, there are creatures up ahead and they're not from around here,' says Kite telepathically.

'Pull over, Jazz, now!' Jet yells.

I pull over, with Jet flying out of his truck and transforming in seconds. I cautiously open the truck door with my senses on full alert and move behind him. Kite lands with a thud beside us.

'Show yourselves, before I light up the forest and burn you to a crisp!' Jet shouts.

Two men walk out with their hands held open in front of them. I recognise them as vampires from King's clan. They have their heads tilted up and mouths slightly open to show their fangs are not dropped. It's a surrender stance.

Using my x-ray vision, I scan through and around the trees. They are alone.

'We know who you are, Queen Jasmine,' one of them says.

'She is not a queen,' snaps Jet.

'Hang on a minute. Who are you to say I'm not a queen?' I snigger, feeling no threat.

'We were at the Nogard Hollow battle but ran as soon as the fighting started. We were not born vamps but bitten by King's men and turned at a mature age.'

'Then you'd know we eradicated all King's clan. So why do you stand before us?' Jet says.

'We didn't know the outcome, as the creatures here refuse to show themselves even though we can sense their elite form,' the vampire says, dropping his hands to his side.

'We have no sympathy for your kind,' snarls Jet.

'We mean no harm and have survived on animal blood without killing them to get it, unlike your dragons and gargoyles,' the vampire says.

Kite growls and blows a puff of warm smoke over them.

'We mean no disrespect. Only to show you we can live amongst you without the fear of us wanting to feed from you.'

'We don't want you here. If Jasmine wasn't here, I would have killed you both by now,' says Jet.

'It's your lucky day, guys. I'll take you back with us but it's up to the clan whether you stay or not.' I hold my hand out. 'I'm Jasmine. You are?'

'You've got to be kidding me,' Jet growls.

'Behave. They are living creatures who deserve to live in peace. Neither you nor I can make the decision who lives and who doesn't, especially when no threat has been shown.'

A vampire steps forward, holding his hand out to me, 'I'm Tom and this is my brother Jack. We were holidaying in England with our wives when we were kidnapped and bitten. That was the last time we saw them.'

'*Probably because you ate them,*' Kite echoes, making Jet snigger.

'We have no special powers as most of the elite do. We were turned accidentally due to the vamps over-feeding from us. We have accelerated speed, slightly amplified strength and a hideous set of fangs,' explains Jack, which are the first words he's uttered.

'So what can you offer the clan? Nothing. You're useless and will be a hindrance. We'll need to constantly have you guarded.' Jet moves in front of me, shielding me from them. 'We already have one useless leech and a few oversized dogs.'

'You have another vampire under your roof? What's his name?' Tom asks.

'Paul has been in my life since I was a child,' I say.

'We met Paul and shared the same blood bank quarters. But we turned soon after he arrived. King would kill anyone who drank a drop from him. He tortured him nonstop due to smelling his queen on him,' says Tom. 'I'm sure Paul will vouch for our story. We want to live amongst the elite creatures in peace.'

'We can never see our wives or our families again. King made sure of that. We have nothing, so that's why we ask to join your clan, your family and hopefully find peace,' adds Jack.

'Since you have nothing to lose, what's to say you won't turn on us?' Jet is still not convinced of their honesty.

Lazarus interrupts my thoughts, asking where I am. Before I can answer, Kite jumps in, telling him I'm bringing home two vampires. I can hear his roar from here and I've got another one hundred kilometres to go.

'You may as well jump in my truck, as our clan knows you're coming. I don't think there will be a welcome mat rolled out, as my fiancé is already blowing his stack.' I smile sympathetically.

'At least I've got someone on my side,' says Jet, walking around the vampire, rolling his blue eyes over them. 'You ride with me.'

'No, I want them to arrive in one piece. Kite can transform and travel with me.'

'Kite can drive one truck while I will travel with you and the leeches,' says Jet.

After a few quick reminders on how to drive, Kite heads off with us trailing behind. The vampires are quiet due to Jet sighing every five minutes while rolling his neck to glare at them. He has only half-transformed to human, keeping his razor-sharp teeth visible as a threat to these already scared men.

Luckily, they don't know too much about the elite, as only the highest of sorcerers can partly change form. It still confuses me how Lazarus partly changed when we were fighting King's men.

True to form, the castle is alive with elite creatures, all in their attack positions. I'm a little offended they thought I'd be stupid enough to bring anyone here who'd be a danger.

I jump out of the truck as soon as I pull up, ordering the two vampires to stay inside until I settle the welcoming party.

Aldore is the first to speak. 'What on hell's earth do you think you're doing?'

'They mean no harm and have no one to support them and nowhere to go. I refuse to turn an elite creature away. It isn't a good feeling, being rejected and losing everything you have.' My mind drifts of to Emily and how she told me no one would support her because she was a vampire, even when she showed to be no threat. I can still hear the quiver in her voice when she said she'd tried to take her life more than once. I never wanted to hear that quiver in someone's voice again.

Lazarus, in dragon form, is stalking the truck, dropping his head so he can see the men inside. He nudges it, making it rock on its wheels.

'Stop intimidating them, Lazarus!'

'He's protecting you since you fail to do so,' says Aldore.

Paul walks past my father and heads straight to the truck. Lazarus growls at him, which he ignores. 'Tom! Jack! You're alive.' Paul pulls the door open and shakes the men's hands. 'Come inside.'

'Um…' Tom looks at Lazarus' huge dragon head which is pushing into Paul's back.

'I remember you both had control over your vampirism or has that changed?'

'They're in control, Paul. Everyone needs to chill and let the two men explain their story,' I say loudly.

With a confident stride, Aldore walks behind Lazarus, giving him a nudge with his clenched fist. Lazarus puffs a mouthful of smoke before stepping back and changing to human form.

'Do you have full control?' Aldore asks the two men, with Lysander moving to his side in gargoyle form.

'As I explained to Jasmine, we have fed on animal blood only and have never once killed one. We were graziers before this happened. We respected and cared for our livestock and find it cruel to kill for no reason,' says Tom.

'I'm Aldore and this is Lysander, who is the head of this castle.' He indicates with his hand for them to step out of the truck. Hesitantly, they do.

'I suggest we change to human form, so no one feels threatened.' Lysander nods, holding his hand out for the men to shake.

We head into the castle with Ash, Jet and Lazarus flanking the two of them. I'm forced to walk behind everyone with Lazarus giving me a fiery glare every so often. Oh boy, I'm in trouble again!

Keira, Kite and her sister Bell stay in dragon form, together with Lolana, who is in gargoyle form, and guard the castle from the roof. Everyone else is in human form, eager to interrogate our new guests.

'How do we know if we're safe around you? We are all creatures and you said yourself you only drink from creatures?' Jarius asks, eyeing the men up and down.

'When we were in King's castle, not once did we drink from humans, nor did we drink from the wolves,' says Tom.

'That doesn't guarantee that you won't,' says Jarius.

'I can guarantee you we won't. You have our word.'

'Your word means nothing to us. Humans who have been converted by force usually become bitter and resentful and eventually turn against their maker.'

'Thankfully, your clan has already killed our maker,' says Jack. 'We have no quarrel with any human or creature.'

The two vampires shoot to their feet, their eyes fixed on the top of the staircase.

'They have angels,' whispers Tom. His fangs drop and, without thinking, I shoot a white sword from my hand and hold it at their throats. One step towards the angels and their throats will be sliced open.

Gabby and Malachi slowly descend the staircase.

'I thought you said you had control,' I snap, pressing the blade into their Adam's apple.

'We do, but the angels can help us! They can withdraw the venom and cure us,' says Tom.

Gabby smiles. 'Lower your weapon, Jasmine. They mean us no harm.'

She and Malachi walk up to them. Gabby looks at me and nods. I notice the two men's fangs have receded, so I withdraw my sword.

'Thank you, Jasmine,' says Tom, before turning his attention to the angels. 'The angles in England refuse to help any elite creature, especially vampires. We've tried so many different remedies, but nothing. We heard Australia had angels who would help the elite. Please tell me we've heard right.'

'There are several pairs of angels in Australia. We are a part of this clan and stand by any elite creature who needs our help,' says Malachi.

'Oh, thank the Lord!' praises Jack. 'I can't wait to hold my wife in my arms again.'

Malachi holds his two hands up in the air, stopping him from saying anything further.

Gabby reaches out and touches Jack on his forearm.

'We can draw venom from the bloodstream and it's said an Aboriginal elder can draw it from a soul. But you have it bedded down inside of you,' says Malachi.

'What do you mean?' Jack says, his eyes glazing over.

'Imagine a tick or leech bedding down inside your system. Your bones, organs, flesh, blood and soul have been taken over by the venom. There is no way of removing it. Once your fangs appear there is no return,' explains Gabby.

'Can you remove a part of it?' Jack asks.

'If we place a leech on you it will drain you dry. It won't stop until it kills you.'

'I'm dead already.' Jack falls backwards onto the couch.

'There is a vampire clan in Australia. I'm unsure of their whereabouts but it wouldn't take long to hunt them out. You may find it more comfortable living with them,' says Malachi.

'No, thanks. We've lived with vampires before. Watching them drain humans made me sick.' Tom moves to sit beside Jack. 'If you angels can't help us, we have nothing and nowhere to go.'

'I believe the vampire clan drink from animals,' says Gabby.

'We need to make a decision whether we want these two elites to join our clan,' says Aldore, looking around the room. 'We must be united in this decision as I won't have angst or negativity amongst us.'

'Jasmine just had a sword at our throats and she said she trusted us,' says Jack.

I drop my head, ashamed of jumping the gun.

'Gabby, Malachi, you can both see the future, past and present. Are these men a threat to our clan?' Aldore asks, placing his hands on the men's shoulders.

'Both of them are as they say. Their hearts are torn with the sorrow of being ripped away from their families. They are no threat to our clan,' says Malachi. 'It is Jasmine's elite instinct to protect us. Together with her ultra-quick reflexes, it makes it hard for her to stop and think before acting. She feels no real threat; it was an impulsive move. If she felt threatened, they would be dead.'

'Sorry about that, guys.' I lift my eyes to see them both nod at me.

'No harm done,' says Tom.

'Huh! Not this time, but I've seen her rip a vampire's head clear off its shoulders and burn it,' sprouts Ash.

'Zip it, Ash!' I snarl.

'We know her strength, as we do all the creatures. All we want it to be a part of something,' says Tom. 'We're graziers and breeders of livestock, and when needed, kill them as humanely as possible.'

'What use are they to the clan?' Jet asks, moving to stand behind the vampires to look Aldore in the eye.

'Ash is useless and he's still here,' says Lazarus, bumping him.

'I wasn't useless when I was keeping your fiancée warm in King's cold castle,' teases Ash.

I ignore the two boys' banter and throw my hand up into the air. 'I vote yes!'

Jet growls and puffs out his chest. I roll my eyes and force my hand higher.

'We vote yes,' says Gabby, holding her hand up shoulder-high, as does Malachi.

'I'll take them feeding with me,' says Paul, raising his hand.

'We could use their skills. I've always wanted to start a cattle and sheep breeding program instead of buying stock from Outback stations,' says Lysander.

'Do you buy them from elite farmers?' Jack asks, intrigued.

Lysander shakes his head. 'We organise for humans to deliver them a fair distance away to avoid the castle and the elite being detected. We then spend weeks mustering them in.' He turns to Aldore. 'It would alleviate the risk of being discovered. It will also make our clan truly self-sufficient. I say yes.'

'I agree with the breeding program and for the men to stay,' says Aldore.

'What about their ability to hypnotise?' Falcon asks. He's keeping his distance. It's the first word he's said all afternoon.

'We've never tried it. I don't even know if we can use that power,' says Jack. 'We've never needed to.'

All eyes shoot to the angels. Gabby smiles. 'They both have the ability to hypnotise and have fangs which can produce venom if required. A vampire's venom acts quicker than a gargoyle or a dingo's venom. But to answer your next question,

Falcon, they only need a drop of blood to survive. Paul, who also is no threat, is the same.'

Falcon's questions continue. 'Who's to say they won't hypnotise an elite into doing something?'

Tom shrugs. 'Who's to say you won't rip us in two and burn us to a crisp?'

'Tom and I lived for, and put pride in, breeding our livestock. The chance to start a breeding program actually gives me hope.' Jack's face lights up. 'As humans, we were good men. That hasn't changed, only our features have. Give us a chance, as we know we would have done if we had met an elite creature when human.'

'I'm hungry,' says Ash. Everyone's eyes shoot to his, most frowning. 'What can I say? All this talk about eating cattle makes me hungry.' He rubs his belly and licks his lips. 'I say yes.'

'I trust the angels' decision so it's alright with me,' says Jet, shocking me.

'Since I don't reside here, I won't vote,' says Falcon.

'I don't want a divide between Nogard Hollow and Elyograg Castle. We are not two clans, we are one,' says Aldore.

'What troubling you, Falcon?' I ask.

Falcon flicks his eyes to Lazarus and echoes, *'You need to keep Jasmine away from the vamps. One bite and she's one of them.'*

'Careful, Falcon. Someone might think you actually care.' I laugh, tapping the side of my head. 'You forget I can hear every word you say to Lazarus, as we are inked.'

Lazarus nods and continues to speak telepathically. *'He's right, Jasmine. One bite and you'll be drinking from me while I sleep. I don't like turning away an elite but having you anywhere near them worries me.'*

'You're being rude to our guests,' says Aldore. 'Speak out loud and share your fears.'

'Are you all telepathic?' Tom asks.

'We are many things and will share with you our powers

when and if we feel necessary,' says Falcon.

I ignore my father's warning and echo, *'Don't be a bully, Falcon.'*

'I wasn't the one with a sword at their throats.'

'They are scared to death. Imagine being in their shoes with no family and no home. We can use them to keep an eye on the stock, especially when those cattle thieves are around.'

Falcon laughs, as it is he and Lazarus who normally pinch the cattle.

Unfortunately, his laughter lets my father know I'm speaking telepathically. 'Jasmine, please share what is so funny.'

'We were reminiscing about when I first arrived and helped steal the cattle.'

'And what has this to do with Tom and Jack joining our clan?' My father's rough tone and creased brow shuts us down.

'I understand your apprehensive, Falcon, but any one of us could bring down these two if need be. As leader of this castle, I will accept them, and I ask you to do the same,' says Lysander.

'What if we give them a trial or let them stay until we locate the other vampire clan?' says Lazarus.

'Finding the vampire clan risks revealing our whereabouts,' says Malachi. 'Not that they are dangerous, but personally, I'd prefer they didn't know too much about us.'

'What if they want to breed?'

'We hate what we've become. I can promise you I'd never give this hideous life to anyone,' Tom says with a quivering tone.

'Falcon, Lazarus, we need your decision. I can hear Ash's stomach rumbling from here,' says Lysander.

'I could eat a horse,' grumbles Ash, flicking his eyes to me. I narrow mine. 'I meant a fat, juicy cow.'

'Fine but if they venture onto our land, I need a warning,' says Lazarus. He then telepathically says to Falcon, *'So I can lock her up.'*

'*I can look after myself, leather guts,*' I echo, with Lazarus raising a questioning eyebrow.

'If Lazarus agrees, then so do I,' says Falcon.

'Welcome to the clan,' says Aldore, slapping them both on the shoulder. 'Gabby will show you your room and the kitchen. I'll organise Paul and one of the gargoyles to show you our feeding grounds. Take the day to settle in and introduce yourselves to the clan. Tomorrow we'll sit down and work out our breeding plan.'

'I look forward to getting stuck into the breeding program. I miss it,' says Jack, standing up to shake Aldore and Lysander's hand. 'Thanks for having faith in us when so many others wouldn't give us a chance.'

'Thanks, guys,' says Tom, who has also stood up. 'I'm excited to get my hands dirty again. When I was human, I'd judge people on their looks or accent. I now know how it feels to be judged, especially when there's no way to change my appearance. It's a lesson learnt a little too late.'

Gabby smiles. 'I'll show you both around. Malachi wishes to speak with Aldore, Lazarus and Jasmine.'

I wonder what the angel needs and glance over at Lazarus, who shrugs his shoulders. Everyone excuses themselves, leaving the four of us.

'Jasmine, would you mind putting up the silence dome? I wish to speak freely and in private,' Malachi asks.

'Of course.' I quickly cast the spell over the four of us. 'Go ahead, Malachi.'

'Aldore has mentioned while you were in England Lazarus could partly change form. Drawing on his dragon skills while still in human form. He also mentioned that together, Jasmine and Lazarus can form and fight as one.'

'Yes, it's true. It confused me at the time, and I forgot about it until now,' I say.

'It is a rare and unique power, but it has been known to happen when two elite creatures are inked and have royal blood. It is the strongest bond two elites can have.

'Together, you are unstoppable and the most dangerous weapon the elites have. It's written in the ancient scripts that only those who have royal blood run through their veins will have these powers.'

I scoff. Malachi takes a breath before continuing, 'I'm not saying either of you have royal blood. I'm saying when joined, your blood becomes royal. My concern is Hudson is having trouble healing the gargoyles that have been bitten by the vampires. They are becoming hybrids.'

'Like Jet?' I ask.

'No, Jet is unique. These elites are still gargoyles with vampirism added.'

'What has that got to do with me and Laz?'

'There's constant talk in the English castle of your victory against King. There is also talk of your joint powers. They are questioning who has the royal blood.'

'What's so good about royal blood?'

'When you two join as one, you become a unique hybrid—a mix of sorceress, dragon and royalty. And you're inked to one another. This is why you can partially transform and join your powers. If a hybrid was to get hold of royal blood their powers would be enhanced to the highest level.'

'Jet is the only hybrid here and he won't hurt either of us for our blood,' says Lazarus.

'It's not him I'm worried about,' Malachi says.

My father growls. 'Hudson is sending the infected gargoyles here for cleansing. I offered for our angels to help remove the venom but if they're already hybrids we're in trouble. I'm expecting them any moment.'

'And you're telling us now?' I narrow my eyes and flick my senses on full.

'Lysander and Lazarus have been told. You have only just arrived home with unexpected guests.'

'The gargoyles won't attack us. It's not in their nature,' I say, ignoring my father's sarcastic tone.

'They're not all gargoyle anymore. Their vamp side will draw them to you,' my father says. 'With your blood combined, they will be as strong as King.'

'Don't even think about asking me to leave Laz. I refuse to do it!'

'I've seen you both fight together and would never ask it of you or Lazarus. But if Malachi has brought this to our attention, I presume the gargoyles are already on their way with the intention of drinking from you both,' my father says, running his fingers through his hair. His eyes shoot up as the howl of the dingoes rattles the castle walls.

Jet flies into the room with Ash storming in behind him. 'We've got guests and they're not my relatives.' His nose sniffs the air.

'And I'm not expecting any of my family either,' adds Ash.

The dingoes howl again and I listen closely to their warning.

'*Six infected gargoyles have landed at the airstrip. They're half an hour out from Elyograg Castle,*' howls Ellie.

'Six infected gargoyles,' I repeat to the others.

'*Two have split from the mob and have headed into the bush. Rhys is tracking them,*' howls Ellie.

'Two have gone bush and the other four are heading here. We have half an hour.'

'You've got to be kidding me! We are being inundated by vampires!' Lazarus jumps to his feet, his eyes swirling red.

'Settle down, Laz. They may come in peace,' I say, quickly switching on all my senses to be sure.

'Do you think it convenient that Malachi happened to mention the hybrids?'

'Malachi?' I search his face for answers as I refuse to ask him about the future and take five years of his life away.

'They may come in peace or...' Malachi stops himself before revealing to the others of our royal bloodlines.

'Come on, boys. Let's give them a welcome they'll never forget. And you stay here,' says Jet, pointing to me.

'Not a chance!'

'Don't know why you bother, mate. She never does what she's told,' says Lazarus.

With a flurry of colours, everyone shoots out the door, leaving me behind. I walk calmly passed Malachi who has remained inside and is making himself comfortable on the lounge chair.

Stepping out of the castle and onto the dusty dirt I'm shoved backwards by Lazarus' two strong hands.

'Stay behind us and that is an order from Aldore,' he says. My father flicks his eyes to me and nods sharply. When did those two become such good mates?

'Most of the elite gargoyles in England didn't have an orgle so they couldn't change form. Jarius, Lysander and Jet, we should change into our natural form so we're seen to be equal,' says Ash. 'Falcon and Corbin, it's probably best to stay in human form. Three dragons on the roof are enough of a warning that we're a strong clan.'

'We're not equal. They've got an extra set of teeth,' says Jarius.

'Stop jumping to conclusions. They may be still in transition and in need of our help,' I say, getting a frowned glare from Lazarus.

'Stay behind us or I'll hold you back myself,' he growls.

The gargoyles are quick to change form and stand shoulder to shoulder with their arms crossed over their chests. Their hard features are expressionless, but their glowing blue eyes are on alert and darting across the land in front of us.

Everyone stands quietly but their senses are switched to high.

'I wonder where the other two infected creatures ran off to,' I say.

'Don't even think about, Jasmine!' Lazarus doesn't turn his head when he speaks to me, keeping his focus on what's to come.

'They could be scared or sick and need—'

'Don't!'

'I'm not stupid. I can take care of—'

'I order you not to approach them!' My father spins his head around and glares at me.

'I wasn't going to anyhow.'

My father turns back around. I childishly poke out my tongue. Who is he to order me?

Lazarus turns with a raised eyebrow.

'What?' I play innocent.

'They're here,' yells Lolana from the top of the castle

Bell and Kite let out a fiery bellow as they stalk the top of the castle roof. Keira flies down and lands behind us. I glare at her as I don't need her protection. The four gargoyles walk confidently across the pasture with their eyes scanning the area. I can hear them whisper to each other to stay calm and that the gargoyles must be in alliance with the dragons.

One of them spots me and regards me as queen. They must also know we can hear them. They are no bigger than our gargoyles and will be easy to take down if the need arises.

They stop several metres away from us.

'We are the elite from Hudson's clan. We've been told Aldore and Ash will help us,' one of them says.

'I am Aldore and this is Ash,' my father says, pointing to Ash, who's puffed his chest up.

'We travelled here in a group of six but two have run off scared.'

'Huh! Told ya,' I say, gaining myself another glare from Lazarus. I'm about to introduce myself but my mouth is covered by a warm hand. I go to move forward, but another warm hand is wrapped around my waist, stopping me.

'I warned you I'd hold you back,' whispers Lazarus in my ear. He must have moved like lighting because, seconds ago, he was standing in front of me. 'Don't even think about shocking me, babe.'

I breathe out an exasperated sigh through my nose. I poke my tongue out, licking his hand. I feel his lips against my cheek, curve into a smile. He slowly releases me, and I do as I'm told.

'Why would they be scared?' Lysander asks, moving several steps over and in front of me to block my view of them.

'We left England as infected elites. During the flight over, we went into transition. They feared you may destroy them as hybrids.'

'Why would we destroy hybrids?' Lysander asks.

'Because with our vampirism, our loyalty changes. We can attack without warning and have vampire venom plus our original gargoyle venom. It's a deadly combination.'

'We have a few deadly combinations of our own,' whispers Jet, turning to give me a wink.

'Ash has trained our gargoyles to attack at will. We are a strong army ready for any invasion,' says Aldore, letting them know they are no threat to us.

'Hudson's plan was for us to come here and be cleansed by your angels and then convince Ash to return with us to England to become the leader of our castle.'

'Hudson's a dog with a bone when it comes to you, Ash,' says Lazarus, moving to the front line.

A loud howl echoes across the land. Rhys has located the

two runaway gargoyles. They're two females and they're hiding in a cave not far from the dingoes' home.

'They're females,' I say and step up beside Lazarus, who muffles a disapproving growl.

'Yes, my queen.'

'She's not a queen!' Ash yells, beating Lazarus to the punch. The gargoyle hybrid takes several steps back.

'I was introduced to you in King's castle as queen. I mean no disrespect.'

'None taken, but call me Jasmine. I must admit I don't remember you or the other three.'

'I'm David. We were forced to cook in the kitchen. You would steal food, which confused me, as I placed ample on your evening tray. The four of us made a pact to turn our backs when you stole food so if we were hypnotised and asked what you were doing in the kitchen we could honestly say, "eating your lunch". We had hoped you remembered us.'

'It was me you were feeding,' scoffs Ash.

'That explains it. You'd have to be the size of a house to consume all that food.'

'I had a lot on my mind. Remembering the cooks was not one of them. Tell me why the females ran away,' I ask.

'One is pregnant with her first child. Since the transition, she is beyond scared for her baby and if the elite will accept it.'

'Which one of you is the father?' I step forward with Lazarus gripping my arm and dragging me back beside him. Ash takes a step forward and slightly in front of me. They still don't trust these hybrids.

'You killed him when you took down King. He stood beside King and became his head gargoyle. He did it to get his pregnant girlfriend released from the blood bank. She became a slave servant and was often fed from when the humans ran dry.'

'Holy hell! She must be scared out of her wits and hate

us with every fibre of her body.' I gasp. 'If someone killed my boyfriend I know I'd be out for revenge.'

'They've gotta catch me first, babe,' whispers Lazarus.

Aldore steps forward, putting his hands on his hips. 'Did she come here for revenge?'

'I don't believe so. We all came here with the hope of being cleansed. And even though we have transitioned we thought it best to still approach you in hope of any help. We've heard…'

'Heard what?' Aldore's body glows a faint blue. He is charging his body with anorics.

'The Aboriginals have healing powers and…' The hybrid's eyes flick to me, as do the other three. 'We know Jasmine has royal blood. It can either enhance our powers or heal us.'

'Royal blood my butt!' Ash laughs. 'Who spread that rumour?'

I jump when Kite drops down from the sky and lands behind the four hybrid gargoyles. Her large dragon form is in attack mode and her tail curled over her back with her sphere pointing directly at them. Her presence is intimidating which forces one of the gargoyles to flash his fangs and shoot out his webbed wings.

'I'll burn them to a crisp if they take one step towards any of you,' she echoes. She rolls her tongue over her razor-sharp teeth, her throat making a hissing sound.

'Stand down, Kite,' says Aldore. But she doesn't, instead, she releases a small flame which falls just short of them. 'Falcon, see to her now.'

Falcon moves quickly to her side, startling her. She bumps him with her shoulder and sends him flying into the gargoyles.

The hybrids roar and open their wings in a defensive stance. Falcon jumps to his feet to find himself face to face with one of them.

Kite inhales and I know she will retaliate if she thinks Falcon is in danger. Lazarus wraps one arm around me to keep me out of harm's way. I use his added energy to cast a solid cloaking spell over the gargoyles and Falcon.

Kite bellows a gut full of fire at them which bounces off the shield I've created. Her sphere is only a metre away from them and I pray it can't penetrate the shield.

'That was quick thinking, babe,' Lazarus whispers. 'Keep it there until Falcon has her under control.'

'Keep hold of me, as I'm drawing through you.'

'I can feel it.' He nuzzles my cheek.

'If you come here in peace like you said, fold in your wings and withdraw your fangs. Otherwise, I'll step aside and let Kite do her best,' Falcon says, inches away from one of the hybrids' faces.

The four panting gargoyle hybrids look at each other before taking long deep breaths to calm themselves. Slowly their fangs recede and their wings fold into their sides.

Falcon looks at me and nods. I shake my head, refusing to remove the shield, as Kite is still licking her lips and growling at them.

'Kite, stand down. Jasmine won't drop the shield until you back away.' Falcon's voice is calm but firm.

Kite rolls her green eye at me. 'There's no threat, my friend,' I say. 'I know you trust me. Go back onto the roof with Lolana.' I smile at her but keep my focus on holding the shield in place.

She pulls her body up, like a cat having a stretch. Her tail relaxes and moves away from the hybrids. Her wings dramatically open and force down to lift her large frame into the air. All eyes watch as she circles us before landing on the castle roof.

I drop the shield and Falcon walks over to Lazarus. Without speaking, he points to his left shoulder. His arm is dangling in an unusual way. Kite must have dislocated it.

With a loud grunt, Lazarus thumps it with the palm of his hand, making a cracking sound.

'Thanks, mate,' Falcon says as he rotates his arm.

'You must be a bit soft if your girlfriend can dislocate your shoulder,' Jet teases while cracking his gargoyle knuckles. 'I would have put it back in for you.'

'I want my arm still attached to my shoulder.' Falcon smiles, rubbing it.

'I'm glad you four stood down. There's been too much bloodshed recently,' Lysander says.

'We are no threat to your clan, but we are on edge with the fear of being caught by vampires again. We refuse to be their slaves and will fight to the death this time around,' says David.

'Unfortunately, there's nothing our angels can do to help you now you've gone through transition. There's no return once your fangs drop,' Aldore says. 'I'm unsure if an Aboriginal elder will be much help as the venom has already latched on. But I'm willing to ask.'

'That is all we ask for.'

'Until then, I must ask you to stay under the guard of Jet and Ash, even though I accept your word that you will cause us no harm. My concern is the two females from your clan and their intentions. You said you believe they mean no harm but you're not positive. As Australia's elite elder, I need to be one hundred and ten percent positive.'

'We understand and accept your orders. I'm happy to join the search party for the two females.'

'That won't be necessary, David.'

'What are the names of the two women?' I quickly step forward, surprising Lazarus, who joins me a second later.

'Alisha is the one with child and Brooke is her friend.'

'You don't need to know their names, Jasmine. The dragons will find them,' Lazarus says, raising his eyebrow, waiting for me to argue.

'Of course you will. I have no intention of finding them.' I smile.

'Follow me, guys. We'll go to the roof as the castle already has a few new guests. If you need to feed let me know.' Jet waves his clawed hand for them to follow.

I'm about to head inside the castle when my father catches my arm. 'I want you to go back to Nogard Hollow with Bell and Kite and remain there until I change the order.'

'King gave me orders! I thought you were my father.' I pull my arm away. 'I'm strong and can easily put those hybrids on their arse if I choose to.'

'I know how powerful you are, Jasmine. It's your short fuse that worries me and your lack of discipline. Your heart guides you instead of using your head and soul.'

'I have just saved the hybrids and Falcon from being burnt to a crisp!'

'Only because you were using all your senses. Too often you're guided by your heart and switch off the sensibility your head brings.' He runs his hands through his hair, obviously frustrated. 'I don't have time to babysit you through this right now. I will call for you once everything is settled.'

'You can call but it doesn't mean I will come.'

I draw on my dragon form and ask the Earth to give me what I need. Golden particles circle around me, while the Earth's energy draws up through my body. My father jumps out of the way, glaring at me. I ignore his stare and keep my focus on the creature I wish to be.

Seconds later, I am staring down at the mighty Aldore, who continues to glare at me. 'You've just proven my point.'

'I now know how Uncle Bill felt when you banished him from Australia,' I echo, before bellowing to Bell and Kite to follow me back to Nogard Hollow.

Just as I'm about to take flight, Lazarus speeds to my

side. My father turns his back and heads into the castle.

'I'll join you soon, babe. I want to make sure everything is settled here before I go.'

I'm about to snap at him but realise he has done nothing wrong. It's my father I'm angry with. I take an extra few seconds to think before speaking. Dragons are irrational and when I'm in this form I need to be stronger than the creature and, as my father has just said, use my head. *Take your time. I'm heading back with the girls.*

He runs his hands over my forearm and rumbles a warm sound. 'You are a stunning dragon, Jasmine. We need to get this wedding organised soon.'

My heart sings and Lazarus smiles up at me.

'I agree. The quicker the better,' I say telepathically, a small puff of smoke escaping my mouth.

Kite lands beside me with an ungracious thud. Bell waits in the air, flying in a figure eight above us.

'Keira is staying behind. Are you ready to go?' Kite asks, keeping her distance from Lazarus' human form.

I don't comment on Keira, forcing my green jealous dragon away. *'Yes, I need to finalise my wedding plans.'*

Lazarus takes a good few steps away from us. I lift my wings high then force them down to feel my four feet lift from the ground. I repeat the action until Lazarus becomes the size of a rabbit. A very tasty-looking rabbit.

Kite and Bell are already flying in front of me, chatting about the wedding and if they're expected to by us a gift since I'm human. With two forceful flaps of my wings, I catch up to them. We glide, telepathically discussing my special event.

'You don't have to get me a present. There's no superstore out here for shopping,' I say.

'I've been to a superstore several times, but Kite's never been. Her fear of humans always stopped her,' explains Bell.

'Was it her fear of humans or her fear of eating them?' We all burst into laughter with flames billowing from our mouths.

As I inhale, I catch the scent of a creature unknown to me. The two dragons continue to talk and laugh but I direct all my senses towards it. It's coming from where the dingoes reside. I'm unsure if it's my human intrigue or the predatory dragon in me but I need to hunt this creature out.

'I'll meet you back at Nogard Hollow. I want to drop in to see the dingoes.'

'I thought we were doing wedding stuff?' Bell sounds a touch disappointed.

'I'll meet you in less than an hour. I want to thank them for the warning earlier today. Plus, I want to ask Ellie to come over and join us. It would be nice to include her.'

'We should come with you,' says Kite. *'Lazarus will take a bite out of me if I let you go alone.'*

'I always visit the dingoes alone. You two go and pull out all the wedding stuff and I'll be there soon. I promise.'

'We may as well feed while you're visiting. I know you hate watching us eat,' says Kite as she dips her right wing to head for the hunting grounds at the rear of Nogard Hollow. *'Don't be long!'*

I dip my left wing and scan the area below. The scent is becoming stronger the closer I am to the river.

The scent draws me towards a place where I have many bad memories. It pulls me to the cold, dark cave where I was held captive in by Attor.

I keep all my sense on high alert as I land in the opening of the cave. The scent is strong and, for some reason, alarming.

I use my x-ray vision, but the thickness of the cave bounces back. I draw on my natural form and within a few seconds, I'm human. My transitions are becoming quicker each time.

I draw in through my nose, collecting the scent and its location. I recognise it—it's a mixture of gargoyle and blood but there's a sweeter aroma attached. It's in the same spot where Demona sat when we were locked inside here. A cold shiver runs over me as I cautiously round the corner.

There are two gargoyles sitting in stone-sleep with half a carcass of a deer. It must be the two runaway females. I approach with caution and keep all my senses on full alert; something my father believes I can't do.

They are both females. I run my hand over one of the creature's wings.

'I know you can hear me. We have met the four members of your clan, who are resting at Elyograg Castle. You have nothing to fear and are also welcome to join us.'

I step back, waiting for a reaction, but there's nothing. I squat down in front of them and look them in the face. Still nothing. I sit cross-legged on the cold cave floor with the palms of my hands open and facing upward.

One starts to crack and break free from its stone-sleep. She takes several long seconds to shake the rubble free from her gargoyle form. She spreads her wings wide open but not in a defensive manner.

'You must be the queen,' she says.

'I am Jasmine and you must be Brooke, as you don't look pregnant.'

'Alisha is in labour. She's trying to delay the process by staying in stone-sleep.'

'That must be the sweet aroma I keep getting. Why is she delaying it?'

'We fear your elite will not accept the newborn now we have gone through transition. We fear your clan may kill it.'

'We don't kill unless we are being threatened. Our clan is not a threat to either of you.'

Alisha's stone features start to crack. She screams out in pain and falls to the cold ground.

I jump to my feet and race to her side. 'What can I do to help? Do gargoyles give birth the same way as humans?'

'Please leave!' Alisha pants. 'We don't know what the newborn will be. It may be pure vampire.'

'You were pregnant before you were bitten so it must be gargoyle first. How do you know it has any vampirism?'

'Because it has been drinking from her internally since the transition,' Brooke says, squatting down beside Alisha.

'Ouch!' Alisha squirms on the ground, holding her large belly. 'Please leave for your own safety.'

'A newborn can't hurt me. Let me take you back to the castle where the angels can help deliver your child.'

'It's too late for that,' screams Alisha.

'What can I do?' I move to Alisha's head and lift it onto my lap. She rolls her glowing blue eyes to me and fakes a smile.

'Pray.' She lifts her clawed hand up and I grab hold of it. 'It's coming.' She screams a deafening roar and clasps my hand until it is blue and bleeding from her sharp nails. Brooke squats at her feet and drags the carcass of the deer closer.

'Gargoyles need to eat after they've been given their chosen soul,' Brooke says, answering my silent question.

'Do you need a soul? We have some in our vault.'

'We have Alisha's father's soul with us.'

'It's coming!' Alisha growls a vociferous roar as the newborn enters the world.

'It's a boy!' Brooke holds up the newborn for Alisha to see.

It looks like a mini-gargoyle, with grey wrinkly skin and beaming blue eyes.

'He's gorgeous,' I gush.

'I need to get the soul. The joining must happen in the first few minutes,' Brooke says, moving towards me with the newborn. 'Hold him off the ground, as the soul must be the first energy he receives. If he draws the earth's energy first, he will never be able to receive it.'

She passes me the sticky newborn, whose eyes light up his face. He studies me, his small hand clasping my finger. He draws it to his mouth and sucks on it as a newborn human would do. I glance up and Brooke is lifting several large rocks. The cave illuminates when she finally uncovers the golden soul. My eyes drop back to the newborn who is content in sucking my finger.

'He's a handsome baby,' I smile at Alisha who is transfixed on her son.

'Thank you.'

Brooke hands Alisha the golden soul. Alisha holds her hands out to me, asking for her son. I remove my finger from the baby's mouth only for him to pull it back in. We all laugh.

'Ouch, he bit me!' I pull my finger out of his mouth and see two small bite marks.

I quickly hand him over to Alisha who places him on her chest and on his back. She lays the soul on his chest. It increases in brightness, matching the glare of the sun. I close my eyes, unable to cope with its ferociousness. I feel a heat cover me, which is a pleasant relief to the cold cave floor. As the heat dissipates, I slowly open my eyes. The newborn is gone and so is the soul. The two hybrid women are smiling and clasping hands.

'He is eating,' Brooke says, nodding to the back of the dark cave. 'He needs his strength as he grows; hence we had the deer here waiting.' There is a small puddle of blood where the deer once was. 'It will take a while so it's best to leave him be. I'll take Alisha to the creek below so she can clean up. It's probably best you come with us as we're yet to see if the newborn has the traits of a vampire.'

'I hope not,' I say, holding up my index finger.

Alisha gasps in horror, 'Did he give you all those bites?'

I lift my hand up and notice a dozen small puncture marks. 'I think that was your hand squeezing mine.' I look closer at the two small bite marks and notice my skin is starting to turn purple. 'This doesn't look good.'

'If it's a gargoyle bit you'll need it taken out quickly,' Brooke says. 'We have two poisonous teeth at the back of our mouths. One bite can be deadly.'

'I'm not worried about gargoyle venom as I've never been bitten by one and presume the venom can be extracted. It's a bite from a vampire that worries me.'

'We won't know if my son has any vampirism until he has fully transitioned,' Alisha says, opening her wings as if testing them. 'You should return to your angels and let them assess you.'

'Promise me you will join the other four hybrids at the castle. I'd like to meet the little fella who bit me,' I smile to cover the anxiety building inside my soul.

'Now we have met you I feel better about approaching your clan. Give me a day or two to let my son mature.' Alisha opens her wings and glides off the edge of the cave.

'Thank you for being so caring, Jasmine.' Brooke smiles before stepping off the cave's edge.

The two women glide down to the river and quickly emerge themselves in the water. I draw on my dragon form but stop when my eyes blur and the cave spins. I gain my focus and try again but the same thing happens. I lift my hand and my index finger is completely purple.

I draw on my gargoyle form, hoping a smaller creature will be easier to form. But my vision blurs and I stagger sideways. I try to call for help and focus on the two women below but it's a haze. I fall to the cold cave floor with my breath escaping me.

'Hmm, what do we have here?'

I glance up to find a teenage gargoyle standing in front of me. 'Help me,' I whisper.

'I'm still very hungry. Should I help you or eat you?'

'You're a gargoyle! You're born to protect the elite,' I murmur as my head hits the wet floor.

'Oh, I'm more than a mere gargoyle,' he says, flashing his vampire fangs. 'I've tasted your blood and I want more. And by the look of your markings, you are going to be delicious.'

My vision blurs and my breath shortens. I use my telepathic waves to alert Kite.

'Where are you?'

'Demona! Cave! Help! Bitten!'

'I hear you, but your message is incoherent.'

The young hybrid walks towards me, licking his pointed fangs. 'I want more!' I gather any strength I have and shock him as he touches me.

He jolts backwards, laughing. 'Is that all you've got, witch?'

I draw again but this time I use the earth's energy to howl to the dingoes. If they hear me, they will alert Elyograg Castle. 'Wow, it looks like you have many talents. You're a cocktail I'm going to enjoy.'

Ellie's howl echoes across the land, telling me Rhys is already notifying the castle of my location. I hear the two women scampering up the cave's face as the teenager lifts me into his arms. My body is limp; I've used all my energy.

Lazarus' angry face flashes before me as the teenager's fangs draw towards my neck. He licks the length of my artery with his cold wet tongue, his breath a cold chill.

I hear my grandfather's words, telling me to shut down my mind. I close my eyes and draw down into my soul. Here I can shut out the world and if I am to die it will be without pain.

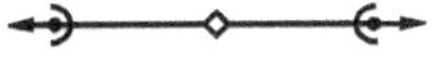

CHAPTER TEN

'I'm telling the truth! I don't know where he went,' yells a female's voice.

'Let me have five minutes alone with her and I'll find out his whereabouts,' snarls Lazarus.

'I warned her to leave before he was born!' The female continues. 'This is why we didn't want to come here but Jasmine assured us we'd be welcome.'

'Well, she's not talking at the moment,' snarls Jet.

I try to open my eyes, but they feel like lead weights. I inhale through my nose and gain the scent of my clan and of the new hybrids. I inhale again and force myself to speak. 'Stop bullying the hybrids, boys.'

'Jasmine?' Lazarus is at my side, grabbing hold of my hand. 'Can you hear me, babe? Can you open your eyes?'

'I'm trying but for some reason, I can't.'

'Gabby?' Lazarus calls for the angel whose presence I can feel. 'Why can't she open her eyes?'

'Let go of her hand, Lazarus,' she says. I feel her palm on me before a calm energy floods my system. It opens my soul and allows everything inside to float freely around my body.

'You can remove the block you've created, Jasmine. You are safe here.' She places her other hand on me. My body lifts off the bed and hovers in the air. It's a vulnerable feeling but one I embrace. A soft aromatic breeze circulates around the length of my body, getting warmer as it cleans my outer shell.

After several minutes, I'm gently placed back on the bed before Gabby removes her therapeutic hands.

I draw in a deep, cleansing breath, blocking out the scent of the elite around me. As I exhale, I force my eyes to open. Gabby's sweet face is the first I see, and then Lazarus pops over the top of her. 'Babe?'

'Hello, handsome.' I smile.

'When will you do as you're told?'

'When I'm dead.'

'You nearly were. The newborn's venom was enhanced due to his mother being a hybrid,' explains Gabby. 'You were lucky it was his milk teeth and not his adult teeth or his fangs.'

'Have you extracted it?'

'I have withdrawn the majority of it. Your system will fight the remaining venom so be wary when changing form or using your sorcery, as it may be affected.'

'I will, thank you, Gabby.' She leans down and kisses my forehead before leaving.

Lazarus is quick to jump into her seat, Jet sitting on the other side.

Jet frowns. 'You're killing me, Aunt Jazz. Can you give me one week where I don't wake up to my senses trying to rip my soul out?'

'I know when someone is inked to another, they can release them. Maybe I can release you from the protective custody hold you have on me?'

'I don't want to be released from anything. I just want you to be safe and do as you're told.'

'Told or ordered?'

'You might want to lose the attitude as Aldore is spitting fire.'

'Huh!'

'You were lucky the newborn didn't bite you a second time,' interrupts Lazarus.

'I can't remember anything, as I shut my senses down.'

Brooke appears at the end of the bed. Her gargoyle form is

large against the men's human form. 'The newborn, or Bronx as he is called, was millimetres away from latching onto your main artery. Together, Alisha and I fought him off you. It was lucky Lazarus and Falcon arrived seconds later as we weren't strong enough to keep him away.'

'Where is he now?'

'He's run off, scared, angry and alone,' says Alisha from the other side of the room. 'I don't condone what he's done but he is still my son.'

'I understand.'

Jet and Lazarus' bodies stiffen before I catch the scent of my father. 'You understand what? That you disobeyed an order? That you put yourself in danger and anyone else who stands by you? That one bite from a hybrid will kill you?' my father bellows from the doorway. 'You understand nothing!'

I refuse to cringe under his rage. I open my mouth only to have Lazarus place his hand over it. I try to bite his hand, but he growls at me. I inhale through my nose and exhale slowly, dropping the tension in my shoulders, pretending to calm down. Lazarus slowly removes his hand with his eyebrows raised at me.

'I liked it better when you were in hiding, mighty Aldore.'

'And I liked it better when you were oblivious to the elite world.'

'I didn't ask you to come here.'

'You did when you brought King to my house! And when your mother died protecting you.'

'Oh, here we go with the blame game. Don't stop there. Blame me for Drake's death, Sky's death and you may as well blame me for Grandfather's death, even though I was a child!'

'You still are a child!'

'No, that's where you're wrong. I will be married within the month and then you can wipe your hands of me. I will no longer need you or the protection of the clan.'

'You will always need me.'

I go to speak but Lazarus grabs my hand and squeezes it hard. 'Stop before you say something you'll regret.'

'Take me home.'

'You're not well enough to go. And the venom is still leaving your system,' my father says in a cooler tone.

'As I said, I'm not yours to worry about.' I sit up and look Lazarus square in the face. 'Take me home or I'll go myself.'

'I'll take you home in the truck. I'm not letting you change form until your system is completely clean,' Lazarus says, standing up and holding his hand out.

I move quickly, kissing Jet on the cheek before bidding the two hybrid women goodbye.

Gabby lectures me on the way out to keep clear of any creature containing venom, which is nearly all elite creatures.

The drive home is quiet, with Lazarus behind the wheel and me gazing out the window.

'Do I have any extra markings?' I ask, breaking the silence.

'No.'

'Are you angry with me?'

'No.'

'What's with the short and sharp answers?'

'I'm concentrating on what's ahead. We have a hybrid lose who wants to drain you.'

'I will recognise his scent instantly.'

'Damn it, Jasmine. You are not hunting him down!'

'I don't plan on hunting anything down. What's eating you?'

'Do you really want to know? Because I have a list.'

'Please enlighten me.'

'You say you're flying straight home then detour when you catch the scent of the hybrids. Your lie has hurt Kite and Bell, who are disappointed with themselves for not going with you.

You approached the hybrids after you said you wouldn't.

'You risked the dingoes' lives! They approached the cave after you called for help. Falcon and I were both bitten by the hybrid when we came to your rescue. Plus, your attitude towards your father is embarrassing and disrespectful, especially as he is our elite elder.'

'You were bitten?' I spin in my seat and search the flesh that isn't covered by clothes. 'Where did he bite you? Which teeth did he bite you with? Have you had the venom drawn out?'

Lazarus gives me a quick glance before he pulls the truck to a stop in front of Nogard Hollow. Bell is sunbaking in dragon form; her red leathery skin glistens in the sun. She lifts her head and blows a small puff of smoke to acknowledge us before dropping her head to the ground like a tired pup.

I jump out of the truck and race around to Lazarus. 'Why aren't you speaking? Are you infected?'

'Lucky for me he was a young teenager and was still learning how to use his teeth. I was bitten by his back gargoyle teeth, resulting in a nasty rash. For some reason, he withdrew his fangs after biting Falcon.' He pulls his t-shirt over his head to reveal the bite mark on his shoulder.

'Oh, babe! I'm so sorry.'

'What part are you sorry for—the lies, Kite, Bell, the dingoes, Aldore or Falcon? You need to think before you act, Jasmine. Your actions have consequences and sometimes it's life-threatening.'

'Is Falcon alright?' I run my hands over his bitten shoulder.

'Unfortunately, he was bitten by the front vampire fangs and the gargoyle fangs. He's undergone the venom extraction. The Aboriginal elder has given him bush medicine as well since this is the second time he has been bitten by a vamp. He is in pain but would do it again to protect you as I would and anyone in our clan.

'And that is the problem, Jasmine. You don't think like a creature, you think like a human which puts you in danger in our world. Creatures are unpredictable and have animal instincts where you don't and never will.'

'You're right. I am human and you will always be a creature.'

'Don't start twisting what I'm saying. You're not going to run away and we are getting married.' He pulls me into his arms and drops his head to rest his forehead on mine. 'I'm asking you to think twice or maybe three times before you act, especially when you're in creature form. As a sorceress, your actions are one hundred percent online.'

He rubs my nose with his, making me smile. 'I know it isn't pleasant for someone to point out your faults and I'm sure you have a list of all mine, but this needed to be said. You're an amazing sorceress who can transform into anything but there's a huge responsibility which comes along with this gift.'

'I have nothing to say. You are right.'

Lazarus blinks several times. His green slit eyes seem unsure of my actions. Normally I'd bite someone's head off if they reprimanded me like he just did. But he is correct in everything he has said. 'I'm not going to argue with you. But I've caught Falcon's scent and it has the sweet smell the hybrids have.'

'It's the venom bleeding out of him. Kite is nursing him inside.'

I lift up on my tippy-toes and press my lips to his. He smiles, before kissing me hard.

He pulls back when Bell murmurs a rumble and rolls onto her back in the dirt. She reminds me of a horse when they need a good scratch. She twists and turns her back to the ground before standing and shaking off any loose dirt. She snorts several times before taking off in the direction of the hunting grounds.

'She is magnificent to watch. She is one of the more graceful dragons around here.'

'What about me?' Lazarus sounds hurt, as he tugs me towards the house.

'You land like an elephant, but you are graceful in the air.'

As soon as I open the front door, I'm hit with a sickly-sweet smell which is drifting from the cave. I sense the two dragons behind the large double doors. Lazarus pushes them open with ease.

'Can you light the lanterns? It's too dark.' Lazarus' eyes reflect like a fox caught in the headlights of a car. He grasps my hand in his.

'I'll cheat,' he whispers close to my ear. I feel the heat draw up my body before a billow of fiery breath shoots from him and lights up the cave. Instead of changing form he uses my earth energy to tap into his dragon powers.

Falcon's large dragon form is curled up like a cat, with Kite wrapping around the outside. His eyes are closed and he is still as we slowly approach.

Kite's eyes are wide open, watching every move we make. She is calm but very protective so I move with caution.

'Hey, Kite. How's the patient?' I whisper even though they can both hear my heartbeat.

He's sweated most of the venom out but is exhausted from the process,' she echoes.

'Is there anything I can do?'

She snorts a large puff of smoke which makes Falcon stir. '*I think you've done enough.*' She's angry.

'I never meant for any of this to happen.' I take several slow steps towards her.

'*That's close enough for now, Jasmine.*'

My heart thuds in my chest; I've hurt the creature she loves and that means I've hurt her. 'I'm sorry.'

'I'm sure Lazarus has explained to you how a dragon connects with another. Once a dragon loses trust in someone it takes more than a mere apology to gain it back. If you slap a dog it will cower away every time you lift your hand. Throwing a juicy bone doesn't erase its memory.'

Moving his tightly wound frame, Falcon uncurls to stretch out his massive dragon form. His scales are dull in colour compared with Kite's and his eyes lack the green glow they normally have. He stretches, pulling his frame upward. His neck curves like a swan, as does his deadly tail.

I keep my eyes focused on the sphere in case he is angry with me as well.

'How are you feeling, mate?' Lazarus asks.

'I'm passed the worst of it. My appetite is back so that's a positive.'

I step back and bump into Lazarus, who wraps one arm around my waist. If Falcon is hungry, I need to keep my distance and my movements slow.

Falcon laughs. *'You're safe, Jasmine. For some reason, you don't tickle my taste buds anymore.'*

'Oh! That's good to know.' I sigh with relief.

'But that doesn't mean Kite won't take a chunk out of you.'

'Have either of you fed?' Lazarus asks.

'I haven't had the energy until now and Kite has refused to leave my side. I'm praying you have, as one of us needs to be in full swing in case of an attack.'

'What attack?' I ask.

'The newborn hybrid is still out there somewhere.'

'His name is Bronx,' I say.

'Call him what you want. It doesn't change the one thing he's after and that is you, Jasmine. He's had a taste and he wants more.'

'He was a newborn then and didn't know how to control his urges. But now he's had time to mature. He may not be a threat to anyone.'

'*Stop thinking there's a silver lining around every cloud. The elite world isn't a fairy tale with a happy ending,*' snaps Falcon. '*I've spent days in pain flushing out that beast's venom. I can guarantee you he is after your blood. When we dragged him off you, he said you had royal blood running through your veins. I don't know or care if you do but he will definitely return to drain you.*'

'You are thinking like a human again, babe,' Lazarus says.

'*I find it ridiculous that you trust the vampires and hybrids at Elyograg Castle. If one of them decides to take a bite out of you, you're turned. I'd even be wary of Jet,*' Falcon says, moving his large frame towards us. He stops when his lifeless green eye is beside us.

'Jet is my family and would never hurt me.'

'*When it comes to greed, creatures take what they want. Luckily, some of us wake up and have regret, like I did when I first met you.*'

'I forgave you a long time ago, Falcon. I hope you can forgive me for this.'

'*It was my choice to stand by Lazarus and rescue you. I don't blame you for the hybrid's actions, but I wish you didn't have such a dramatic life.*'

I run my hand over Falcon's scaly face. His eye slowly closes as if he's enjoying my touch.

'Once upon a time you were my drama. Go eat, my friend.'

'*Have you eaten, Laz?*' Falcon asks.

'Not since we rescued Jasmine. I wanted to be beside her while she slept.'

'What? You won't heal that bite on your shoulder if you're not in your natural form. You should have eaten,' I say. 'Go with them and eat. I sense Xandria is here so I'll hunt her down for some girl talk.' Kite bellows a golden flame from her mouth and paws the ground with her front foot. 'I'd love it if you would join me after eating, Kite. We've brought our wedding forward so I've got to finalise the plans and your opinion means the world to me.'

'I'll think about it,' she says before taking off, leaving behind a dramatic swirl of dust.

Falcon follows her with a noticeably slower take off. Lazarus pulls me into his arms and kisses me.

'We have cattle grazing next to the corral. I eat there so I'm close by. Can you stay out of trouble for the next hour?'

'That depends if Xandria leads me on a wild goose chase.' I reach up and kiss his warm lips.

He winks before stepping back, clearing the way for his enormous frame. He smiles a sexy grin before the earth circles around him in a whirlwind of red particles.

Within seconds, he is standing in his true handsome form. He nuzzles me with his warm nose before rubbing his head against me. I run my hand over his neck and down his large belly. I continue to the end of his tail, stopping short of his sphere.

I walk around the other side and glide my hand along his scaly length. When I reach his head, I open my arms and lay my body between his green slit eyes. He rumbles his approval.

I press my lips on the scale central to his head. His warmth floods me and I feel the build-up of energy I get when we make love. He shakes his head and I step back, laughing. 'Good idea, babe. If I shock you in dragon form you may singe all my hair off.'

He blinks before opening his wings. I step away and allow him to take flight. He circles me once before heading out of the cave. He is a magnificent creature and I'm so happy I have the elite creatures in my life.

I follow my senses to find Xandria in the kitchen with a glass of wine.

'Since when do fairies, or any elite creatures, drink alcohol?'

'Since my boyfriend grew fangs! And since we've become inundated with vamps, wolves and hybrids.' She lifts the wineglass and pours the remainder of its contents into her mouth.

She holds it in her mouth for a few seconds before gulping it down. 'Ah! 2002 was a good year for the Barossa Valley.' She spins the empty bottle on the table in front of her.

'Alcohol isn't the answer.'

'Coming from a woman who ran away to the Outback and hid inside a bottle of Jack!'

'Yes, I ran away and drank to forget and that is why I can tell you alcohol won't solve your problems.'

Xandria leans over to the cupboard while keeping her petite bottom on the chair and pulls out another bottle of wine. She unscrews the top and pours herself another glass. 'I'm depressed, angry, annoyed, sad, scared and to top it off, feel guilty. Sit and have a glass of red with me. I need a friend.'

'If it stops you drinking the whole bottle, I will gladly have a glass. But only one glass. Last time I drank it nearly started a war amongst the elite.'

'I remember that day well, when Jet and Laz were at loggerheads over you. It must be nice to have creatures love you.'

'Paul loves you, Xandria. I thought you were coping with his vampirism.' I take a small sip of the red wine and it's delicious.

'I was but now there are more of them to deal with, plus the hybrids. The vamps are human first—they weren't born under elite rule. Once they realise their strengths they could turn on us or humans.'

'You must have some kind of powers to protect yourself.'

'A fairy's power is a ball of fluff compared with the rest of the elite. We were last in line when they were giving out powers. I have nothing to protect myself with unless I erase everyone's memories and make them think they are a goldfish.'

I take another sip of my wine, with Xandria topping up my glass. I shake my head, but she continues to fill it to the top.

'Once Paul has settled the two new vamps at Elyograg Castle, he can come over here. You could use this as your meeting place. I can protect you when you're with me and I'm sure Paul will do the same.'

'How are you feeling after being bitten?'

'I'm conscious of what I say and do as there is still venom in my system.'

'I can smell it and it's disgusting.'

'I can always rely on you to tell me how it is.'

She laughs. 'That's what friends are for.'

I catch the dragons' scent moments before I hear them returning to the cave. I hear them transform and then walk in our direction.

'We've got company.' I flick my eyebrows towards the door, moments before the three dragons walk in. 'How was the roo?'

'You're slipping, Jazz. I had roo with a side of deer.' Falcon licks his lips. 'Great combination; you should try it.'

'I'll pass. Do you feel stronger after eating? Can I get you anything?'

Lazarus rumbles a groan. 'I liked it better when you two didn't like each other.'

Falcon rolls his eyes. 'I'm running on half the cylinders I normally do but eating always makes me feel better.' He smiles and wraps his arm around Kite, who is keeping her distance from me and is extremely quiet.

'Do you want to join us in a glass of wine, Kite?'

'I need to head into the cave with Falcon. He should be resting in his natural form.'

'You stay here with the girls. I'm happy to go with Falcon. I need to get back into my natural skin for a while,' Lazarus says.

'Why don't you have a break from babysitting me and

enjoy some girl time?' Falcon kisses Kite on top of her head. 'Laz and I need to discuss the new arrivals and the newborn hybrid. The conversation will bore you.'

'Only if you don't need me.'

'Great! Come sit down and let's go over the last-minute details for the wedding.' I smile.

'That's our cue to leave,' Falcon says, kissing Kite on the cheek.

Lazarus walks over to me, staring at the wine in my hand. He leans down and kisses me slowly on my lips then licks his as if tasting the wine. He cocks his head and flicks his eyes back and forth.

'I like you in this skin,' I whisper into his ear.

'I like you in any skin. I thought you made a vow not to drink again.'

'One glass won't hurt me.'

'You've had more than one glass.' His warm breath coats my ear and neck.

'It's annoying having a fiancé who has heightened senses. Go shred your skin, dragon.'

'Make this your last glass. I don't want to find the house burnt down and Kite and Xandria turned into toads.'

'Ye of little faith!'

'No, I just know how my wife-to-be thinks.' He nibbles my ear before kissing my cheek. 'I'll slip in beside you late tonight. I'll be a while, as I need to reboot.' He smiles at the two other women before heading for the door. 'Just have a sip, Kite. We need you at your best, just in case.'

'I'll be waiting,' I whisper seductively. Lazarus hisses through his teeth, giving me a quick wink over his shoulder before disappearing.

'You two are sickening, you know that?' Xandria says, grabbing a glass for Kite then refilling mine.

The three of us finish off the bottle of wine and stupidly open another. We decide we want to go to Melbourne to find a wedding dress and the bridesmaids' dresses. Instead of driving we would fly there in dragon form with Xandria riding on one of our backs. For some reason, we all found it hysterically funny.

By the end of the night, Xandria is sprinkling fairy dust all around the kitchen, making us sing and dance like ten-year-olds.

I make it to my bed, just, leaving Kite, who heads down to the cave with the boys. I pray she can transform properly. Xandria is sleeping on the kitchen table covered in her fairy dust.

'Here. Drink this. It will help clear your head.' Lazarus hands me a fizzy orange drink.

'Thank you.' I sit up, taking the glass from him.

He has a disgruntled look on his face. 'I asked you to take it easy.'

'I didn't hurt anyone, did I?'

'That's not the point, Jasmine!'

'Oooh, Jasmine is it?'

'Just the other day we had a discussion about being responsible and thinking before we act.'

'We were having fun and no one got hurt.'

'For a human, it's fine to drink alcohol but not for an elite creature. Kite was a mess last night. Lucky for her, we were both in the cave to stop her from flying out to eradicate the newborn hybrid. She then wanted to take on the vamps and the wolves!'

'She was happy when I left her.'

'As soon as she transformed into her natural form, her creature instinct took over and switched on the predator in her. A very drunk and dangerous predator.'

'I didn't realise she drank that much.'

'The three of you drank three bottles. Do you ever see us sitting down to have a beer at the end of the day? No, and there's a good reason for it. Elite creatures need to have their senses clear and in control at all times. What would have happened if the newborn hybrid had come here last night and Falcon and I weren't there?'

'I wouldn't hear him because I was passed out.'

His eyes start to swirl red and his brow pulls in tight.

'I get it, settle down.'

'Falcon and I are heading out to search for any sign of the hybrid. Do you think you can behave for a day?'

'The girls and I were going to head to Melbourne to look for wedding dresses.'

'You're taking Kite, who doesn't cope being around humans?' Do you think that's a clever thing to do?'

'She has to learn someday. I can keep her under control.'

'Like you kept her under control last night?'

'We are going to look at dresses, not to drink.'

'Wait until we've hunted down the hybrid. Then I'll take you shopping for your dress.'

'I want to shop with the girls. They're excited, as neither of them has been to a bridal store. And since I'm the only human here to have a wedding, Paul excluded, they probably won't ever have the need to.'

'Because they are creatures?'

'Yes, because they are creatures.'

'That's exactly why they shouldn't be amongst millions of humans.'

Xandria walks into my bedroom holding her head. 'I've spent many days being around humans. I can help calm and quench Kite's thirst.'

'You need to clean up the kitchen. You've left an overload of dust in there. I nearly exploded,' growls Lazarus.

'It was feel-good fairy dust. It should've made you happy, if anything,' she says, leaning against the wall.

'If he was happy in the kitchen it definitely wore off by the time he got to my room.' I take a sip of my fizzy drink, keeping my eyes low.

'I had a reason to be angry.'

'I'll go clean it up. I need coffee.' Xandria turns to leave but suddenly stops. 'Between Jasmine and me we can help Kite. You do trust us, don't you, dragon?'

I slowly lift my eyes to his which are staring down at me.

'Don't try and start a fight between Jasmine and me. She knows I trust her but sometimes her judgement is done through human eyes and not an elite's.' Lazarus rubs his head with both hands in a frustrated motion. 'I'll agree if you promise to keep low-key and visit a bridal store on the outskirts of Melbourne. And stay at your father's house. He still has it under a cloaking spell.'

'Agreed,' I say.

Xandria smiles before heading out. 'Bugger, I was looking forward to riding to Melbourne on the back of a dragon.'

I snigger but stop when Lazarus' brow pulls together. 'Low-key means you all go as humans and none of you change form. Actually, I'm adding to our agreement, and you're not to use any of your powers the whole time you're in Melbourne. Except your cloaking spell.'

'Agreed.'

Lazarus narrows his eyes and sits on the edge of the bed. 'Why are you being so agreeable?'

'I want a wedding dress. I want to marry you the human way and the creature way. I want my husband-to-be to trust me as much as I trust him.'

His features relax, his heart skipping a quick beat. 'You need to keep that heartbeat under control. I may remember how delicious it sounds next time I'm in dragon form and find it difficult to control myself.'

He pounces on my lips and kisses me passionately and with meaning. He loves me.

FALCON AND LAZARUS leave in search of the hybrid while I help Xandria and Kite clean up the kitchen. We try to re-bottle Xandria's fairy dust but end up in tears of laughter.

We are interrupted when Jet enters the kitchen. 'By the shocked look on all your faces, I presume Laz didn't tell you that I was coming along for the ride.'

'No, he didn't. But if you want to tag along with three ladies, you're welcome.' I walk over and kiss his cheek. 'Shopping with the girls is super fun.'

'He also told me you'd try and put me off.' He smirks and folds his arms across his chest.

'All aboard!'

IT'S NOT LONG before we are driving over the rough ground, heading for Melbourne. I stop overnight at our usual campsite, knowing it's safe for Kite to change form and hunt.

It takes another full day before we arrive at my father's house. Jet heads out to scan the property for anything unusual.

I have an eerie feeling when I open the front door. My senses are switched on full alert. I can't hear anything and sense the house is empty.

I head towards the lounge room, passing my parents' bedroom. My feet stop and my body freezes. My mother's scent hits me hard. My heart thuds painfully in my chest.

A warm hand rests on my shoulder. 'Is there anything I can do?' Kite whispers.

'I thought I'd forgotten her scent. The scent I've stored is tainted with blood.'

I walk into my parents' bedroom and pick up one of her

favourite scarfs. I lift it to my nose and draw deep and long. 'I miss her.'

'I know how you feel,' Kite says. I lift my eyes to her and they are filling with tears.

'I'm sorry about your father and brother. If I'd known…'

'We should all get some rest,' Xandria says. 'We've been given only one day to find the perfect dress.'

I wrap the scarf around my neck and nod to the two women. 'I'll show you where to sleep.' I give Kite my room as I want her to soak up my scent as much as she can. If she does lose control, I need her to know which human I am. I slip into my parents' bed and do the same; soaking up my mother's loving scent.

Jet walks in and plonks his gargoyle form beside the bed. 'It's all clear outside. Go to sleep, Aunt Jazz. I'll keep watch.'

I smile before reaching over to rest my hand on his shoulder. With my other hand clasped around my pendant, I drift off into a blissful slumber.

THE THREE OF us girls are awake and dressed ready to go before the sun has fully risen. I start driving towards Melbourne city, unbeknownst to the others. 'I know I agreed to stick to the local stores, but Melbourne has a wider variety of dresses,' I say.

'I won't tell Lazarus if you don't,' Kite says.

'You've gotta be kidding me?' Jet glares at all three of us. 'In and out. That's all we are doing.'

'I'm in!' Xandria says from the back seat of the truck. 'We've got the strongest, smartest and most intelligent hybrid to protect us.'

'Don't play on my ego.' Jet turns to snarl at the fairy. 'I already know I'm the strongest.'

'Have you eaten enough to keep in control?' I say, turning my head from the road to glance at Kite.

'I can handle it.'

'You'll hear the deafening sound of a million beating hearts, all of them out of control and filled with anger, fear, hate and love. It will be a rollercoaster for your senses,' Xandria says.

Kite licks her lips. 'I can handle it. Falcon wouldn't have let me come if he didn't think I could handle it.'

'Did you not hear me?' Jet's clenched fist hits the dashboard. 'This has trouble written all over it. Damn it, Jazz, can't you just do as you are told?'

Xandria leans between the two front seats and gasps. 'Look! Too late Jet. There is the city.'

'Wow, it looks like a concrete jungle. Do any gargoyles reside there?' Kite leans forward with wide eyes.

'I don't know. There are several buildings with gargoyles, but I've never looked close enough to see if they are elite. And even if they were, we are here to shop for a dress. I'm not here to meet the relatives.'

'You're being selfish and putting these two and me in a dangerous situation.' He leans over so his face is close to me. 'Turn around.'

'Aren't you a little curious?' I flick my eyes to his face and see him mulling over the situation. 'We will be in and out within the hour. I'll keep us under the cover of my cloaking spell. No one will know we're here.'

Xandria sighs loudly and I know she's about to bait Jet. 'I've been amongst many humans and Kite believes she's under control. That leaves the hybrid and his ability to control himself.'

Jet turns his shoulders to look at her. 'If I didn't have control, you'd be wingless. Is there a store on the outskirts, saving us going into the heart of the city?'

'Yes, and I can get us there in five minutes.' I smile and reach over to clasp his hand. 'Thank you. I love you.'

'I'm only agreeing to this because I'm with you. You can explain this to Laz when we return.'

I park the truck in an underground car park, close to the bridal store. My senses have been on full alert since leaving home and are inundated with vulgar smells once we step out of the truck.

Kite coughs and shakes her head several times. She scrunches her nose up like a dog that's sniffed another dog's butt and regretted it. I hand her a pair of sunglasses to cover her dragon eyes. It takes her a few minutes to adjust to wearing them. Jet pulls out a pair and slips them on.

Xandria and I walk either side of Kite as we exit the underground car park. Jet walks behind us. I know he has a large build but it's the first time I've noticed how tall he is. He can easily see over the top of us. Kite freezes and grabs our hands. Her chest is rising and falling at a rapid speed.

People are everywhere, rushing to get to work on time. Her eyes are darting around and I fear I may have done the wrong thing. With my spare hand, I flick her nose.

She shakes her head. 'What's that for?' She releases my hand to rub her nose.

'I wanted you to stop concentrating on what's happening around you.'

'Well, it worked. Now I want to bite your hand off.' She smiles.

'Are you coping or should we leave?' Jet asks.

'Amazingly, I'm coping. It started as a head-rush of beating hearts. But now it's become annoying, like someone continually beating on a drum.'

'Fantastic! Let's go shopping,' Xandria says, already walking away from us.

I turn Kite to face me and scan her face.

'I can handle it,' she says, nodding at me.

I look up at Jet. 'Don't worry about me, I'm fine. Worry about yourself when you get home and explain this to your fiancée.'

As we follow Xandria I start to chuckle.

'What?' Kite asks.

'I once flicked Laz on the nose. He was taking in my ex-boyfriend's scent so he could hunt him down when I wasn't around.'

'I'm amazed you still have your hand attached to your arm. He has a shorter fuse than me.'

'He didn't bite me, but he did burn my ex's car.'

'That's what we dragons call true love.'

'I call it jealousy.'

'I suppose you can call it that as well.' She laughs as we enter the bridal store. She slowly scans the store and her smile increases as she takes it all in.

'Over here, girls!' Xandria has her arms full of brides' dresses. 'There's so many to choose from.'

Before we take a step further a small stout woman pops up in front of us. 'Can I help you, ladies, oh, and a gentleman?'

'I'm looking for a wedding dress and three bridesmaids' dresses. I also want six tuxedoes.' I search my pockets for my list. 'Here's a list of the sizes I need.'

'Surely the groom and his groomsmen will want to try them on.' She smiles as she takes the list from me.

'The men don't have time. All I need is six tuxedoes with shirts and ties, please.'

'Speaking of time,' says Kite, tugging on my arm, 'we are also short on it.'

Kite gives me an awkward smile. I spin my head around to see if anyone else is in the store. It's empty. I use all my senses to see if anyone is approaching. It's clear. I frown at her, unsure of what she is trying to tell me.

'I sense elites close by,' she echoes.

'I sense nothing. I think you may be a little paranoid. But I'll make it quick.'

'If you would be so kind as to get those for me while I try on some dresses,' I say, smiling at the woman.

'Of course. There is a private dressing room for you and your bridesmaids over there.' She points to a set of large red velvet curtains. 'And the gentleman can sit in the front waiting room.'

'Terrific, but the gentleman comes with us.' I gently grasp Kite's elbow and tug her towards the dressing room. Xandria, with her arms full of dresses, forces her way through the velvet curtains.

Kite runs her hands over the curtains before stepping through. There are several comfortable-looking chairs surrounding a small elevated circular platform which Jet falls into, sighing. In front of the platform are four humongous mirrors, allowing the bride to see her dress from all angles.

'Here, try this one on first. I know it's not white, but antique pink will go great with your olive complexion and dark hair.' Xandria has dumped all the dresses onto one of the chairs except for one stunning dress. 'You try this on and I'll go and find some bridesmaids' dresses. What colour do you want?'

'Something that goes with antique pink, I suppose.'

'Great! I'll be back soon.' Xandria skips out of the dressing room just as the small woman walks in.

'Can I offer you some champagne?' She holds a bottle of champagne and three glasses, stopping in front of Kite.

'No, I don't drink alcohol,' Kite says.

I interrupt and move to stand in between them both. 'Coffee would be great, as none of us drink alcohol.'

'Of course.' She bows her head. 'If you're going with the antique pink, I'd recommend the groom being in something a little softer than black. Say a grey.'

'I agree,' says Xandria, bouncing back into the room with an armful of dresses.

'Sure. Make but them a dark grey. Jet can try his one on.' I nod to the woman as she walks out of the room.

'I've got a nice pair of jeans.' Jet says.

'But you will look dashingly handsome in a suit.' I smile as the shop assistant hands him one.

'I suppose it won't hurt to try it on.' He stands and heads towards a free changing room.

I turn to Kite, who hasn't moved a muscle since we entered the dressing room. 'How are you coping?'

'I sense gargoyles close by, but they're no threat. I presume they sense me and want to know what a dragon is doing smack-bang in the middle of their city.'

'I sense them too and agree there's no threat.' Jet sticks his head out with his nose in the air sniffing.

'Relax, guys. No elite creature will show themselves in the city. This is supposed to be fun,' says Xandria, handing her a lilac-coloured dress.

'What's this?' Kite asks, turning her head towards me.

'I want you to be my bridesmaid.' I grin.

'Me?'

'Yes, you.'

Kite takes me in her arms, squeezing me tightly. 'I'd love to be one of your bridesmaids!'

'I'm one as well,' says Xandria, who has already slipped on the bridesmaid's dress and is zipping it up.

'I'm asking Lolana as well. Laz has already asked Jet and will ask Falcon and Ash before we get back. I'm getting two extra suits for my father and Paul.'

'I was excited to go to a human wedding but now I'm ecstatic!' Kite releases me from her warm, tight arms, strips down and pulls on the lilac dress.

I do the same and once the dress is on, I step up onto the circular platform. I draw down into my soul and speak to my departed loved ones.

'Hello, my daughter.'

'I always pictured this day with you standing beside me,' I say.

'I'm always standing beside you.' I feel a soft squeeze of my hand. I look into the mirrors that surround me. My mother's form is faint but visible. Beside her is Grandfather, whose smile is large and warm. My other hand is softly squeezed. Sky is also standing me.

'I miss you all so much.'

'We are always with you, Jazzle,' says Sky.

'You are going to be a beautiful bride,' says Grandfather, wiping an elusive tear away.

'The colour suits you,' my mother adds. *'Antique pink is my favourite colour.'*

I turn slowly to see the back and sides of the dress. It's held on by two shoestring straps but fits firmly to my torso. The breast is daintily beaded with small crystals down to my waist. The back of the dress is cut out and scallops over my bottom. From my hips down, it flows out elegantly.

'Should I be wearing white?'

Sky chuckles. *'I think "traditional" flew out the window once you decided to marry a dragon.'*

'I suppose you're right.' I stop admiring the dress and take in the features of my loved ones. *'I wish you were with me on my wedding day.'*

'Your father will be by your side,' my mother says. *'You need to mend your differences. He loves you. He will always care for you even when you are married and under Lazarus' protection.'*

Grandfather puffs his chest before speaking. *'You promised me you'd never let darkness enter your life, that you'd keep the positive energy flowing through you. When you fight with your father, you're letting the dark side in. You're letting the venom of evil dictate to you.'*

'I want to be taken seriously and not treated like a child.'

'Your father and the elites close to you all respect you as a sorceress. Your ability and strength are not questioned. It's your dark behaviour that is questioned,' Grandfather says.

'I felt betrayed by him. Everyone knew he was Aldore except me!'

'Surely you can understand we wanted to protect you,' Mother says. *'Every day it took all his powers to keep you hidden. All we wanted was for you to have a normal human life.'*

'Your father gave up everything to protect you and give you some type of normality. Don't punish him for caring and protecting you from the elite life,' Grandfather says.

'I'll fix things with him when I return,' I say, knowing what Grandfather says is true. *'I love you all.'*

'We love you. And I approve of the dragon, not that he bothered to ask for my blessing,' huffs Grandfather.

'It's a bit hard to ask for your blessing. You are...'

'Just let him know I approve.'

'I'm sure Lazarus will sleep better knowing my deceased grandfather won't haunt him.' I chuckle. Grandfather's lips curve into a cheeky grin.

I feel my hair being tugged and lifted. Kite has moved behind me and has twisted and wrapped my hair into a bun. The frosted vision of my loved ones fades.

'Are you okay?' she asks. 'You look like you're miles away.'

Xandria laughs. 'Don't you dare say she's "away with the fairies".'

'I'm fine.'

Kite moves to stand beside me on the platform. She removes her sunglasses before pulling a few strands of hair down on either side of my face. She runs her eyes up and down my dress then stares into the mirrors in front of us.

'This is the one.' She smiles.

Xandria steps up onto the platform on my other side. 'She's right. This is the dress.'

The bridesmaids' dresses complement my dress beautifully. They are right. These are the dresses.

Jet walks out from behind the curtain, tugging at his tie and jacket. 'Don't know how men can wear these uncomfortable ties. I feel like a dog wearing a collar and lead.' He stops and stares at the three of us on the platform. 'You look… human.'

'You're supposed to tell a bride she looks beautiful,' says Xandria.

His eyes roll over me, stopping when he reaches my eyes. 'You're always beautiful to me. The dress is lovely, but I like it best when you're wearing torn jeans and a floppy t-shirt.'

The small shop assistant is overwhelmed when I explain I want to take all the dresses and suits today. She asks for a few hours to get them organised.

'What are we going to do for the next couple of hours?' Kite asks.

'We could shop more or eat,' says Xandria, who is sniffing the air. 'Yes, we definitely need to eat.'

'How are you coping?' I ask Kite.

'So far so good. I'm happy to eat, even if it's boring human food.'

'I have an idea!' Xandria's smile grows. 'Let's go to Crowne. We can eat seafood until we burst.'

'You've been to the casino before?' I ask.

'I've been here once or twice.'

'What's a casino?' Kite asks.

'You will love it,' says Xandria.

'I suppose we could go as long as you feel in control, Kite.' Jet says. 'I sense no threat.'

'Let's go!' Kite says before walking off in the wrong direction.

Watching Kite walk through the crowded streets of Melbourne makes me laugh. Her nose twitches as she takes in every scent she can. She reminds me of a dog going for a walk.

Unsure of her reaction, I grab her hand as we walk through the entrance of the casino. She stops statue-still, and slowly turns her head around then back the other way.

'Oh, my! Look at all the shiny flashy things.' She moves closer to the line of poker machines. 'I want that one.' Then she moves to the next one. 'No, I want that one.'

One of the machines close by gets a large win, triggering flashing lights and a loud annoying tune. 'This one! I want this one.'

The man sitting at the machine glares at Kite. 'Nick off.'

'No! I want this one,' snarls Kite.

I flick her nose and quickly move my hand away in case she takes a bite. She growls at me but at least I gain her attention.

'I forgot you like shiny gold things. This is too much for you. We should leave.'

'Can we take one with us?'

'No, honey. These are full of venom. They look shiny on the outside, but they drain you just like a vampire.'

'It smells like the devil died in here.' Jet's nose is screwed up.

The man sitting at the machine spins around in his chair. 'I said nick off!'

Xandria moves in between the angry man and Kite. She leans forward and whispers into his ear. With her free hand, I see her sprinkling a pinch full of fairy dust. The man's features soften before he calmly turns to play the machine.

'Maybe we should head to the buffet,' says Xandria, grasping Kite's hand in hers. She escorts her to the buffet which, thankfully, is away from the glittery machines. There are rows and rows of seafood. Kite accidentally dribbles as she walks up and down the aisles, unsure of what to do.

I grab two large plates and walk her and Jet to the start of the buffet.

'Here are your plates. Walk along and take as much as you want.'

'I wish I could change form. I'd eat all this in seconds,' Kite says.

She overfills her plate which raises a few people's eyebrows. Jet grabs another plate, filling it. Xandria grabs a table at the back of the restaurant, giving us a little privacy.

Jet pushes his two empty plates away, picking food out of his teeth. He sits back, folding his arms across his chest, and scans the room.

Kite devours her plate full of seafood and heads off for another. Lucky for me, she has forgotten about the poker machines.

I smile with joy as she piles oysters up on one side of her plate then layers prawns on the other. I don't have the heart to tell her she is supposed to shell the prawns before eating them. She downs them, shell and all.

As I finish my first and final plate, Kite is heading up for her third plate. Her pace is getting faster and faster. *Kite, you're supposed to be human and need to walk casually.*

She smiles, nods and slows down to a crawl.

Jet shoots to his feet as Kite stops and her posture stiffens. A young man in his twenties is walking around her in a slow calculated stride. I draw him in and instantly recognise the scent of an elite. If my senses are right, he is a gargoyle.

Xandria is oblivious to anything—her food and her own

voice keeping her occupied. Jet and I quickly approach Kite, who hasn't moved a muscle.

'She's with me, mate. You'll have to find another attractive lady,' Jet says, draping his arm over Kite's shoulder.

'I mean no disrespect to any of you,' he says, bowing his head.

'We need not have this conversation here. In public with human eyes,' I say.

'Our concern is why your lovely lady friend is here,' he whispers then smiles.

'We mean no harm and will be leaving within the next hour.' I lean closer to Kite's ear and whisper, 'you can breathe. He seems to be alone. There are others on the rooftop, but they are all calm as I'm sure you can sense.'

'You know I come in peace, so may I join you at your table?'

'Yes.' I turn and open my hand, indicating for him to go first towards our table.

'No!' Kite and Jet snap in unison.

'What's wrong?' I ask.

'I want to keep eating,' Kite says.

Jet huffs and moves to stand in front of the young elite. 'We come in peace but don't mistake it as our weakness. I will snap the neck of an elite if need be.'

I gently push Jet aside. 'There's no threat, so settle down.' I turn to face Kite. 'Go get another plateful and I'll walk our guest back to our table. Calm yourself before you return.' She nods then walks slower than a snail to the buffet. I try not to laugh.

Xandria lifts her head from her plate when I return with the human gargoyle. 'Well, hello. I didn't see him on the buffet. Is there another one for me?'

Jet plonks down in his chair with his chest puffed.

He pulls out my chair and I graciously sit down. He sits beside me and cocks his head.

'Is everything alright?'

'I'm trying to work out if I've seen you before,' he says.

'And who might you be? Why have you approached us?' Xandria gets straight to the point.

'As I explained to your beautiful friend here, we sensed the dragon and are curious about her presence.'

'She is no threat to your kind and, as I said, we will be leaving shortly,' I say.

'We sensed no threat. Hence, I was nominated to approach you. My clan live amongst the buildings of Melbourne. We rarely get visitors and when we do, they are usually not welcome. Your arrival has caused quite a stir.'

'May I ask your name?' Xandria asks, fluttering her eyelashes.

'Call me Tyson. Where is your clan located?'

'Elyograg Castle and No—' Xandria stops when I reach over and pinch her arm.

'Does it matter? We're leaving soon.'

Kite returns and sits between Xandria and me. She doesn't seem to trust Tyson.

'This is Tyson,' Xandria says to Kite.

'I heard,' she says, eating her prawns whole.

'Humans peel their prawns,' says Tyson.

Kite flicks her eyes to me with a look of embarrassment.

'I don't,' I lie to keep her calm.

'I've heard of Elyograg Castle. Isn't that where Australia's greatest sorceress lives, under the protection of all the elite?' Tyson asks.

'She was there but has now gone into hiding,' I answer.

'It is said her father was the great Aldore. Is that true?'

I laugh. 'I think someone is pulling your leg, Tyson. Anyhow, how many are in your clan? Are you mixed or just gargoyle?'

'Mainly gargoyle. We have clans on the outskirts of the city which cater to the other elites. What about Elyograg Castle? Do you cater for all elites?'

'Yes, we cater for all the elite which makes us an unbeatable force.' I want him to hear and repeat that we are a clan that can't be beaten.

Interrupting our conversation is a loud burp from Kite. 'I'm done. Let's go.'

'It was a pleasure meeting with you all. Next time fly up to the rooftop and meet my clan,' Tyson says, standing up and helping to pull our chairs out. 'You will always be welcome.'

Jet huffs and shoots to his feet.

'If I could get up there I would.' I smile.

'Oh, I'm sure you could. I sense something special about you and it's not just your beautiful looks.' He leans forward and brashly kisses my cheek. 'Have a safe journey home, ladies.' He kisses Xandria on the cheek and attempts to kiss Kite, but she holds her hands up to stop him. He bows and smiles at her. He shakes Jets hand, stopping to take in his features.

Xandria and I grab a hand each of Kite's and drag her quickly through the casino. Jet walks behind her with his hand firmly against her back. It's a relief when we get to the bridal store and the dresses are ready for us. I pay and get Kite to the truck as quickly as I can. Her constant nagging about wanting a poker machine was starting to grind on my nerves.

'Did you notice Tyson and several other gargoyles followed us to the bridal store but stopped when we got into the truck?' I asked.

'He is doing his job. There's no threat here but the stench reminds me of the vampires back home. I was starting to think the city was full of leeches,' Jet says.

'I suppose they're protecting what's theirs,' Xandria says.

'I'd do the same,' says Kite. 'Do humans peel prawns or was he trying to embarrass me?'

'Most humans peel them. But if you barbecue them the shell becomes crunchy and edible.' I smile not wanting her to feel embarrassed.

'I found the shell quite edible.'

'Your teeth are little sharper than a normal human. How are you coping?'

'I'm proud of myself for coping amongst the humans. But I would like to change form to stretch my wings.'

'It will take the rest of the day and night to get to a safe area for you to change. Why don't you sleep and I'll wake you when we arrive?'

'I think I'll keep my senses wide open until we're out of the city.'

'Relax, Kite. I'm switched on.' I glance over to Jet. His eyes are darting back and forth, taking everything in.

CHAPTER ELEVEN

OUR TRIP HOME is without drama. We arrive at Elyograg Castle as dusk falls. Lazarus is just returning from the hunting ground. He is quick to change to his human form and is opening my truck door as soon as I park.

'I missed you.' He smiles.

'Not as much as I missed you,' I say, returning the smile.

'You've got five minutes before the hens' party starts,' Kite says.

'What's the hurry?' Lazarus says, helping me out of the truck and wrapping me in his warm arms. 'You've had her for two days.'

'The human tradition says the groom shouldn't see his bride the night before. She is supposed to spend it with her bridesmaids, drinking, eating and watching strippers,' says Xandria, who has her arms full of bridal wear.

'Strippers?' Lazarus squeezes me tight. 'Did anything out of the ordinary happen?'

Jet huffs. 'My first outing and I was stuck with a bunch of girls, shopping.'

'We tried on dresses, ate seafood and drank coffee. Nothing unusual about that.' I roll up onto my tippy-toes and am about to kiss his lips when Kite pushes me backwards.

'No kissing before the wedding. You only have to wait one more day!'

Kite drags me inside the castle and into the large lounge area where everyone has congregated. My father moves quickly to my side and kisses me on top of my head.

'He's allowed to kiss her,' mumbles Lazarus.

'How was your trip?' my father asks, smiling down at me.

'Uneventful,' I answer.

'Thank goodness,' Falcon and my father say in unison. It makes us all laugh.

'I need everyone to try on their suits and dresses so I can do any alterations. I don't want any arguments, just your obedience,' Xandria says. 'Laz, Falcon, Paul and Ash, I'll do you guys first. Jarius, Corbin and Lysander, I want you to put your old suits on so I can make sure you look reasonable.'

Xandria walks off with the men obediently following. Whatever power she has, I want some of it.

Lolana jumps up from the sofa and wraps her arms around me. 'How'd the shopping go? Can I have a sneak peek at the dresses?'

'You can have a sneak peek at the bridesmaids' dresses because one of them is for you.' I smile.

'What are you saying?'

'I would love you to be one of my bridesmaids.'

Lolana squeals and wraps her arms tightly around me. Her strength lifts me off the ground.

'Come and I'll help you try your dress on. Plus, I have so much to tell you about shopping and eating seafood,' Kite says to Lolana, who is still squealing with excitement. She eventually puts me down and follows Kite upstairs.

It leaves me and my father alone.

'I'm glad we're alone. I want to apologise for the way I've been acting. I know what you do is to keep me safe,' I say.

'Living amongst the elite isn't the easiest. It tests your patience. Plus, you've been bitten and left to fight the venom. I've always known you love me.'

'I was hoping you'd still walk me down the aisle tomorrow.'

'It would be my pleasure.' He kisses the top of my head.

'I'm asking my cousins to the wedding. I know you don't want me near them, but they are family. Wolf, dragon, gargoyle or sorcerer, we are family.'

'I too have had time to think and I'm happy for you to see your cousins. But I'd ask you do to it while I'm around. I'm uncertain of a wolf's traits and can only go on what I saw with my brother.'

'If you hadn't banished him, and instead had supported him in his transition, you'd know.'

'I agree. I was young, naive and over-protective of you and Sky. It was a judgement made with my human heart and not my elite head. I contacted him several years later, asking him to return home, but he had settled down and had a family. He has since passed away so I can't ask him to forgive me. I must live with the guilt of turning my own brother away.'

Lysander races down the stairs. I get a whiff of a scent I had recently picked up.

'We have a visitor,' Lysander says.

'I know the scent. It's not threatening.'

'I sense that too,' he says.

The three of us move quickly to the front door. There is a truck a short distance away heading in our direction. Lysander moves towards it, leaving us standing on the castle's porch.

When the truck pulls to a stop, he walks to the driver's door.

'I'm Lysander, the head of Elyograg Castle.' He shakes the man's hand as he steps out.

I inhale deeply and his scent hits me hard.

I sense Lazarus close by. 'Jasmine, where are you?'

I walk back into the lounge room where Lazarus, Xandria, Kite and Jet are sitting comfortably on the sofa.

'Do we have a guest?' Xandria asks.

I'm about to answer when the front door opens and Lysander walks in.

'Tyson? What are you doing here?' I ask.

'You know this gargoyle?' Lazarus asks with a questioning brow.

'We met at the casino in the city.' Xandria smiles, oblivious that she has just dobbed me in.

'Casino? City?' Lazarus' eyes narrow and start to swirl red.

'He was admiring Jasmine's beauty,' Xandria says, adding fuel to the fire.

'Really?' Lazarus growls.

I turn my attention away from my angering fiancé and towards our guest. 'Why are you here?'

'We need help. You mentioned that your clan is unbeatable.'

'Unbeatable?' Lazarus says.

'How can we help?' I try to ignore Lazarus, but his body is radiating a fiery heat.

'It looks like I've arrived at an inconvenient time. Maybe I should come back in a few days.'

'We are preparing for my wedding. I won't be here in a few days. Please, sit and tell me what you need.' I open my hand to indicate that he should sit on the lounge chair.

Kite comes skipping into the room then stops when she spots Tyson.

'Please tell me you brought me one of those shiny poker machines,' she says. 'Or some of those crunchy prawns.'

'Poker machines? Prawns?' Lazarus is beyond angry. 'You told me you stayed on the outskirts of the city! Jet, you've got a hell of a lot of explaining to do.'

Lysander interrupts. 'How can we help, Tyson?' He again offers him a seat and this time he takes it.

'There are humans who have captured several elites. They've had them since birth, torturing and killing their parents. We are unsure how to approach and disarm the humans.'

'How is it that we've never met you before yesterday? There was a call-out for all gargoyles to help in the battle against the Europeans,' Jet asks.

'We had our own problems to deal with. Bringing them here wouldn't have helped you in your fight. I apologise on behalf of our clan for not standing by you.'

'But you expect us to stand by you?' Lazarus asks.

Lysander brushes off Lazarus' question. 'Is your problem now resolved?'

'Somewhat. It's difficult living amongst so many humans and, with the increasing number of vampires in town, it makes it difficult to keep hidden. They drain humans then hypnotise them so they forget what has happened. The humans end up in hospital with flu symptoms.

'Several of my clan are working alongside the doctors, trying to keep a lid on it. We've had to reveal ourselves to a number of humans in order to help the infected ones.'

'So what can we do to help?' Jet asks.

'I know you have a powerful sorceress here. I've come to ask for her help in rescuing the gargoyles,' Tyson says.

'She's unavailable,' Lazarus snaps.

'I can help,' Jet says, sitting down opposite Tyson. 'Tell me more about the situation.

I quickly sit beside him, intrigued by what Tyson has to say.

'Don't you have wedding stuff to organise, Jasmine?' Lazarus asks.

'You're Jasmine?' Tyson's eyes widen. 'You're the sorceress we're looking for. You were in Melbourne and no one knew.' He rubs his hands over his face several times. 'How stupid of me! I should've at least asked your name. I sensed you were an elite but...'

'I don't want to sound rude, but I was in the city for my

own personal reasons. I had no intention of meeting the relatives. When you approached us it was unexpected, so we left soon after, as you and your clan saw.'

'We only followed you to your truck,' Tyson says.

'We know,' Kite says, tapping her nose.

Jet coughs to gain Tyson's attention. 'Tell me more about the captured gargoyles.'

'As I mentioned, we revealed ourselves to several humans. Two male humans took advantage of our situation and lured several of my clan into a trap. They drugged and kidnapped them. Two were female gargoyles, who were pregnant. After the babies were born, the humans tortured and dissected the females until they died. They still have the young gargoyles in captivity.'

'I presume the young gargoyles haven't received golden souls,' Jet says.

'We are unsure, as their mothers died close by. We pray they've taken their souls. If they haven't, they'll be uneducated and untrained. They would be terrified.'

'Can you give them a soul later in life?' I ask.

'A soul can only be accepted by a newborn. A gargoyle without an elder's soul is…'

'It's a tough start but we can help train and educate them here. Do you know where they are?' Jet asks.

'It's a day's drive from here. The exact location is unknown, but I can ask the dragons near home to help.'

'That won't be necessary. We have our own way of sniffing them out,' Jet says.

'So you'll help us?'

'Give me a few days to plan our attack. Plus, Jasmine and Lazarus are getting married tomorrow,' Jet says.

'Good idea! Then I can come along,' I add.

'You, my dear aunt, are going on your honeymoon. I, along with Ash, can deal with this situation,' Jet says.

'Jasmine, the sorceress, is your blood aunt?' Tyson asks with Jet smiling and nodding. 'And you're a gargoyle. So that makes you a hybrid.'

'One that should be keeping himself hidden,' I snap.

'I thought we were the first clan to have a hybrid,' Tyson says. 'The father of one of the newborns was a dragon.'

'Please don't tell me the hybrid is one of the captive gargoyles?' Jet says.

'Sadly, yes.'

'An uneducated, untrained hybrid is a recipe for disaster. I'm amazed it hasn't escaped or killed its captors by now. The humans must have subdued it somehow.'

'That's what we are hoping for. Our biggest fear is the humans are training it to fight for them.' Tyson stands up and begins to pace the length of the double sofa. 'With the vamps on the increase and the fear of a hybrid attack, we are continually on alert.'

'It would have been nice to know you had a hybrid at the start of the conversation,' growls Lazarus. 'Are there any other surprises?'

'You didn't disclose your hybrid. I'm still unsure of what powers he holds,' Tyson replies.

'All you need to know is that, together with Ash, I'm the one who can help you.'

'Thank you.' Tyson stops pacing and sways side to side.

'When was the last time you ate or were in stone sleep?' Lysander asks.

'A week, maybe longer.'

'As we've mentioned, we have a wedding tomorrow. You're welcome to attend or spend the day rebooting your system. But first I'll take you to our hunting ground so you can eat.' Lysander stands.

'I think it's wise to stay in my true form. I can't ask for help and not be at my best. I wish you all the very best for your wedding.' Tyson places his hand on my shoulder. 'You'll be a beautiful bride.'

Lazarus smothers his growl, making Tyson smile.

'Follow me,' Lysander says, nodding his head towards the front door. 'I'll be back in an hour, Jet. We'll discuss the rescue in detail when I return. Make sure Ash is here.'

'I'll head out and find him.' Jet quickly leaves the castle.

'Come on, girls, we need to have our hens' night,' Kite says, with Xandria jumping on the spot, clapping her hands with excitement.

'Jasmine will be with you soon. I want to have a word with my beautiful bride,' Lazarus says in a cool tone.

The two women skip up the stairs and enter my bedroom. When I hear the door close, I stand with my hands on my hips, ready for Lazarus to growl at me. He raises an eyebrow as if to question me.

'We were only in the city for a few hours. Kite handled the situation perfectly. No one was hurt.'

'You took a dragon into a casino!'

'She loved it… a bit too much.'

'I asked you if anything out of the ordinary happened.'

'Nothing did happen.'

'I think meeting Tyson should have earned a mention.'

'I didn't think meeting him was important enough to mention. Big strong Jet was with us. Plus, it was you who told him who I was, not me.'

I take slow steady steps towards him and stop when we are close. He inhales a deep breath, then relaxes the tension in his shoulders when he exhales.

'You didn't ask if I went into the city so technically, I didn't lie.' I lift onto my tippy-toes so our lips are centimetres apart.

I'm about to kiss him when Ash and Jet burst through the doors.

'Oi! You're not supposed to be kissing or even seeing each other before the wedding.' Ash smiles, happy with his interruption.

I drop to my heels and shrug my shoulders. 'I'm not supposed to marry a dragon but I am.'

'I've given up on trying to stop that but this I can stop.' Ash turns his head away from us and whispers. 'Kite, come down and drag the bride-to-be away.' Kite is instantly at my elbow, dragging me up the stairs. I turn to see the shocked look on Lazarus' face.

Ash walks over to him and slaps him on his back. 'One more day and she'll be all yours.'

Lazarus smiles. 'She's already mine.'

'I love you,' I whisper as I climb the stairs. I hear Lazarus' heart skip a beat.

⤫

I WAKE TO the smell of a freshly cooked breakfast. 'Mmm, that smells delicious.' I sit up in bed as Malachi draws my curtains and lets the morning light sneak in. 'You're spoiling me.'

'A bride should start her day with a healthy meal. It's her day to be spoilt.'

'You and Gabby have made sure of that. You've been cooking for days. Thank you.'

'It's our pleasure. Do you still want to go for an early morning ride?'

'What better way to start my special day than riding Blue Boy.'

'I'll get your horse ready for you.'

Malachi turns to leave my room, but I stop him. 'I know you and Gabby are our clan's angels and it's your duty to care for everyone. But I want to thank you for being my friend, especially when I didn't deserve you.'

'Maybe I should be thanking you. Before you came here, our lives were quiet and mundane. You've definitely livened things up.'

'Thank you, Malachi.'

He leaves with a smile on his face. I eat my breakfast before skipping down the stairs towards the yards.

'Don't go getting into trouble, Jazz,' Ash says, walking up past me.

'Aren't you supposed to be in stone sleep?'

'On my way.'

I skip down the remainder of the stairs and exit the castle. Blue Boy is standing patiently beside Malachi. I throw my leg over his back and am soon heading towards the river. I relax, letting my legs loosely flop against my horse's belly. My eyes are closed, my mind is blank and my senses shut down. I'm at peace with myself.

Blue Boy stiffens underneath me; something has caught his eye. I grab a handful of mane as Jet's gargoyle form lands in front of us.

'What are you doing out here?' Jet asks, folding his wings in.

'I'm having a quick ride before the wedding. What are you doing out here?'

'I want to ask the dingoes for their contact in Melbourne.'

'I'm concerned about you revealing your powers to another clan.'

'What's the use of training and having these powers if I can never use them? If I have the ability to help an elite in danger, I should.'

'I noticed your powers have increased. In the battle, you used your powers whilst flying. I need to be connected to the ground to use mine.'

'I draw it up into my body and hold it there. Then, when flying, I release it from the pit of my gut. I can also partly draw on my dragon form, which allows me to fire anorics.'

'It makes sense. I can throw a flame whilst in dragon form so I don't see why I can't partially form and do the same. I should try it.'

'Don't go practising now. Lazarus will gut me alive if you hurt yourself today.'

'Speaking of which, I'd better return or my bridesmaids will hunt me down.'

'Don't take this the wrong way, but I'm glad I'm handing over the reins to Laz. Once you connect as his partner in dragon form, it releases me as your guardian.'

'I thought you liked protecting me.' I smile.

'I will always have the desire to protect you, but the urgent need will be gone.'

'You're leaving me and heading into Melbourne and into the lion's den.'

'The lion is a kitten compared with you, Aunt Jasmine.'

'I love you, too. Go find the dingoes and I'll see you at the wedding.' I collect my reins and turn Blue Boy towards home.

'We will always love you.'

I know when he says 'we', he means Drake and himself. He opens his wings and, with a dramatic downward thrust, he lifts into the air. He has more powers than he is letting on. Gargoyles can't take off from the ground. They glide from a height.

KEIRA CATCHES MY arm as I'm about to leave my bedroom. 'I was hoping for a quick word before you marry Laz.'

I look down the hallway and spot Jet. He must have heard Keira and tucks himself behind a pillar. *I'm here if you need me, Jazz.*

Let's see what the cow wants. I smile. 'Of course, Keira.

'In private, please.' I pretend to use my cloaking spell. 'I'm leaving before the ceremony.'

'Oh, I'm sorry to hear that.' I couldn't sound more sarcastic.

'You think you're special but you're nothing but an unskilled witch.'

'Well, this unskilled witch is marrying the dragon you're in love with.'

'A human marriage means nothing to an elite. Being inked to another is the only connection a dragon has.'

I pull my t-shirt to the side exposing my marking. 'Lucky for me I have both.'

'Enjoy the short time you have together. Bronx has tasted your blood and he wants more.'

'How would you know?'

She slides her t-shirt down, revealing her yin-yang marking. Along it is Bronx's name. 'We have been together for the last month. He salivates at the thought of draining you. I rejoice at the thought of him doing it.'

'We will kill him then kill you.'

'Do you think Lazarus will help kill me, a dragon from his clan? His feelings for me are deep-rooted and will never be compromised by the likes of you.'

'Where is Bronx?'

'I'd rather die than reveal where he's hiding.'

Jet steps out from behind the pillar. 'I can make that possible.'

In a millisecond, she is gone. I shake my head trying to take in what she's has revealed.

Jet wraps his arms around me. 'Are you OK?'

'I knew Bronx was out there, but I always thought it was a juvenile thing he did when he bit me. I suppose I was wrong.' Jet rubs my back. 'I couldn't give two hoots about her, I'm glad she's gone. But I've got to think about Laz and his feelings.'

Lazarus interrupts. '*You left your cloaking spell down. I presume on purpose. I heard everything. Let's enjoy our day. I'll notify Lysander and Falcon of the situation.*'

'*Jet's here and he saw the whole thing. He will handle it. I'll see you soon, my handsome fiancé.*'

CHAPTER TWELVE

My father squeezes my hand when my heart thuds hard in my chest. I've caught a glimpse of Lazarus at the end of the aisle, looking handsome in his suit. My nerves dissipate when I smile at him and he smiles back, giving me a cheeky wink. The groomsmen look pristine in their suits, except for their shoes. They're all barefoot.

The setting is stunning, thanks to the hard work of my bridesmaids. We chose to be married beside the river where several large weeping willow trees create a dramatic background. It's also close to the resting place of my mother and my cousin, Sky.

My bridesmaids have laid a pale pink carpet for me to walk down, with a dozen white chairs on either side. The chairs running down the aisle have flower arrangements attached. I know the angels have been growing them for some time. There is no music being played. The sound of the running river, birds singing and critters chirping is our orchestra.

With my arm folded through my father's, we follow my three bridesmaids in their lilac dresses down the aisle. They step to the side, allowing me to stand beside Lazarus. My father smiles before kissing my cheek and placing my hand in Lazarus'.

'Look after my girl,' my father says, shaking his free hand.

'You can count on it,' he says before turning his eyes to me. 'You take my breath away.'

He leans forward to kiss me, but Paul quickly interrupts. 'Not yet, Laz.'

Paul starts the ceremony, which is a blur as my eyes are

glued to Lazarus'. Paul taps the top of my hand, gaining my attention, and places a ring into it.

We've decided to use the dragon ring Lazarus gave me when he first proposed. He made a matching one for himself. The design is perfect, with the dragon wrapping around the finger with the tail holding a small diamond and a ruby sitting at its mouth.

'Do you, Jasmine, take Lazarus as your husband?'

'I do.'

'I do too,' says Lazarus, leaning in to kiss me.

'Not yet, mate.' Paul laughs. 'Do you, Lazarus, take Jasmine, as your wife?'

'I do. Can I kiss her now?' Paul smothers his laugh and shakes his head.

I hold Lazarus' hand in mine and place the wedding ring on his finger. 'You are my inspiration and my soul's fire. You are the magic in my days. You provide a safe haven for me and protect me against all. I vow to stand by you, even when your jealous green dragon comes out.' I smile and Lazarus chuckles, but quickly regains his composure. 'When I am with you, I am whole.'

Lazarus smiles, his eyes flicking back and forth between mine. He lifts my hand and slowly slips on my wedding ring. 'The day I met you, you ruffled my scales. Your beauty, strength and stubbornness captured my heart. Your knack for getting into trouble and starting wars excited me and drew me closer to you. So close, you became inked on my heart.'

He lifts my left hand and places it over his heart. I can feel it beating under my palm. 'I'm proud to stand beside you as your husband and as your dragon. I vow to disembowel, shred, rip apart and burn any creature who tries to take you from me. I'll kill—'

Paul clears his throat, gaining Lazarus' attention. He shakes his head ever so slightly.

Falcon, who is standing beside Lazarus, echoes, '*Keep your speech light, mate. No killing or disembowelling anyone. This is a happy occasion.*'

Lazarus nods then locks his eyes with mine. His heart beats quickly and in time with my own. He smiles before taking a deep breath. 'Gosh, you're beautiful. I'm a better man for meeting you.'

'You may kiss your bride,' Paul says.

'Oh yeah,' Lazarus breathes before pressing his warm lips onto mine. He kisses me long and passionately, his arms pulling me in tightly.

'Everyone, please help me congratulate Mr and Mrs… Lazarus and Jasmine, as husband and wife,' Paul says, tapping us both on the shoulder. 'That's if they stop kissing.'

Lazarus looks down at me and smiles. 'When do I get you all to myself?'

'After we eat. The angels have prepared an amazing banquet. We can't leave yet.'

'We're married.'

'Yes, Lazarus. I am your wife.'

He kisses me quickly before everyone approaches us. My father grabs me first and hugs me tightly. Then my three bridesmaids, Lolana, Kite and Xandria, squeal and skip around me, all taking turns to hug me. No doubt I will be covered in bruises, as they don't realise how strong they are.

Ellie and Rhys are next to approach and congratulate me with a kiss and hug. I spot the two young dingo pups happily playing in the background.

Ash surprises me by picking me up and cradling me in his arms, forcing me to wrap my arms around his neck.

'Has anyone told you how beautiful you are?' he says, nuzzling my cheek. 'I'm happy for you and Lazarus. He is a good man and will protect you, not that I'd admit that to him.' He locks his glowing blue eyes to mine. 'I love you. He's a lucky man.'

'I'm the lucky one.' I smile. 'I love you too, Ash.'

'Can you put the bride down so everyone else can congratulate her?' Falcon says.

Ash rolls his eyes before gently placing me back down on my feet. Falcon, Corbin and Jarius all take turns in picking me up and spinning me around. Maybe it's an elite tradition to squeeze and spin the bride. I'm not far from vomiting.

Eventually, Lazarus has me back in his strong warm arms. I take my time to look around at my extended family. They are smiling and chatting happily. I glance over to the river's edge to find Lysander standing beside the ghostly image of Sky, my mother and Grandfather.

Lazarus kisses the top of my head. My life is complete. We have the ultimate bond and it's not just the diamond-encrusted dragon rings that circle our fingers, it's deeper than that. Our bond runs through our blood and is deep within our souls. We are inked.